MURDER BY THE BOTTLE

MURDER
by the
BOTTLE

Ed Whitfield

MAGUIRE
CRIME

Published by Maguire Crime
an imprint of RedDoor Press
www.reddoorpress.co.uk

ISBN 978-1-913062-70-5

A CIP catalogue record for this book is available from the British
Library

Cover design: Clare Shepherd

Typesetting: Jen Parker, Fuzzy Flamingo
www.fuzzyflamingo.co.uk

Printed and bound in Denmark by Nørhaven

For all Bacchus's party boys and girls of the once mighty
Blackheath 306

Contents

Letter to Hugo Morley, C/O Maugham and Meer   ix

PART ONE: THE OLD WORLD   1

I A Breach of Trust   3
II End of Termagant   9
III A Stroke of Blue Pencil   12
IV Circle and Wye   17
V Artless   25
VI Petra   30
VII Ragesh   38
VIII The Three Tests   48
IX The Cradling   61
X Welcome to the Gallery   69
XI Dinner at Boondoggle   81
XII Denial   92
XIII Goodbye, Old World   100

PART TWO: THE NEW WORLD   113

I The Shock of the New   115
II Over, Under and Through   122
III Thirty Feet   128
IV The Puss and the Plan   136

V Murgatroyd   143
VI Good Housekeeping   158
VII Missing Seconds, Lost Days   167
VIII Art Unbound   178
IX A Trip to the Cellar   185
X The Waiting Room   198
XI The Inquisition   204

PART III: THE WORLD BEYOND   221

I An Evening with Cassandra   223
II Scraps   230
III The High Price of Borrowed Time   238
IV Decapitation   251
V Drinking Alone   266
VI Point of Departure   270

POSTSCRIPT   281

Acknowledgements   303
About the Author   305

To Hugo Morley
C/O: Maugham and Meer
37 Tottenham Court Road
London WC1E 3NA

Dear Hugo,

My name is New Shockley but you know me as Keir Rothwell. The media continue to deadname me. So much for investigative journalism. With my old life behind me, I'm free to speak out. I feel a tremendous sense of relief and find I have a lot to say. However, all around me – in print, on television, online – the impress of who I was remains. The police hunt for him, the public loathe his caricature. I share their disdain for this fictive monster. Meanwhile, the commentators, you amongst them, wonder where this fiend resides. Will you see him again? If so, on whose terms? I wish you luck looking for a man who does not exist.

I've ingested a lot of nonsense about me, Hugo; a full English of tabloid lies. Caught between my teeth: prolefeed and fictive testimony from jealous peers. What you have in your hand is the reply – my memoir.

Why send it to you? Is it our shared affiliation with a now melancholy seaside town? No. Rather, I respect your critical faculty. I trust your wits. Your name had a bearing on my decision to study art at Perrangyre. You should feel no guilt about that – it's a note in the margin. The town's people, not you, were responsible for their fate.

I wanted to send my account to a discerning brain, someone who'd see past the moral panic, the eulogising and the hysteria – the stuff that gets baked on after the fact.

I want people to know what I felt, what I thought, what was said; I want them to understand that so-called monsters are made not born, and that each person who's selfish, cruel, ignorant or base takes their turn as creator. This is not about ego. I'm nothing. But my art matters. It deserves a shot at being understood by those capable of taking it on. Else, what was any of it for?

My artistic ambitions always included writing but I never had a story I could tell. Now I have *the* story. I can't defend this manuscript in person for obvious reasons, or contact agents, or any of the privileges granted to the non-hunted. But I hope once you've read it, even if you can't empathise with me, you'll endeavour to understand my perspective, perhaps encourage others to do the same.

I hope you'll forgive some of the indulgences – the novelistic conventions, for example, and the deferring of details up to the point I became aware of them. But I wanted the story to unfold for the reader as it unfolded for me. Wisdom after the fact is all very well but it does not reproduce reality.

You'll pass this letter and the book that accompanies it to the police, no doubt. Feel free. It won't lead anyone to my door. Manuscripts are easily sent to third parties. They can be printed from anywhere, posted by anyone. Bear that in mind.

Perrangyre's changed since you left in 1965 – a lot and not enough. If more like you had stayed, maybe what occurred would never have happened. Still, that's fantasy. Here, in as much detail as I can give, is the truth.

Sincerely,

New Shockley – Artist

The Four Objectives of the Licencing Act 2003

1. The prevention of crime and disorder
2. Public safety
3. The prevention of public nuisance
4. The protection of children from harm

PART ONE

THE OLD WORLD

I

A Breach of Trust

It was the phone call that poisoned everything. It had been long anticipated and dread had taken hold like fungus in a neglected toenail. Maisie meant to hurt me. She'd been planning it for months. My father, when talking about his first wife, slurred that a man knows these things. If she recoils when you reach out to brush her hand, if her eyes drop when you talk up the future, if you discover that your favourite rows – the kind that smash glass and crush plasterboard – have tributaries that flow into small talk, you're in trouble. Beware the unspoken, he said.

Mother, never Mum, says I sound just like him. Until recently that's where the similarities ended. But now I know his pain. I can add it to the long list of things no young person should know. I've been saying nothing for years. You have to do that when your affair's illicit and shameful. Well with that phone call those ugly things were going to be said at last.

'Keir, I'm at the studio. I need to see you. Straight away, please.' Maisie's voice, once honeyed, was tart.

'Sure,' I said, trying to sound strong, 'give me half an hour.' The journey took fifteen minutes but I needed some thinking time. The ascent to the art school is quite a tableau. Few students get to work on the periphery of a cliff face. Perrangyre throws these scenes at you, like fresh bread for the gulls.

Minutes after the call I was plying the coastal path, rehearsing my lines, daring to imagine her replies. I was pre-humiliated, incensed that the succubus on the hill was prepping to lumber me with dead metaphors like sad eyes and a broken heart. As an artist I spend all my time fighting cliché, yet here I was, tailored to wear the very worst.

When I reached the school entrance there was a tramp blocking my way. The wind was up and he seemed to circle with it, like a fart trapped in an eddy. He wore a sandwich board with 'SAVE THE WORLD' emblazoned in red – a dull carmine, old blood. I pushed past him. 'It's too late for that,' I said, 'far too late.'

At the studio doors I hesitated. The coastal wind had violated my hair. I straightened it as best I could. New glasses were removed and stowed.

Maisie was sitting on a paint-flecked table, leaned back and loose. Her arms were stretched behind her. She looked playful. It felt all wrong. I tried to look past the sexual sadism – the morello cherry hair and blush lips she'd contrasted with a virginal-white outfit. But this was Maisie, a tease or nothing. Maybe she feared being nothing. I know I did.

'So, what are we doing here?' I said. This was my self-harming debut and I wanted to do well.

She sighed. 'Keir, c'mon.' She hadn't spoken to me like this since the early days. I was just a boy then. She was a celebrity, the woman who appeared on late night TV and discussed the arts, sometimes making points you could understand; the artist magazines profiled again and again; the self-titled Chair of Artistic Innovation at this sandbox of higher learning. The condescension came naturally. As I'd grown into myself and started to speak up, it tapered off. Now it was back.

'You know what needs to happen,' she said. I swallowed and hoped she hadn't noticed the beads of sweat or the nail canopies, bitten back and splintered. All gooseflesh was safely hidden, draped in a fine suit jacket.

'It doesn't have to happen, does it?' This was maudlin stuff. I'd have dumped me. She fingered her neckline.

'Keir, you're sharp and you pay attention to what goes on around you. That's one of the things I like about you. What other people miss, you get. You've got an old brain. Most twenty-year-olds are impossibly trivial. But not you. So stop pretending. You know it's over. Let's say our goodbyes and part on good terms.'

Maisie was right. I did have an old brain – the kind aged in a barrel. She understood that about me immediately. It's what got me noticed. I looked my years, but behind the eyes she saw sediment – accrued experience. I've never liked my generation. All my heroes are my parents' vintage or dead. Maybe it's envy. My lot are so carefree, aimless and cosseted; the most infantilised iteration of humanity that's ever lived; and in the midst of this gene pool there's me, pissing out, feeling about a hundred years old. My mother jokes I'm living life backwards, so when I'm thirty-five I'll be joyful, and at fifty I'll be bounding up staircases like an idiot, putting on silly voices and pretending to know about things I don't, rather than pretending not to know the things I do.

'I don't think I'm ready,' I said.

'Well I'm sorry but things have moved on,' she said.

'What things?'

'You for a start. You've become a different person.' She was right but this was the first time it had been presented as a problem.

'I'm still me,' I said, which sounded ridiculous then and does now. Maisie's frown confirmed as much.

'You're not the Keir Rothwell of old,' she said, 'you're New Shockley – the artist. Isn't that what you keep telling me? You have a persona. One that's attracting a lot of attention.' At last, I thought, we get to it – the imminent threat of discovery.

'Soon,' she went on, 'you're going to be public property. You'll be judging prizes; you'll be dinner party conversation. When that happens, you won't care about me any more. I know because I had a "me" once.' Wilfully underestimating my feelings was Maisie's neat way of dismissing them. I used to think it would stop as we crept towards parity.

'You haven't changed,' I said, 'more's the pity.' She laughed.

'Keir, we were never going to walk down the aisle together. We had a great time, but it was of the moment. My profile's built since I've been here, there's a lot of people watching my every move. The school wants me to do more. I can't be embarrassed and I don't do fairy tales.' No, I thought, you're more a noir kind of girl.

'I love you,' I said. Maisie's face palsied and I realised that whatever she'd expected me to say, this uncharacteristic grab from the well-rummaged bag of stock platitudes wasn't it. The look of disgust, the creeping surprise, reminded me of Mother's face, the day she found me oiling my length. Odd that I should think of them both.

'I have to go,' she said, getting up. She was halfway to the door when she stopped suddenly, as if she'd forgotten to unlock my manacles.

'Oh, it goes without saying, but this remains our business. There's no statute of limitations on our official secret, understood? If asked, I'll deny it and I'll be believed.'

'The benefit of being a practised liar,' I said. She snorted and was gone.

It didn't take long for me to reach my own studio. Just within the threshold I paused and cast a tearful eye over the work displayed on walls, on tables, on plinths. This was a year's graft, the product of walks with Maisie, workshops with Maisie, pillow talk with Maisie. I circled around the pieces, certain I'd throw up. How empty they looked, how derivative. I reached out to touch the head of a sculpture, a prop in a piece of video art, and felt deep loathing and a pain that began in the gut, quickly rising to the base of my throat. Wherever I looked I saw her – the byproducts of lies and false promise.

I felt disorientated, chemically drunk – a sense of clouding, of burning coal in my sinuses, the return of something old and rotten. I'd forgotten this boy, this precursor to the artist, the kid yet to flirt with civilisation, who now took control where I stood. He ripped the canvases from the wall, tearing, putting a foot through. He tore into towers of copper and plaster; punching, splitting – smashing against chapped pillars until there was nothing left but twisted wireframes and half-picked scabs of hanging bits. A screen cracked and lights left their mooring, strangling fixtures that came loose and fell away.

Finally, myself again and exhausted, I crouched. The

world around me was detritus. I got up and surveyed the damage. Glass crunched underfoot while the waves beyond the window offered a solemn contrast. I had nothing left and was just hours away from having to present these broken wares to an expectant school – the final act in a now fruitless year.

I was going to need a new project, a new reason to be.

II

End of Termagant

Even with a generous dab of Vicks rub in each nostril, the reek from the mound was penetrating. As I pushed on through to the presentation hall, my surprise piece mounted on a rusty trolley that squealed like a kicked dog, I looked to its head and noted dark liquid leaking through the cloaking shroud.

Leaving the confines of the warren and now exposed to the long gallery space that connected the studios with the main hall, I tried to ignore the eyes fixed on the moving slab from those on each flank. My sweat, which my body replaced as fast as I could sweep it from my brow, was in my eyes – they were stinging; there were salty droplets on my lips. I stared ahead, pushing forward, the dreadful whine of each wheel rotation stark in this vast echo chamber. I feared being stopped by an inquisitive gawper at any moment, a bored student breaking from their work, determined to take a peek at mine. I feared discovery.

On I went, closing the distance, intent on reaching the main hall's double doors. On a normal day the central lobby would be a maelstrom of creativity; eccentric peers, with their moth brooches, surf hair and retro-rags, building monuments to themselves. But this was the end-of-year open day, a time to nakedly present work in full view of discerning visitors. They were here, programme in hand, turning from the mermen sculptures and desiccated lemons on time lapse, to follow my trolley. I took the strain and avoided their gaze. I kept moving.

I hit the doors to the auditorium and heads turned, bemused audience members registering the reek from beneath the cloth. I had the crowd's attention – faces had changed. The murmurs became a cacophony. I pushed forward, keen to mount the ramp and get on the stage. In the adjacent slips I noted three empty seats, one reserved for me, the others for my parents. Perhaps it was better they hadn't come.

The front row was alive with expectant tutors, gesticulating, waiting, exchanging comments in each other's ears on work already seen. At the foot of the ramp I glanced across and saw dusty Dean, Professor Trevenna, who still made currency conversions from pounds, shillings and pence. He rose to talk to me but I pushed on. Next to him, an empty chair. Maisie's chair. The cloth covering the trolley was now saturated. This thing had to been seen and quickly. I prompted the stagehand with a gesture and she announced my handle, 'New Shockley'. Applause. I pushed the trolley up the ramp and on to the stage, the stink tarring the back of my throat. Eyes in the hall blinked out of sequence. The room was mine.

I focused on Maisie's unclaimed spot. 'Ladies and Gentlemen,' I began, my voice breaking, 'I give you, *End of Termagant!*' With that the shroud was torn from the mound. There were gasps, coughing – some retching from the front row. A joke broke out, 'It's the moronic Prometheus,' but make no mistake, the atmosphere turned – it turned over. I looked to my labours. Man alive. In the gloaming I'd noted its freakish personality. Now, in the full glare of the afternoon, it was monstrous. There was no denying it. No looking away.

The rot played its part. The spoilt meat, the bulk of its vaguely human form, had shifted. The splints that held the dismembered joints together were partially visible, like exposed bone. The wine coloured hair was matted while the eyes hung loosely from gouged cavities. Much of it had split and browned. It was indelibly horrific.

'I believe this work speaks for itself,' I said, emboldened by the crowd's reaction, 'but if anyone would like to know more – if you insist on a bit of explication – then I'll be around. Art can be opaque sometimes, like a partner at the end of a relationship. And sometimes we need answers. And sometimes, if we don't get them, it causes a real stink. Thank you for listening.' Walking off the stage I caught a new onlooker in my peripheral vision, a latecomer who'd missed the meat of my presentation.

Maisie stood by the slips, staring up at the artwork. The skin under her eyes seemed loose, like the crease in an unbuttoned blouse. Some of the crowd followed my gaze and looked to her. There were eruptions of embarrassed laughter throughout the hall. Art was bound to life. This audience understood.

I gave her a smile, just a little upturn of the lip, and gracefully made my way down. At the foot of the ramp I felt temporarily elated, only for thick saliva to suddenly collect in my mouth. Bolting for the double doors, ignoring the rising crowd, I made the flip side, just in time to see a waterfall of porridge break on the polished floor. Gallery spectators turned to sneer.

'Return to your art,' I said, 'I'm not an exhibit.'

11

III

A Stroke of Blue Pencil

Professor James Trevenna picked a mint from the tin on his desk and lolled it round his mouth. He contemplated first me, then which of his many questions would open our hastily called meeting. His secretary, whom I knew he felt up, demanded I be there at two o'clock, prompt. I arrived at twenty-past.

'Keir,' he began, 'I'd like to understand what happened yesterday. I'm hoping you'll do me the courtesy of being forthright.'

'Do you really want to understand?' I said, noting a number of atmospheres bearing down on the room. 'There's a lot you should kn—'

'First things first,' said Trevenna, cutting in, 'what happened in the studio?'

'The studio?'

'Yes, we thought we'd been vandalised, that kids had got in, but Maisie tells me you had a creative disagreement and destroyed it – a year's worth of work. Is this true?' The audacity of that woman.

'The police were called,' Trevenna continued, impatient for a reply, 'they found remnants of your, for want of a better word, presentation – dry blood, hair. They were treating it as the scene of a violent assault, a burglary gone wrong with an as yet unidentified victim, until Maisie intervened. She had to do a lot of talking on your behalf. There was a detective present, for God's sake.' I felt stinging pain behind my pupils, needle-like.

'Did you give them my name?' I said.

'I'm sure it came up,' said Trevenna. He began to choke on some wayward saliva and forced himself upright.

'We couldn't contact you,' he said, composing himself, 'and then you show up in the main hall, on the most important day of the year – a day when we have press in attendance, with that ghastly meat effigy, which I have to say was grotesque. For one awful moment I thought you'd brought a body on stage. Now I'm hearing a lot of salacious nonsense in connection with the thing.' An expectant stare; a plea for reassurance.

'It's not nonsense,' I said. The mint Trevenna had been gently lifting to his mouth was dropped back in its tin.

'Consider very carefully what you say next,' he said, 'because there are no second chances now.' This was it – the chance to put stones in Maisie's pockets and walk her out to sea. I wondered what the old man could handle. A storeroom fumble? Bare breasts clashing over open paint pots? The weight of the words on my lips was felt by both of us. A relationship between student and celebrity lecturer was a reputation-lancing story in a provincial town. This was an abuse of privilege, a grubby episode the fevered tabloids would spin down to depravity. The school's constitution forbade it for a reason. When had it begun? How many years? The more there were, the lewder it became. I felt my cheeks flush and the room start to buckle.

13

'Look, I don't know what she's told you,' I said, 'but you have to underst—'

'I'll tell you what I understand,' said Trevenna. 'Maisie's one of the region's most prestigious artists. She's highly respected. A lot of students at this college rely on her mentorship and some have funding attached to it.'

'Money's not the issue,' I said.

'Is that right?' said Trevenna. He now reached for another mint and this time it connected with his wet dog tongue. 'Let me educate you. Maisie isn't just a tutor. I can replace a tutor tomorrow. She's sponsorship and media recognition. Her picture is on the cover of the prospectus. The man she stands next to in that charming family portrait is me. If she's approached you, if you were propositioned in some way, of course I must know about it, but if there's something else going on here – if you had a go and she sent you packing, or if this is a fantasy that's got out of hand…'

He said more but now I struggled with my cues. I knew the script – every beat and line, but the still potent memory of Maisie's face as I left that stage broke the bonds of those well-crafted sentences. The words wouldn't come. From my open mouth poured fudge.

'I know how important she is to the school,' I said, 'but I can't allow you to ignore this.' Trevenna's head cooked from the inside.

'*You can't allow?*' he repeated slowly. 'Well I can't allow a thug to remain enrolled here, do you understand?'

'What are you talking about?'

'I'm talking about the damage to the Yankel Feather studio. The destruction of college property. The school owns the copyright on your work and all the materials used therewith; in other words, everything you destroyed belonged to us. I'm talking about recalling the police and their man,' he fumbled for a bit of paper, 'Murgatroyd, and prosecuting you for criminal damage. I'm talking about defamatory remarks against a member of staff who's brought in millions. I'm talking about a student who no longer fulfils the requirements to advance so is entirely dependent on the good grace of this office to continue! Is that clear enough for you, Mr Rothwell?'

End of Termagant, a piece built from butcher's bits, the bounty from Maisie's hairbrush and old glue, may not have been a year's work, but it had integrity. I'd worked hard those past nine months, so hard my fingers bled, but everything built was a collaboration with a fraud. Now I knew Maisie had nurtured those ideas, offering a dug to suck, because it flattered me – it bought my silence. There was no way to know where sincerity ended and self-interest began so I had to write off the lot. But now it was bungeroosh filler I had nothing to offer in my defence, only the truth. And one truth, I realised, with Trevenna's threat to recall the police still warm, could easily unearth another.

'Fine,' I said, 'I'll leave. I want no part of this degenerate set up.' Trevenna rose to his feet and gestured towards the door.

'I think it's for the best,' he said tonelessly. Despite myself, I registered surprise at his agreement. No pause for thought. No negotiation.

'One thing though,' I said. 'Is this line you've taken something to do with having a natural sympathy with the likes of Maisie?' He tensed.

'What?'

15

'Well, it's just your secretary, Jane – is that her name? I hear you've been cracking on to her for years, really ruffling the skirts. I'll bet when it comes to forcing yourself on a vulnerable, younger woman, you're a tenacious bastard, aren't you?'

With that Trevenna pushed me towards the door. When that didn't work he moved around and began pulling on my jacket. The sound of my shoes scuffing the floor underscored his pig-like grunting.

'Careful,' I said, 'maybe I'll call the police myself. Show them some marks.' He released me. I couldn't call them, of course, but I enjoyed the flash of panic in the old man's eyes as I left.

IV

Circle and Wye

The first time I saw Kerry Lasky she was mapping my body with a charcoal pencil. I'd been life modelling for extra cash back then, before Maisie started to take care of things. I was going to need a vocation now. The weekend following my summit with the Dean, we sat in my flat at Fore Street; Kerry regarding me as she had back when, with scarlet cheeks.

'They threw you out?' she spluttered. 'Seriously? No one's thrown out; you'd have to kill someone and even then they'd probably give you a second chance.' Kerry had a way of empathising that few understood. 'Can't you appeal? You've got a year to go, they can't do this, can they?'

'They can and they have,' I said. 'I have nothing to show for the last year, it's all gone, so I can't go on and even if I could, my alleged conduct breaches the code we signed when accepting our place. In other words, unless they have a change of heart and invite me to return, perhaps because Maisie has a pang of conscience and decides to confess on the same day Trevenna hangs himself for molesting his secretary, I'm fucked.' Kerry huffed, as though planning an assault on the three little pigs.

Instead of swine there was Robin Eep. Robin the great painter, Robin the sculptor of wireframe faces; Robin, who once bound a couple of dining chairs with masking tape and called it a study in dualism. Robin: Kerry's occasional bedmate. He was studying the TV.

'Your problem is that you let other people control the situation,' he said. 'Why would you allow that? I wouldn't.'

I reached across and turned off the television, silencing Peter Falk. His indomitable pursuit of Louis Jourdan had reached its apex, with the latter's food critic wearing a forlorn expression that mirrored mine.

'I was enjoying that,' said Robin.

'We've both seen it a hundred times,' I said.

'Turning off *Columbo*,' said Kerry with mock solemnity, 'things must be serious.'

I collapsed into my armchair. Kerry had burned some incense. The smell masked the damp odour but couldn't hide the peeling walls. I liked my little home on Fore Street, I liked the inelegance and its agedness, but now I had nothing else.

'Oh New,' said Kerry, 'if you drank I'd offer you a drink.' Kerry called me New; a sign she respected my art. Robin, who was keen that no ego be built higher than his own, made a point of sticking to 'Keir'.

'If I drank I'd need one,' I said. Kerry smiled. Robin patted my arm.

'Chin up,' he said, 'you don't need the school, anyway.'

'You should have seen the look in the old man's eyes,' I said, 'fear, jealousy, disgust – it was all there. He never wants to see me again.'

'But we do,' said Kerry, 'c'mon, we're the Circle, aren't we? Indivisible.' The Circle was the name Robin had given our little group. It was nice to belong to something and better than being a square.

'Perhaps this is your chance to get started on your novel,' said Robin, reaching to the wall and disdainfully fingering my collection of battered books and so-called cult movies. Pulling out a DVD case, he saw Roger Corman's name and pushed it back quickly.

'What novel?' I said.

'Didn't you say you wanted to write, that you had material?'

'No, I said I'd love to write but I have no material.' None I could use, anyway. Behind me the kettle was boiling. 'Perhaps I should earn the expulsion,' I said. 'I could burn the place to the ground with those hypocrites inside.' It was a joyful little fantasy and for a moment I allowed it to play in my head. I saw a storeroom door turned to splinters by my boot, a grab of flammables and the dousing of surfaces. I saw a match head ignite, a wall of flame, metal yawning and splitting, wood blackening, canvases bubbling, blistering busts – improved by the burn, and in the midst of it all, amongst the roar of the flames and the violent dance of orange and yellow, two writhing figures, one decrepit, his chicken skin crackling, the other thrashing, yelling, a hand shielding each of her faces; faces transmogrifying into charcoal.

'OK, you provoked them,' said Kerry, the words awkward in her mouth like broken teeth, 'and you shouldn't have gone anywhere near Maisie, women like that are poison, but they can't do this to you for fuck's sake.' I liked Kerry when she was animated and indignant like this, so I liked her most of the time. It's likely she was born righteous. She was unburdened by shyness, unsoiled by doubt. She was a rich tapestry of colour from her auburn bed hair to her ankle-length indigo coat. I loved to look at her and she knew it. God knows what she saw in a nihilist like Robin.

Robin's hand had been stuck to a bottle of ginger wine for close to an hour. Having diluted what remained with his saliva, he now reached out and tried to force it into mine.

'Break your embargo and have a bit of this,' he said, 'it may loosen you up.' Those who didn't drink were ridiculous to Robin, like people who thought their automatous pets could understand them.

'No, I don't think I will,' I said. The ornate bottle was left on the coffee table. It looked expensive, better than Robin's usual gut rot. I heard the flick of the kettle switch and jumped up to stew my tea.

'The school would have to act if you had evidence Maisie was screwing around with the students,' said Kerry, 'you can't be the only one.' I stopped stirring. It's not that Maisie cheating was a ridiculous idea, there was no point pretending otherwise. But she and I had been so *involved*, there didn't seem to be room for anyone else.

'I'd know if she was seeing someone,' I said. Robin looked at his toes.

'Would you?' said Kerry. 'Really? It's not as if you were living together or in each other's pocket twenty-four seven. She managed to keep you secret for what, two years? I mean, sure, some suspected but nobody *knew*, New. If she could do that, couldn't she be keeping someone else?'

'Kez, you'll upset the delicate balance of Keir's mind,' said Robin, reaching for his bottle.

'But it's possible,' said Kerry. It was indeed possible,

but the thought made my hand quiver as I lifted the teabag from the mug.

'I think you should follow her,' said Kerry, 'you know, at a discreet distance. See where she goes. See who she meets.'

'Stalk her, that's a great idea,' said Robin, 'you could infiltrate her bedroom, upholster yourself so you look like the furniture, and wait. Who knows what you'll find out? If you're lucky, she'll sit on you.' Kerry frowned at Robin and I took the opportunity to laugh, though I'd already decided that a little jaunt around town wouldn't do any harm.

'Well we'll see,' I said, 'but I have to re-enrol somehow, there's no way in hell my parents would understand this. No way.'

'I wouldn't even think about going back,' said Robin, enjoying himself. 'You made your point, they got it – leave it there. The school doesn't make you an artist. It's either in you or it's not. It can be directed but it can't be taught.' This was typically reductive stuff from him; I was being invited to disagree, to say something about cultivated intelligence, about peers. I skipped over the trap.

'What are you doing there, then?' I said.

'The place has resources,' said Robin, 'facilities. I need a space.'

'Well so do I; I need a lot of space.'

'Knowing when to back away from a bad situation is crucial,' said Robin, 'think about the hassle you've already had, think about having to bump into Maisie every day. Now I think of it, remember Wye Stammers?' Kerry coughed, like she'd inhaled a particle of Magda Goebbels.

'Wye Stammers?' I said.

'Oh you must remember him,' said Robin. 'Wye me? The guy who could make a wolf nervous? He was obsessed with rooks – he drew hundreds of the bloody things. He'd bolt from a room, sometimes mid-conversation.'

'I have no idea who you're talking about,' I said.

'Well anyway,' said Robin, 'everyone thought he was lonely; desperate for a bit of attention.' The storyteller sat upright. 'But there was nothing to the guy. Not a bad bloke if you found yourself trapped with him on the bus and forced him to talk, but missing something. He was a world away. Anyway, one day he invents a mental health crisis.'

'We don't know he invented it,' said Kerry, 'he was probably a bit disturbed.'

'Nah,' said Robin, 'he needed a little human interest. I don't think he was ready to go to uni. By all accounts he was fine to start with but rapidly went off after a few weeks of term. He was probably depressed. So he goes online and tells people he's suicidal. Seriously man, he went for it – "I'm desolate, I have no purpose, I can't escape my demons", all this shit.'

'He wasn't right,' said Kerry, 'he wouldn't approach me.'

'Right,' said Robin, 'and Kerry gets on with everyone.' Not you, I thought, not initially. Declaring her to be his muse had made the difference. She never asked for proof. Vanity needs none, I suppose.

'What he imagined would happen,' Robin went on, 'is that people would come online and say, "Are you OK? Can I help?" and a few people did, he pushed the buttons of some who, like him, were loners and didn't mind being co-opted into the fantasy, because it's a connection I suppose.

But many more smell a rat. They're like, "do it, you decide when, fuck this life!" It was brutal.

'So what starts as trolling becomes a campaign, basically. Wye's getting the interest, only unfortunately it's all centred on one idea: that he should top himself. So eventually he buckles, right – he's had maybe a hundred calls to kill himself a day for a fortnight, so taking the fantasy to what I suppose is its next logical stage, he says "I'm going to do it, on the bridge, Saturday, midday" – he actually makes a social media event out of it.'

Kerry shook her head, recalling the incident with less relish.

'He invites people,' said Robin, 'you must remember this, Kerr.' I waved him on. 'So anyway, the day comes and I suppose he thought, despite being trapped in this performance, no one would take it seriously, and that maybe, the only people who'd turn up would be the genuinely concerned – people who'd pull him back, take him under their wing and say, "It's OK Wye, stick with us, you'll be all right", but on the day hundreds come – I mean, it's like a summer parade or something, and there he is, the idiot, nervously perched on the bridge, with people chanting, "jump, jump, jump!" They're actually daring him to vault into the river, and believe it or not he jumps! He goes in!

'Now I don't know, I'm not a shrink, but it's pretty obvious he believed, even then, that he'd be OK, that someone would pull him out and that by jumping he'd prove he meant it. But if you're going to jump into a river, you better think about the current. We'd had a week of storm-force weather, I mean gales and torrents, and he was literally swept away – I mean, gone, just like that. There wasn't even time to toss someone in after him. They pulled him from the bank near the Latch Key a couple of hours later. Dead.'

Kerry bit her nails.

'It was awful,' she said, 'just awful. Don't you remember it, New?'

'No, I don't remember it at all,' I said. 'Anyway, how can anyone know what goes on in someone's mind? You assume it was a stunt but maybe he wanted to die.'

'I don't think so,' said Robin.

'You don't know,' I said.

'All right,' said Robin, 'why, no pun intended, did he take his watch off before he jumped? They found it neatly laid out on the bridge stones.'

'Rob,' I said, 'it's a charming story, but how does it help me?'

Robin smirked. 'OK, here's the moral,' he said, 'the only reason Stammers is dead is because he became trapped in his own snare. He didn't know when to cut and run. He should have gone his own way. It's the only allegory I've got, so try to project your circumstances on to it.' Robin would have been happy for me to give up, of course. Like a young Gore Vidal, a little piece of him died whenever his friends were successful.

'There but for the grace of God, go Wye,' I said. Robin smirked. I turned to Kerry, hoping the joke had lightened her mood, but she was a world away with her thoughts.

V

Artless

A while ago I discovered that if you stood at a certain angle to the art school, perilously close to the cliff edge, you could get a direct line of sight into Maisie's office. She was high up by request, to enjoy the ocean panorama. But this meant looking in required putting distance between you and the granite edifice and there wasn't far to go until the grounds of the school gave way to a precipitous drop; a fall that famously claimed the founder's daughter back in the 1920s.

I'd been standing there for aeons, the wind high and circling, and felt vulnerable, as though a sudden gust would send me to the rocks at any moment. Worse, there was nothing to see. She'd been sitting in view of her window all day, occasionally breaking off to talk to visitors, but no one of consequence. You didn't need to be in the room to see how dry the exchanges were; each visitor looked robotic. As the temperature dropped and the futility of the exercise became acute with the cold, the compulsion to be in that room, talking to her myself, became all-consuming.

Hard stepping the school corridors, I thought about my situation. I had to fix it, else life would become cheap and grey. I couldn't go back to that. Ascending the staircase to Maisie's bolthole, I imagined the next life – meandering around, knocking into people, rubbing up against situations, powerless. I'd been so certain of the future, I knew its shape and texture, but now I couldn't see it, just the entrance to my ex-lover's room. Her name, proudly displayed with her pompous title, built a stock of anger that forced the door. Maisie was at her desk. She looked up from a document.

'Oh,' she said, taking a long breath, 'I wondered when you'd come. Are you here to finish me off? There's a first time for everything.'

'Hello,' I said. It felt measured, an adult opener. We could be adults, couldn't we?

'I'm busy, Keir,' said Maisie, regarding a document, 'so say whatever you need to say, then go.'

I tried to modulate the tone of my voice but the adrenaline added a quiver, like an invisible agent had plucked my vocal cords.

'I need your help,' I said, vulnerability thought to be a good option, 'I need to come back and I think you owe me.' Her face fell and kept on falling.

'You try to humiliate me,' she said, 'undermining everything I'm doing here, turning me into a bit of lewd tittle-tattle, and you think I owe you something? What could I possibly owe you?'

'Your job,' I said. The words were two blows from a ball-peen hammer. She dropped her paper. 'I could have pulled the trigger with Trevenna,' I went on, 'I could have gone into details that would have shaken the false teeth out of the old man, the kind of things that only a real lover and not some student fantasist would know, but I didn't, I saved you. I gave them an out, and they swept me away and waved you through, so yes, you owe me, you owe me another chance.'

Maisie laughed. It wasn't the endearing chuckle I'd grown to love, rather pointed, shrill.

'My hero,' she said. 'There I was, thinking you'd tried to get a little childlike revenge, only to pull back when you realised no one would believe you, but no, you were looking out for me. Aren't you a sweetheart? Well thanks for thinking of me, gallantly intervening so I can continue to do the job I worked fucking hard for. Perhaps now you'll piss off and let me get on with it.'

'What am I supposed to do?' I said. 'Where am I supposed to go now? I can't go home, you know that.' My background had always been intrusive to Maisie. Rare cameos in conversation had been met with a quick change of subject, or a dismissive line like, 'Would it really be the end of the world?'

'For my father, yes,' I said. 'What you have to understand is that my dad's need for a drink isn't an endearing yet incidentally ruinous little vice. He *drinks*. Can you understand what it's like to live in a house with a functioning alcoholic? Watching the moment, around the same time each day, when the poison he's been tipping down him since lunchtime finally kicks in. The eyes become heavy, there's a certain sluggishness, the speech slurs, and then comes that little edge to the voice, the bite. Then Mother looks over to me. Because I'm the comfort. If I meet the stratospheric expectations placed upon me, there's the possibility of deliverance – a better future. If not, there's nothing.'

Maisie looked past me to the wall clock behind. She'd heard this speech before, though had never listened.

'Keir,' said Maisie, picking up her document, 'what

27

you do and where you go is your business. No one forced your hand here, no one ever does. You just can't help yourself. You have to take people on. Well actions have consequences.' My future was in the balance and all she had to offer was fortune cookie fare. Hands that had long turned to fists came down on her desk. She got to her feet.

'All right, that's it – go, please,' she said. I leaned into her.

'Taking people on as you put it, not holding back, that's what makes me a great artist – it's the will to challenge. It's the reason I'm here. I can't go back to being a spectator; I can't just consume. I have to create. I came here to do a job. I have to finish it. Otherwise there's nothing for me. It's oblivion, understand?'

She pushed her way past me, throwing open the door and gesturing for me to step through it.

'Goodbye, Keir.' Teacher was dismissing me yet again.

'Listen,' I said, holding out a hand, 'I'm lost, Maisie. I don't know how to do anything but this. Even if you hate me, this is my life. It took a lot for me to get here. More than you know, actually. This can't be it.'

She studied me. The grip on the door handle didn't falter, however. In her hardened expression I thought I detected a moment's sympathy, a flash of maternal concern.

'I don't decide if you get to come back,' she said finally, 'and I can't see you if you do. But destroying that work, great work, that's going to count against you. You pissed in the font, you know that, right? I hope for your sake you have something else; something you could present to the appeal board in September. Maybe they'd give you a hearing, if you're all you're cracked up to be.'

'Trevenna will never give me a chance without a good word from you,' I said, 'you know that.'

'He's retiring,' said Maisie. 'April Zuccaro's taking over. You don't know that because nobody does yet. April likes you, always did, and fortunately for you she was on sabbatical when you put up that misogynist monstrosity of yours, so perhaps she'll be disappointed, but she'll only be hearing about it second hand. If you experiment with being humble, the way you can be when you forget to perform, you could charm her. You can say you had an episode. She's a sucker for an artist's breakdown. She's had her share.'

This, I realised, was as good as it was going to get. It was time to go.

'If you can't go home,' she said, as I meandered to the doorway, 'stick around, earn some money and work on your portfolio. Then maybe you have a chance. Make it good though, Keir. I mean, the best you've ever done, you understand?'

'And what about...' I mouthed the word 'us'; a model of discretion. I was in the corridor now.

'Forget it,' she said, lowering her voice, 'forget it or it's going to leave a mark. Just know that if it does I won't be the one crying over it. I won't be lonely. You're playing to an empty hall now. Get off the stage.'

I watched the door close.

VI

Petra

Believe that my talk with Maisie dissuaded me from following her. It felt pointless after that. The logic of regrouping, rebuilding my portfolio, earning some change, seemed inescapable. Pitching to April Zuccaro, a woman I knew to be human, whatever that meant, felt like a pretty good idea. My belle was right on the specifics; April liked me, she laughed at what she assumed to be jokes, and better yet she had a history of mental instability. If I could get in a room with her sometime soon, a salvage operation was on the cards. I was contemplating this, standing next to Lau's Chinese on the Causeway, enjoying the breeze and taste of seaweed, when Maisie honed into view.

She looked like the sirens you saw on plates in the town's tourist shops, drawing the eye with nautical blues and greens. Better still her hair was damp, as though she'd stepped from the shower minutes earlier. I watched her from the safety of Lau's walk-up as she stopped to check for something – a piece of paper from her coat's inside pocket, perhaps a spell to entice sailors, then pause to complete whatever thought had crystallised in her mind.

She pulled her hair from behind her shoulder and brought the length down over a conspicuous nipple, brushing it with her hands. I'd seen the tick many times but never accompanied by such unquenchable carnal yearning. Temporarily drunk, I almost forgot to follow her, but now a terrible thought crowned. Kerry's warning, that if Maisie kept me for a couple of years then why not someone else, punched me in the gut. She and I had our fixed days; times passed off as regular appointments. Today, Saturday, wasn't one of them. As Maisie moved down the thoroughfare, jostling for position amongst the summer visitors, I was compelled to keep pace. Could she be meeting someone? The weakest part of me needed to know.

Keeping both a discreet distance and firm eye on my quarry was hard work. The interlopers, fresh from the branch line train and nearby holiday village, imposed the city discomfort of bunched and rubbing humanity on the narrow street; a channel designed for meandering fishermen and their carthorses.

In winter it was possible to stand alone on the same cobbles and hear the howl of the coastal gale pass between the Regency houses and their granite stone successors, the odd empty beer can rolling in stops and starts along the gutter. But this was a morning when the disorientating din from figures weaving behind and in front of Maisie, as she banked on to Teetotal Street, drowned out everything bar the cry of the gulls and the splutter from the endangered minibus.

Once I'd navigated the turn, the line of people thinned out. I was forced to slow my pace as Maisie slowed hers. Crossing to the other side of this tiny artery, I stuck to my line of shops – the identikit galleries, the tourist dives; the town eating itself – ready to duck into one at a moment's notice should she turn around. A few more yards and she finally stopped, once again fishing out her little slip of paper. I slid into an adjacent entrance way, looking through the convex window that lined the passage to the street beyond. Maisie pocketed her slip and took a sudden turn, gliding into the shop opposite. A second later I was back on the street, taking position in front of it, lining up to get a good look at the place, when I felt a strong and familiar hand on my shoulder.

'Why, hello there,' said Robin, 'fancy bumping into you here.' Did I look as vexed as I felt? Probably.

'Where the hell did you come from?' I said. 'I can't really talk, I'm in the middle of something.'

'You look like you're standing in the street to me,' he said, pulling a brown bag from one of his long coat's bottomless compartments. 'Fudge?' He held out the goodies. 'You've got to try this, I got it from Christie's, it's incredible.'

'I'm following Maisie,' I said, 'she's across the way.' Robin laughed.

'Oh for God's sake, Keir,' he said, 'I'm sure Kez was kidding and if she wasn't, she should have been. What are you expecting to see, some Kit Musculature-type emerge and start groping her in the street? Did she ever touch you in the street?' Robin knew the answer.

'We never had weekends,' I said, 'never. I've known the woman two years and I have no idea what she does with her downtime.'

'Or who,' said Robin, biting off a corner of fudge. 'Are you sure you don't want a bit of this?' I turned desperately towards the shop.

'Robin, please,' I said, 'she may come out at any moment.' He looked across the street.

'She may have slipped out while we've been talking, do you want me to take a look?' I nodded. Robin drifted across the road, feigning amusement and pretending to tiptoe. He looked through the shop's window, making exaggerated head movements, only to swing around with mock disappointment. 'She's not in there,' he said.

'What?' I moved to join him, checking the façade of the Victorian shop front beyond. 'In Vino Veritas' was brilliant burgundy, a wine joke no doubt, and the name was proudly displayed on the masthead in a calligraphic font. It was unlike any of the pastiches on the high street. It had, dare I say, character. I peered through the window. A sign, 'STAFF WANTED', made it hard to see past an incomplete pyramid of bottles, but eventually only the silhouette of a female figure behind a crimson curtain was discernible. Without needing to take a second look, I knew it wasn't Maisie's. I'd lost her.

'Don't worry,' said Robin, 'she probably didn't see you.'

'It hardly matters,' I said, 'I was being ridiculous. I barely know what I'm doing any more.'

'Perhaps it wasn't a wasted experience,' said Robin, 'look' – he pointed to the sign – 'they need staff, you need money. It's not a bad place this, I've bought the occasional bottle from them, you could do worse.' I must have grimaced because he went on, 'Look, it's the beginning of the season, they'll need people. Anyway, the company wouldn't be too bad, take a look.' He motioned with his head towards the window. I turned to see a girl's backside gently pressed against the glass. A moment later the rump was retracted and replaced with a bangled hand that placed a final bottle on top of the pyramid display. I moved a little closer and watched as the figure disappeared behind the bloody partition. The shadow of the retreating form became more opaque as the body between the curtain and the light source behind it withdrew, becoming diffuse, finally fading to nothing.

'I'll see you later,' I said, giving Robin his cue. The door to the wine shop was glass with a wire mesh protecting its surface. A poster depicting Parisian caricatures quaffing what I now know to be cheap table wine, welcomed punters. A handwritten sign above the threshold warned them to 'Mind the step.' I went inside.

The interior of the shop was a curious assault on the senses. As the door clunked behind me, the mesh rustling against the glass, I stepped up into a world suffused with sawdust and resin. The wood floor was covered in the former while the latter rose from the varnished counter that ran along the shop's right flank, ending where the curtain began. That was as far as customers went. The left of the shop, from the door to the halfway mark, was divided into giant cells. This manmade honeycomb housed specially selected wines. Each came with a long strip of card on to which someone, the same someone who'd scribbled the 'Mind the step' warning, had ineloquently written out some tasting notes. The first read 'Cape Longhorn Pinotage – a full and spicy delight that will liven up spaghetti bolognese.' I tried to imagine someone leaving their house focused on livening up spaghetti bolognese but couldn't.

The remaining bins, I now know them to be bins, alternated red and white until they gave way to mixed shelves. Some of the bottles that filled them were neatly spaced; others looked disturbed, groped then rejected.

Many of them had a plastic cardholder hanging off the bottleneck like a loose tie. There were a few lonely cards in place. I brushed the left flanking bottles with the tips of my fingers until, at the bottom of a far shelf, nested between two dusty whites, I saw Robin's favourite brand of ginger wine. I plucked it. The glass was embossed, old fashioned. An elegant product for a shop with a certain cachet. I wondered if Maisie came often. I'd take the risk.

I hadn't heard the movement of the curtain behind me. Now came the voice. 'You all right there? Can I help?'

I swung round. Her top half had a certain elegance, the fine lines incongruous with the potato and swede accent. She had a long neck, not quite the full swan but in competition, that cocked to check the shelf behind me. Eyes that were the colour of rock pools, with housing that was just a little frayed, like the beachhead, fell to the bottle in my hand. Waves of long hair, like those on the chalk drawings of mermaids you saw in the pubs, were hooked back behind her ears. As she did so I noticed yellow and brown tinges on the fingertips. I watched the bangle I'd seen in the window slip down her wrist. A tarnished wedding ring clung to her finger with such force that the surrounding skin looked pinched.

'I hope you can help,' I replied, a moment needed to recall the question. 'I see you're looking for people.'

'The sign never lies,' she said. And with that she walked over to a box of six bottles, dragging it off the counter and towards the bins.

'Well you might have got someone and forgotten to remove it,' I said. 'Are you the manager?'

'No no,' she said, 'not me – I'm just a humble servant.

The man you want is Ragesh. He's not here today; he's romancing his better half, lucky buggers. Do you want to drop in tomorrow?'

'I can do,' I said. She stood tiptoed, holding the box awkwardly with one hand while pulling out its contents with the other and pushing the heavy bottles to the back of the top shelf.

'Great,' she said, 'well I reckon you'll be OK, Radge is pretty easy going and he can teach you all the wine stuff if you don't know. When I came I only knew red and white.'

'You don't say.'

A moment later, without warning, she lost her footing, causing the remaining bottles to slip from their cardboard coffin and smash. The dark contents quickly mixed with the sawdust.

'Are you OK?' I hope I sounded sincere. I moved to help, but she waved me away as though taking a pot shot at a nuisance fly.

'I'm all right,' she said, 'I just slipped, I don't need a knight in shining armour, thanks.' Maroon faced, she steadied herself and surveyed the spill. The shop had an almost imperceptible tilt and the liquid had started to collect against the wall.

'Oh God,' she said, surveying the deep red puddle, 'looks like someone's been murdered, doesn't it?'

'OK, well as I'm here I'll take this bottle,' I said, now feeling obliged to buy something.

She tried not to look at the spillage as she started to run the purchase through the till.

'Don't worry,' she said, 'if you can do the hours, Radge will sort you out.' Was I worried? I didn't feel it.

'That's great,' I said. I watched her carefully as she quickly rolled my prize in paper, sliding the bottle into an open bag.

'If you could tell him I came in and I'll be here tomorrow, I'd appreciate it, I'm Ne- Keir. The name's Keir.'

Her embarrassment bled away, a wry grin taking its place.

'Are you sure?' she said. 'Sounds like you forgot it for a moment. I'm Petra. Definitely Petra.' She extended a hand.

Looking back, I don't recall if I shook it or not.

VII

Ragesh

That night my bed became a theatre of preternatural horrors. I struggled to sleep, my confused senses, addled by fatigue, tormenting my brain. I saw movement in the half-light, felt the mattress crawl and the touch of something smooth, like a cockroach shell, against my hair. The surrounding walls darkened, then swayed, marked by shadows I couldn't source. In time I slipped away and dreamed of Maisie. It was disjointed, spatially ridiculous, but there she was, interstitially present, nested between the darkened, cubist dimensions of what looked like the school, her partial face fluidly breaking off and mixing with the gloom like the mercurial globules trapped in a lava lamp.

Dreams of this kind have a long finish, they bleed into your day. The images had no anchor and no waking key, but I reasoned, throughout the uncanny morning that followed, that the unconscious was a kind of artist, conflating images and ideas, toying with structure and symbolism, in order to challenge the receiver, testing their wits. Nevertheless, the dream left my cuticles frayed. A couple bled. I felt this was the closest I'd get to knowing how it felt to be a woman followed home. I wondered how many nights like that were to come.

The aura of the dream lingered as I returned to In Vino

Veritas that afternoon. The air was superheated and humid from days of punishing sunshine, and the shop was equally stuffy, with no air conditioning to speak of. Things had changed since my last visit. Shelves that had been modestly populated were now full and the wine in those dedicated bins had been reordered into perfect rows, anticipating inspection. A fresh layer of sawdust had been applied to the floor, with eddies and other bristled patterns pointing to a fine-haired broom.

Petra wasn't there but the owner of the broom was; I found him crouched behind the counter, pushing a CD into the player nested beneath.

'I'll be with you in just a moment,' he said and propped the broom against the counter. 'Lisa Ciplinski, you a fan?'

'I don't believe I've had the pleasure,' I said.

'Ah, an incredible voice – vintage stuff this – late sixties, wait until you hear it. This is her album of Ruben Royer compositions. A perfect marriage of performer and songwriter. Royer's a poet, a wit. But Ciplinski's pipes, oh my God.'

The CD played and I had to agree, the orchestral bombast, the wry, sensual vocal – my host had a great ear.

'I like it,' I said, 'I can't believe I've never heard this, it's just my sort of thing.'

'A man of taste,' he replied.

He rose to his full height and I got a proper look at him for the first time. He was Asian, that is to say of Indian extraction, somewhere like that, and he was lean, not athletic but a man who looked like he went for a run from time to time. He was unpretentiously dressed in a faded T-shirt and grey tracksuit bottoms. I liked him immediately.

'At the risk of racially profiling you,' I said, 'I'm going to assume you're Ragesh? I'm here about the job.'

He smiled and fired back, 'Nah, I'm Rupert, Ragesh is in hospital – he's come down with lung fungus – got it from bats shipped over from the mother country.'

As I opened my mouth to offer a half-hearted apology, he said, 'No, just kidding, yes, I'm Radge. And you are?'

I laughed, a burst cut with embarrassment and relief. 'Keir – Keir Rothwell, I was talking to Petra yesterday, she told me to come in and have a chat with you.'

'Old Zeller, huh? Yeah, she's a good girl,' he said, 'she's spirited, you'll work with her a lot as there's only her and Fabian at the moment, well three of you once we've got you going. So what do you know about wine?' I knew it made people drunk, obnoxious – sometimes aggressive.

'I know what I like,' I said.

'Good answer,' said Ragesh. He re-clasped the broom and walked round to face me. 'Most people say "nothing" or "red and white", but it doesn't matter too much because provided you've got a mouth and a memory I can teach you the basics; enough to get the Great British Public through their mealtimes and breakdowns, anyway. You a student?'

Oh, the pathos.

'I was,' I said, 'well, hope to be again, I don't know yet – I studied Art up the road, mixed media – so I do painting, drawing, sculpture, film; I'm diverse.'

Ragesh's eyes narrowed.

'Hmmm, an artist – great, yeah, we can do something with that – we'll need the window decorated for the summer, as well as a few of the blackboards; that's not where Petra and Fabian's gifts lie, at least I don't think so, anyway – you said "was", "hope to be again", have you taken a year out, what?'

'They invited me to leave,' I said. Ragesh laughed.

'You were chucked out? How do you get kicked out of art school, did you paint the place puce?'

'Something like that,' I said, 'suffice to say I'm between ideas and need somewhere to lie low and make money while I work out how to make them see the error of their ways. I have to stick around. It's complicated.'

'Isn't it always?' said Ragesh, a warm smile on his face. 'Well this is definitely the right place for a man between ideas. Some of us have been between the ends of that dumbbell for some time. When can you start?'

'I'm not getting any richer, so how about now?' I said, and with a handshake the deal was done as Lisa Ciplinski's sardonic voice improved the air with the words, 'I turned my back on humanity, a dream that became a calamity.'

***

My induction into the world of wine was rapid, comprehensive (from the layman's point of view) and only occasionally interrupted by the imposition of customers. Ragesh did his best to get them in and out at speed, going as far as putting a bottle in the hands of those indecisive quaffers whose tastes were better known to Radge than to themselves, while others were palmed off with our special selections; the wines the owner had insisted on importing, perhaps because the shop and its sisters in St Ives and Perranporth had made a deal with the producer.

Ragesh kept me to himself initially, scheduling Petra

41

and Fabian to work on alternate days, fast-tracking my education in the tasting fundamentals. Lesson one: differentiating between wines 'wasn't all bollocks'. My tutor told me to taste with the whole of my trap, rather than 'flushing it down your throat'. He talked about a wine's tannins, bandying terms like 'mouthfeel' and 'body'. We discussed acidity and its machete-like ability to cleave through creamy sauces. We talked about colour, barrel aging, astringency, and the gamut of grape varieties, many of which sounded like alien planets – Pamid and Xinomavro being something you apparently put in your mouth, rather than terraforming for human colonisation.

My new boss was picky when it came to the bottles he took home. He preferred Burgundy to Bordeaux, and I was not to trust anyone who thought otherwise. When it came to sparkling wine, I was to champion traditional fermentation and reject the tank method. It didn't matter if I didn't understand the distinction. He did, and he knew what he was talking about. A Super Tuscan wasn't a comic book character, but something to be discovered. Dornfelder was Germany's dirty little secret and worth sharing, though only with the unstuffy and innocent. Self-anointed experts need never know.

Viticulture, Ragesh explained, was like sex; everyone thought they knew about it, but actually only a select few could make each encounter worthwhile. There were fewer masters of wine in the world than committed socialists, and chances are I'd never be one, not ever, unless I gave years of my life to the task and was prepared to subordinate everything to the will of Bacchus, the Roman God of Wine, whom my new boss professed to worship, twinkling eyes and mock genuflection included.

'You're a child of Bacchus now,' he told me. 'He alone chooses the customers. Each is a test of our knowledge. If we do well, we're rewarded with women and song. If we fail, it gets bloody. Anyway, the thing is to know enough to bluff.'

My education was spatial as well as technical. Ragesh believed that in order to serve the amorphous mass he called 'the punters', one had to be able to navigate the shelves, that rich mosaic of artwork, producer, appellation, region by another name, grape and price, with indomitable authority.

'Your job,' he said, 'is to match wine – perhaps to food, often to expectations. Sometimes it's about flavours, sometimes textures, other times you're looking to partner a bottle with a personality. How does the punter see themselves? Are they quirky, serious, self-important, easy-going? When you get it right they leave the shop with their bottled essence in a bag. They want a lifestyle guru. That's why they come here. If they want a drink, they go to the off-licence.'

Ragesh wanted to know more about me. His interest seemed sincere, not the scooping up of biographical bits to form judgements, so I played along and gave him the unclassified parts: my career suicide, Maisie's soft deviance (and other euphemisms), destroying my work, *End of Termagant*, Trevenna. My new boss looked shocked in some places, amused in others. They were all the right places.

'You and the sacred lacquer have much in common, young man,' he said, going on to explain that like my art career, wine had once been ravaged by the machinations of a parasite. In wine's case a louse called phylloxera temporarily threatened to make Europeans teetotal. A cure of sorts was eventually discovered: the grafting of an unpalatable foreign root to the diseased vine, thereby protecting it from annihilation. When I asked how that helped me, Ragesh said, 'I haven't a clue.' He was compelling, like a great game of cards.

Late into my induction he found me hunched across the counter, glum and munching on a bag of Mason's, the gourmet peanuts we used to tempt decadent punters. My finger circled the Gamay grape on a chart of varietals mocked up to look like the periodic table. Normally I'd have straightened up, tried to look busy, but maybe I wanted to hear the inevitable question.

'What's up, young man?' he said. 'You're miles away.'

'This is the only chance I've had to think of late,' I said, 'and most of what there is to think about is pretty ugly.'

'You've got the greatest shop job in the world,' he said, 'what more do you want?'

'I want Maisie,' I said. 'I feel stupid saying it – childlike, actually, but I can't help it. She's the only thing that's mattered to me for a long time. To make matters worse, half of me is standing here, hoping she'll walk in – just so I can talk to her. The other half dreads it in case she comes with some lunk. I followed her here, you know. That's how I found the place.'

Ragesh was silent for a moment. 'I don't know her by name,' he said, 'is that the reason you're here?'

'No,' I said, 'well – maybe that got me through the door, but no, I promise you I want the job – I need it.' My new boss smiled.

'Everyone's shacked up with the wrong person at some point,' he said, 'your perfect woman could walk through those doors tomorrow.' I thought of Maisie as she once was – warmer, gentle; the paradox who made me feel human while hiding me like a stash of sticky porn.

'I hope so,' I said.

Ragesh smiled. 'I haven't known you long,' he said, 'but I'd say you were wise beyond your years, and wise people usually work out a way to make things better.'

I couldn't remember the last time I'd felt consoled. That made the moment more poignant somehow.

'I'm not wise,' I said, my eyes watering, 'just battle hardened. And tired.'

'Give yourself a break,' said Ragesh, 'you're a good guy, things will work out for you.' I tried to smile.

'Yes,' was all I could manage.

★★★

Ragesh was the best boss I could have hoped for under the circumstances. His unassuming manner and apparent sincerity alchemised platitudinous bullshit, turning it into a philosophy I could buy in to. 'This job is about graft', 'always let the dog see the rabbit' – greetings card stuff but I lapped it up. I needed it.

More than that, in those first shifts, he built me up. He made me feel like I was more than a prop behind the counter. He took me seriously. A few days in, he caught me meandering around, filling quiet periods by straightening rows of bottles, taking a breakage to the back office graveyard, the necropolis beyond the red curtain, to join those smashed by Petra the week before, even sweeping the floor with what I imagined to be a dead stare. We had a fateful conversation.

'I'm sorry it's so quiet,' he said, 'I did Monday in here with old Zeller and it was non-stop, I don't understand it. I want you to meet the regulars. We get them all in here – the mad and the bad, even the police.'

'The police?'

'Oh yeah, there's a detective who comes in every now and again, a real character – he's great fun. He's told me a few stories. It's a small town but you'd be amazed what goes on.'

'Well I'll look forward to meeting him,' I said, feeling an ache in my chest – creeping heartburn.

'Listen,' said Ragesh, 'I may have a little job for you if you're interested?'

'Sure,' I said, glad of the change of subject, 'what do you need?'

Ragesh motioned to the lines of bottles. 'Now you see those?' he said. 'What do you notice about them?' I surveyed the shelves. They were, to my untrained eye, unremarkable.

'They're a façade,' I said, 'if I get too close I'll notice it's wine bottle wallpaper?'

'No, sadly those bottles are there, we need to sell them,' he said, 'the problem is they're not labelled up – they don't have tickets, you follow?'

'Not really, no.'

'Well in the box below the counter you'll find old cards for the bottle necks, wine tickets we call them. Anyway, most just have the wine, price and a generic description on them; we pull the details from the guide if we're not sure.' I looked behind the counter and sure enough a crumbling book was wedged between some old CDs. It was ancient according to the date on the broken spine.

'Do the descriptions change much?' I said.

'Nope,' said Radge, 'they're pretty consistent, but there's no substitute for first-hand tasting notes. One year may be better than another, yes?' Looking around I could see that half the bottles were ticketless.

'You're a creative sort of bloke,' he went on, 'articulate, erudite I dare say, and I reckon you're imaginative, being an artist and all, so here's the deal. I want you to write descriptions for each wine. Take your time, consult the guide if you need to, we'll taste a few, within reason, obviously, we can't take the piss, but I want you to entice the punters with a bit of sparkling prose. Really draw them in. You up for it?'

Oddly enough I was.

'Won't Petra and Fabian want to do some?' I said, anticipating the answer. Ragesh affected to clear his throat, as though suppressing a chortle.

'They do a few,' he said, 'but they'd rather drink it than write about it, you with me? It shows, unfortunately. I need something that will grab the punter by the throat. I want you to get them thinking about the wine, surprise them, make their eyes bulge.'

This was a pleasing image.

'Surprise them?' I said. 'I think I can oblige.' And that afternoon, with Ragesh ferrying stock from the cellar to the shelves, I blew the dust off the wine guide, considered my quarry and got to work.

VIII

The Three Tests

Petra Zeller was laughing in her way, using her nose and throat to pass incredulous gas. She throttled the neck of an Italian white, the Mondovani Pinot Grigio, and read its new description, first with a scowl, as though inspecting a mangled limb, then with an explosion of indiscriminate laughter. She turned to me and said, 'Are you serious?'

'Always,' I said.

She read aloud from the card. 'With a flavour that's opaque, like the best people, a wine on to which you project your sensory fantasies, like a thalidomide child complaining of pain in the fingertips, it's little wonder that Pinot Grigio is the people's wine – it's whatever you and your uncultivated friends want it to be: another winner from the birthplace of fascism.

'I repeat,' said Petra, 'are you serious?'

'According to the guide it doesn't taste much of anything,' I said, 'only the Pinot Gris – the New Zealand stuff – or the Alsace version brings out the grape's flavour.'

'Are you autistic or something?' she said, her voice spiking. 'We have to sell it, you cock.' Was that the aim?

'Look,' I said, 'the old tickets were dry as dust. This one's true.'

'It insults the people most likely to buy the wine,' protested Petra.

'Do you really think it will make any difference?' I said, moving to stand in front of the shelf holding the bulk of my new tickets. 'I've been here over a week now and I've sold more of that than anything else. It's bomb proof. We could say it was a cancer risk and still sell out every weekend. It probably is a cancer risk, actually.'

Petra was inspecting the shelves, arching her long neck to get a look at the cards behind me. I watched as she silently counted the number of new entries. How many were there, she wondered – thirty, forty? In fact, during a quiet week with Ragesh, in which he'd kept the public occupied while I scribbled away at the far end of the counter, I'd managed a half-century. I'd written until my wrist ached.

'Jesus Christ,' she said, 'are they all like this?'

'If you mean, are they written in the same style, yes,' I said. 'Radge wants the whole shop done. He wants me to write the tickets. I'm just keeping myself interested. There are only so many variants on "redolent of cherry" and "oak notes" you can write before your hand issues a fatwa against your brain. Radge wanted them to stand out. They stand out. The guide is dry, dull. These aren't dull.'

Petra was pulling out bottles now. Holding them as if she'd picked up a dead rat by its tail. She read from another card – Garson's Zinfandel Blush, late of California.

'When you think of great wine your mind turns to France, New Zealand, Lew Zealand and maybe the other Muppets, but don't forget about California, the region that's cornered the market in sweet wine that coats the nostrils with the smell of an old tyre yard. Don't leave your wine snobbery at home, bring it here and exchange it for a bottle of this fruity, saccharine swill. Not dry, not a dessert wine – it doesn't really know what it is. Perhaps you'll decide and tell us.'

Petra left the bottle out of place, precariously balanced on the edge of the shelf. My muscles tensed. She plucked another and read the ticket aloud, her tone aping a teacher trying to humiliate a child by sharing their sub-standard homework with the rest of the class, deputising the kids as bullies.

'The Deed, Malbec, South Africa,' she began, pausing to study my face as I tried to recall what I'd written. She waited for a nod and continued, 'South Africa atones for apartheid with this glorious wine, unashamedly made from crushing dark skins underfoot.'

'Indeed,' I said.

'You're kidding, right?'

'No.'

'Anyway,' I said, 'wouldn't you buy that, based on that description?'

'No,' she replied, 'I might wonder about the person who wrote it!'

'Well I'm giving the punters a little more credit,' I said. 'I'm going to assume they'd like something interesting to read for a change. Radge must be such a man, because he said they were fine.'

'He saw this one?' she said, suspicious, 'and the one about an old tyre yard?'

'He read plenty,' I said, 'and looked happy.'

She carelessly stowed the bottle in its nook. 'I'd just be careful is all, people may not get your unique brand of wit.'

'Oh, but you get it, right?' I waited with mock expectation, the question lingering like a flatulent episode.

'Sure,' she replied finally, 'but I'm not the one you have to worry about,' and with that she retreated to the back office.

'I'm not so sure,' I said, addressing my chest.

The curtain rustled again and Fabian Stroud emerged. He was graceful, moving with great precision, his carriage stiff, his clothes bound to him like a second skin. This was my inaugural shift with the three of us and Fabian had made me feel welcome by flaying the skin from my face with his curiously large cat's eyes on first meeting, then spending most of the morning cocooned in the cellar.

'And what were the two of you gassing about?' he said, his voice fluid and fruity, as though constituted from our discounted summer wine.

'The new wine descriptions,' I said, 'Petra was just saying how pleased she was with them.'

'Really?' said Fabian. He rubbed his glistening hands together; the moisturised remains of a back office grooming.

'Have you read any of them?' I asked.

'Yes,' he replied. Any hope that he'd deign to comment further soon evaporated. In silence, he moved buoyantly across the shop floor. I smiled as I remembered Radge describing him as 'a panther on its hind legs'. Radge had undersold my new colleague.

'You and Petra becoming fast friends?' he said at last, straightening the bottles she'd replaced.

'She's a character,' I said, 'full of vim.' He chortled.

'Lovely girl,' he said, 'doesn't know a thing about wine, but she's very gregarious with the customers, they respond to that. You know, the ones that value that sort of thing.'

'But you don't?' I said, sensing an opening. His pointed face turned to mine.

'What's important is knowing what you're talking about,' he said flatly, 'that's what the serious customers appreciate. We don't have many of those here, of course, but I grin and bear it; one day I expect to be dealing with a more exclusive clientele.'

'Oh?' I said. 'You plan to work in Truro?'

He grimaced. 'London, dear boy; a firm like Berry Brothers. Somewhere distinguished. A place where one can sell sparkling wine to connoisseurs; people who appreciate the craft, rather than students vying for a decadent piss up.' And with that he continued to fiddle with the bottles, pushing them, pulling them, twisting them this way and that, the remainder of the hour turning in silence.

★★★

I was alone on the shop floor when he came. His face is so familiar to me now, it's hard to remember a time when it was anonymous, just another punter meandering between shelves. But this one was different somehow. I knew it from that first moment.

He was in his late thirties, but had the buoyancy of a man my age. He seemed to hop from bin to bin, barely making an impression on the sawdust carpet. He was lithe in every sense, and his movement triggered a half-forgotten memory of a character I'd seen illustrated in a book as a child. He was vibrantly dressed; and although looking like a guest at a country house, trumped stuffiness. He might have been an earl's incorrigible nephew. He arched his head and stared at me.

'Good afternoon,' he said, with a voice cracked on Cornish coves, 'you're new, aren't you?'

'New Shockley, yes,' I was tempted to say, but didn't. Instead I smiled, enjoying the private joke. 'I am,' I said.

'What have you done with the others?' He was stone faced and a moment passed before he relaxed into a grin. I took my cue.

'They're out back,' I said, 'I'm Keir, can I help?' The visitor seemed to contemplate the question.

'Oh I'm OK,' he said, 'just browsing.' He began to turn to the shelves before changing his mind and swinging round. 'Have we met?' he said.

'Unless you've seen me in here, no,' I said. Now Petra emerged from behind the curtain. She glanced at the two of us, feigning shock.

'What have you done, Rothwell?' she said. 'Mr Murgatroyd, are you here to arrest him over his wine descriptions?' Murgatroyd, our visitor, laughed. Petra, turning to me and taking a moment to enjoy my confusion, said, 'Mr Murgatroyd's a detective, Keir. But mainly a lover of Northern Rhône, isn't that right, Mr Murgatroyd?'

'I can't deny it,' said Murgatroyd. Now he turned back to me. 'Keir Rothwell, that's your name? Now I'm sure I know you.' I saw Petra's eyes widen a little.

'Maybe you've seen some of his art,' she said, smirking. 'He used to be an artist.'

'I am an artist,' I said. 'It's something you are, not something you do,' and with that Murgatroyd, who'd been holding the waist of a bottle he'd almost subconsciously plucked from the shelf while we spoke, brought it down on the counter with near-shattering force.

'Of course, the art school!' he said. 'The attack that wasn't – that was you.' I tried to look relaxed, like I'd been recalled from a wedding reception, but Petra sensed my discomfort. 'I knew I'd heard the name recently – Keir, it's distinctive, there aren't many Keirs in Perrangyre, maybe none, except you, of course. But yes, Keir Rothwell, I know the name.'

'What's this?' said Petra.

'I destroyed my work,' I said, 'it was a kind of protest.'

'You did a little more than that,' said Murgatroyd, 'I spent the whole afternoon at that studio. We were treating it as a break-in and assault until a colleague of yours set us straight. Lucky she did. It looked like a cyclone had torn through that room. We found blood, all sorts.'

'I'd just used raw meat in something I was working on. I'm sorry to have wasted your time,' I said.

'Oh, it wasn't a waste,' he said, 'I got a little tour, got to see a few of the galleries. I didn't really understand much of it. I don't know a lot about art, but there were some great minds on show. It was the best violent scene I've been to, I think. But yes, the damage; you must have felt very strongly.'

'I did.'

'I hope you don't always get that angry,' he said, sliding the bottle towards the till, 'there's a lot of glass in here.' Petra was staring at me now.

'The destruction was part of the art,' I said, 'no anger involved.' Murgatroyd took the answer with an upturn of the mouth.

'Just that bottle then please,' he said. I put it through the till. He grabbed it without waiting to be offered a bag and extended a hand towards Petra. 'I'll see you again.'

'OK, bye bye,' said Petra, breezy and oblivious to the sudden atmosphere, 'don't forget to bring the cuffs for this one next time.'

'Let's hope that's not necessary,' said Murgatroyd, 'nice to put a face to a name, Keir – don't break anything.' And with that he was gone.

'Watch yourself,' said Petra, 'you'll be in his black book now.' I tried to stay composed.

'Was that really necessary? How the hell do you know about the school, anyway?'

'Radge told me,' she said, 'but he left the vandalism bit out. I hope you're not mental, it's bad enough taking it from the customers.'

'I don't want to be discussed, do you understand? My business is my business.'

'All right,' said Petra, 'calm down, we don't want another protest.'

'Does he come in a lot?' I said.

'Murgatroyd? Every now and again. Great name, don't you think? The first time Radge told me what he did, I thought he was kidding. He looks a bit flamboyant to be a plod. Appearances can be deceptive as they say,' and with that she returned to the cellar, leaving me to hope the detective's next visit would fall between my shifts.

Looking back on those first few weeks, I'm inclined to think I rode my luck. As time went on some increasingly overfamiliar faces could be seen ogling the tickets, regarding them at arm's length, but saying little. 'What does it mean, "The perfect partner for an Armitage shank"?' I'd explain it was a joke about vomiting. Or someone might ask, 'What is GCSE level enjoyment?' But it was easy to parry such questions, and as the days went on a sense of invulnerability began to build.

I surprised myself, caring more and more about the words scribbled on those small white cards, taken aback by the pride I felt as their numbers swelled – 100, 200, 300 – an entire shop written by me, my signature everywhere; a gallery had sprung up around us. I was starting to feel useful again, quietly getting off behind a fixed smile. Then, my luck changed.

It shouldn't have been me that day, that's the irony – tragedy – pick your word and nail it up. Ragesh had called me late in the afternoon. Rosa, his wife, had asthma; he needed to be at home. Could I cover? I could and so began an evening shift with a crestfallen Petra tethered to me for a third consecutive day. I don't do counterfactuals; they're fruitless, fictive, but I've thought about that shift a lot.

He'd darted in to escape the rain; a brooding beast, sodden from his unprotected head to his clomping feet. He swept globules from a poor mane of receding hair with swollen fingers, and the drops ran down and made their escape from the tips. He looked vulnerable, embarrassed, a man who needed more than a drink. The world had failed to snap into place for this sponge and he was furious.

We watched him creep from bin to bin, shivering, trying to find comfort in the shop's warm interior. He muttered, pulled clothes away from wet skin and tried to focus on the shelves, alert to us watching his every move. He touched a few bottles, pulled them out, surveyed the backs then replaced them. Finally, he stopped in front of a bottle of

Lakewater Special Reserve; a sparkling wine for a man who'd lost his spark. He stank of damp wool and spirit. I watched him read the ticket, I saw him hunch, and when at last he turned to us, his eyes heavy and face part-fallen, like he'd suffered a mini-stroke, I knew we were in trouble.

I looked at Petra. She was leaning forward on her stool. The tension seemed to have its own gravity, it was pulling her towards the visitor. I turned back to him, now with the Reserve in his hand. He was rereading the legend, 'Because you're special… and not in a mentally retarded sense either.' The words had percolated into his sodden consciousness. His mouth opened just slightly. A small pool had formed around his scuffed shoes. I deduced it wasn't urine from excessive mirth.

'What do you have to say about this?' he said.

'It's a lovely bit of sparkle,' offered Petra. I winced.

'I don't care if it's made of mermaid's tears,' he said, glaring at Petra, 'what do you have to say about this?'

'Just a joke I think,' said Petra. I felt sorry for her; I knew she had no idea what was written on the card. I opened my mouth to interject but he was already on her, moving closer. Petra was off her stool and backing away.

'Think this is funny, do you?' said Mr Rainstorm, breaking into a snarl. 'You won't when I slap that smile off your face.'

'That's it,' I said, 'you're out.' He turned to me.

'What?'

'You don't threaten my colleague, you're out. Off you go.' He was moving towards me now. The tip of Petra's thumb was clasped between her teeth.

'Did you write this?' he demanded.

'Yeah,' I said, 'I wrote it just for aggressive drunks like you. Glad you noticed, now off you pop.'

'You wanna see aggression?' he said, holding up the bottle, 'because this is a disgrace. I've got some aggression for the person who wrote this.'

'I'm willing to bet you've got some for everybody,' I said, 'women, kids, everyone you meet when you've had a few.'

'Keir, stop it!' said Petra. She turned to Mr Rainstorm. 'Sorry, you have to go or I'm calling the police.' Rainstorm stared at Petra.

'Shut your fucking mouth or you get this.' He waved the bottle at her.

'Man, you're an angry guy,' I said, 'what's wrong with you? It's not enough to be obnoxious, you've got to be a thug too? I just love your kind; you're all so obvious and useless. I hope you're sterilised. Are you sterilised?'

Petra had opened the door and was now shouting over the rain, ushering the soak towards the torrent.

Mr Rainstorm was squinting now, trying to punctuate his thoughts.

'Bring me the manager,' said our guest.

'I'm the manager,' I said. Petra shot me a look. She was wired; it was rather wonderful.

'You?' he said, lips upturned. 'I don't think so, you're twelve. Get him here, now, before I batter you.'

'You shouldn't assume it's a he,' I said, 'but in this case you're right, it's me, and I say the description you're holding is the best I've seen for that wine, so either buy it or piss off.'

'What did you just say to me?'

'I said buy it or piss off.' I now collapsed the distance between us. 'We've all been very impressed by your peacocking and as you see from my Cheshire Cat grin I'm absolutely petrified, except this is routine for me, I've dealt with people a lot more imposing than you, and I've been threatened before, it's no great shakes, you get used to it. What people like you never get used to, is what they get in return.'

He lurched towards me, bottle raised and Petra, showing hitherto hidden dexterity, vaulted across the shop floor and got between us, pushing him back towards the open door, demanding I retreat to the netherworld beyond the red curtain.

'You've got a smart mouth,' he bellowed at me, 'we'll see what you have to say when I come back and shut it.'

'In that event I doubt I'll be saying anything,' I said, 'the drink's a real logic killer, isn't it?'

He was in retreat now. He dropped the bottle, which didn't break, and allowed Petra to back him to the threshold, fixing his gaze on me as he went. As a prop that facilitated saving face, allowing Mr Rainstorm to withdraw, Petra was magnificent.

The sound of sweeping, violent rain filled the shop.

'I'll be seeing you again,' he said, pointing at me as Petra shepherded him into the storm.

'Excellent,' I said, 'we'll have to make it clichés at dawn sometime.' The door was closed. He was gone.

'Jesus,' said Petra, 'you really know how to wind people up, don't you?' She broke into relieved laughter. 'He was an arsehole though.'

'And then some,' I said.

'I wouldn't worry,' said Petra, 'I doubt he'll be back. The poor sod probably won't remember any of that tomorrow.'

I nodded, unconvinced. Returning to my spot behind the counter, I felt a strange sensation grip me, a sense of uncanny emptiness to accompany the dissipating adrenaline. Later that night, hauled up in bed and mapping the topography of my ceiling, I realised, with quiet resignation, that this internal void wasn't fear of Mr Rainstorm returning. It was the fear he wouldn't.

IX

The Cradling

When the history of Perrangyre is written, assuming someone's moved to write such a pamphlet, it's likely the Sunday following my argument with Mr Rainstorm will be marked as significant.

The Circle had congregated, the normal pleasantries and inanities exchanged, but this weekend there was a new topic on the agenda: the self-righteous wine drinker. Typically, Robin had a view.

'Your mistake was to argue with the man,' he said, 'you had a perfectly good alternative.'

'Oh really?' I said, nonplussed at this second-hand wisdom. 'What would you have done?'

Robin locked his fingers, slowly arching them back to cushion his head. 'Why didn't you just review him on one of your wine cards?'

Kerry laughed. I did not.

'That's a great idea,' chirped Kerry. 'New, you could do it for all your customers. It would literally be a new concept,' she spelt the words out on the air with the tips of her fingers, 'the perfect wine for the socially retarded.'

'No,' said Robin with a sneer, 'my beloved hasn't quite grasped the nettle; I'm saying you review him personally, forget the wine; "this wine's very much like your archetypal misfit who comes in from the rain, a half-drowned idiot, and shows the nth degree of humourlessness – full bodied, tasteless, a waste of time" – etcetera, etcetera.'

'Might he not read it?' I said, playing the Robin role in the conversation I'd had with myself the night before.

'You'll probably never see him again,' said Robin, 'it's not for him, anyway. It's for you. You'll know it's there, you get the last word. One day, long after you've jacked it in, if he returns and reads it, knowing the man described is him, well that's just beautiful.'

'Does it matter if New has the last word?' baited Kerry.

'It matters to him,' said Robin.

'You can ask me,' I said, 'I'm just over here.'

'So that's what you should do,' Robin continued, 'use the wine critiques – let off some steam; they won't know what you're talking about anyway, they'll just think you're weird. It'll get you through the summer with your brain intact.'

Robin had seduced me with his malice; my heart and soul was on board, but was there a point to any of it? It felt bitty, petty even; satisfaction would be short-lived. I had to forget about this and crack on with my portfolio. In fact, Robin's would have remained an interesting little aside in an otherwise wasteful Sunday conversation had I not buried my better judgement and agreed to a drink with Petra the following evening after work.

The Mr Rainstorm incident gave Petra and I common cause for the first time, the wind well and truly changed as the new week began. Whatever my view, Petra usually argued the opposite. Indeed, she did so with such infuriating, ignorant zeal, that I privately modified Zeller to Zealot and began to use her new moniker when she wasn't around.

But now we rounded on our sodden nemesis with ripe glee and, from there, some of the worst regulars. There was the porcine bore, thrift bastard and survivor of a cranial bleed to no great benefit, Brain Haemorrhage Guy. Shaky mustard stain on lapel and public school curly-haired argument against hereditary wealth, Drunken Lawyer, who wore his family's financial backing, the pressure of not being good enough, and some dried mucus on his sleeve. Demanding, bra-eschewing, Obnoxious Katherine, grown from a culture of pure arrogance, who had no time to fuck around but some to bend over at the counter, aerating plentiful tits and getting off on your reaction. My eyes widened while Petra's rolled. The list went on.

Now it was us against them, not us against each other; our truce signed on common ground. It felt good, natural even. It was perhaps inevitable that one of us would get carried away.

'It's a slow night, what do you say we close early and go for a pint?' said Petra. I agreed. Perhaps we were both carried away.

Petra's venue of choice was the nearby London Inn. I'd walked past it a dozen times, never tempted by the dingy interior, bellowing clientele and pop tones blaring from giant wall-mounted speakers. I followed Petra inside and found myself squeezed through a rectum of tightly packed, writhing lower hominids, hunched over half-empty pint glasses. They drank the discharge from rusty pipes. As we pushed and twisted our way to the bar, the landlady noticed my companion and acknowledged her with a raise of the head.

'All right Petra, darlin',' she said, 'how are you? How's your Ian?'

Petra mumbled a response. I'd asked Fabian about this Ian, having caught a few glimpses of a wedding ring. She'd dismissed a direct question, 'So you're married then?' with a simple 'yes'. Stroud described him as 'mountainous' and 'brooding'. Now, with Petra's blood thinned by cheap white wine, I pulled the thread.

'So tell me about Ian,' I said.

Petra swayed a little, before steadying herself, propping her head up with her hand.

'Why do you want to know?' she said.

'Are partners off limits?' I said. 'You've never talked about him, that's all.'

'He doesn't like me talking about him,' she said, rubbing the base of her throat, 'he can speak for himself.' This was provocative stuff.

'Happy marriage is it?'

'What?'

'Are you happily married?' I said, slowly sipping a pint of coke syrup and barely carbonated water.

'None of your business,' said Petra.

'That's a no, then.'

'Jesus, you never stop, do you?' She topped up her wine. 'We're fine. We're very similar actually, had a bit of a whirlwind romance as it happens. He was my brother's mate. I'd known him for years, since I was ten, but we got close when my father died. He was really there for me. I'd never have got through it without him.' I imagined the coke syrup turning my tongue black.

'You must owe him,' I said. Petra was looking through

64

her drink to an imaginary world beyond; a planet of good choices, attentive males.

'I do love him,' she said, 'despite the problems.'

'What problems?' I said. She looked up from her glass.

'Nothing,' she said, 'the usual stuff, things lost in translation. He has his ways, his ideas about things, and I have mine. We can't always be on the same page.'

'I thought you said you were similar?' I was pressing now but couldn't let go. Perhaps it was the sugar. Petra sighed.

'That's right we are,' she said, 'we're cut from the same cloth, think the same things are important – family, home, doing our own thing.'

'So what's the problem?' I said. She licked the residual drops from her glass.

'Sometimes I don't think he likes the way his life turned out,' she said. A protective hand hid her eyes from view. 'He can be teasy…'

'Sorry, what?'

'Teasy,' said Petra, 'ah that's right, you're not Cornish, are you? Not from around deez parts as they say. Bloody tourists. He's bad tempered, irritable, you know, like you.' I ignored the provocation.

'Why don't you split up?' I said.

'What?'

'Yes, if it doesn't work, why not? If you don't make each other happy any more…'

'Who says we don't?' said Petra, awoken from her slump.

'Isn't that what you meant?'

'No, it fucking well wasn't!' She toyed with the now empty bottle, clutching my arm as though it were a life raft.

'What about you?' she said. 'I suppose you've got a posh girlfriend from that art school.'

Radge hadn't told her about Maisie. Good old Radge. 'Not any more,' I said.

It was Petra's turn to regard me like a bug on a slide.

'What happened?' she said.

'I honestly don't know.'

As we ran up this dark alley stained with blood and urine, the conversation turned to my destroyed work, an act of desecration Petra thought most amusing.

'Why did you do it, because of her?' she said.

'I had little choice – it was about artistic integrity, amongst other things.'

'Huh? What the hell does that mean?'

'Enough,' I said, 'if you want soap, watch TV.' Petra reached out and punched my arm. It hurt.

'Hey, why don't you call up the school and tell them you've made some new art at the shop, maybe they'll take you back.'

'What art?' I said. 'What are you talking about?'

'Your tickets,' said Petra, 'they're all arty and different, aren't they? You could label up the whole shop with your shit and call it…' she pretended to ponder the question like it was a philosophical quandary, 'wine shop!' And with that she dragged herself up laughing and stumbled towards the toilets, apologising to those she fell into on the way.

I sat alone at our table, warming the base of my pint glass. My muscles tensed, my teeth started to tap. Robin's prescription for dealing with Mr Rainstorm was repeating on me, churning my gut. I realised that somehow, improbable though it was, he and Petra had conceived. I heard the cry of the newborn, those first exhilarating signs of life. As I waited for Petra to return, the idea gained form and weight, and the world around me was downgraded to blended shapes and an ambient gabble.

Maisie had said that a return to the school meant creating something new, the best work I'd ever done. I'd listened, suspecting insincerity, but felt paralysed without my muse. But now, thanks to Robin and Petra, I could see a design for the first time, the foundation for a working installation that would reorder the mundane and everyday, turning blithe consumerism into an act of directly mediated iconoclasm.

The work would retain the name of the thing it consciously deconstructed and remade; it would be called 'In Vino Veritas'. This wasn't a joke, not an amusing bit of situationism, but a direct attack on the complacent, who crossed the threshold in search of reassurance; those plugged vessels of symbolic sophistication, the wine, acting as crutches for fragile identities.

Yes, they'd come to feel safe but would leave dissembled and empty. Such a piece would feed itself. The reactions of the clientele would condition it, shape it, add meaning. The vulnerabilities expressed would inform the next generation of wine tickets, then the next, then the next.

April Zuccaro, new Dean of the Art School, would visit at my invitation, see what the shop had become, know that every card was a commentary that informed the whole and would recognise, as the unwitting customers could not, that she was standing in the most urgent, indeed the most relevant exhibition in town, and behind it all, me: the man her institution had shamelessly ejected.

Maisie had been inducted to the teaching staff for less; she was, in Trevenna's words, sponsorship and media recognition. How could I be worth less to the school once this headline-grabbing piece was live, just a mile from its revered estate? How could the admissions board ignore it?

As Petra continued to empty herself, I pushed my glass away, leaned back and dreamed of what was to come. There was an eruption of laughter, enough to turn heads; musical mirth that sank into the brickwork permeated the dark wood and smothered the wailing from wall-mounted speakers. It was the sound of a man back in control, answerable to no one but himself.

X

Welcome to the Gallery

The next morning I cantered to In Vino Veritas. As I pushed through the door with gusto, almost tripping on the step to the shop floor, I found myself face to face with Murgatroyd, bag in hand, apparently on the verge of a welcome exit.

'Why, hello there,' he said. The space I needed to move round him was stacked with cases that Petra, sunken-eyed and pale behind the counter, had yet to move. I was trapped.

'Mr Murgatroyd, hello,' I said, trying to sound cheerful, 'got everything you need?'

'Enough to be getting on with,' he said. I took a step forward, expecting him to stand aside. He didn't. 'Have you managed to mend any fences with the art school?'

'Not yet,' I said.

'Well I wish you luck with it.'

'Thank you.' He now allowed me to brush past him. I was halfway to the curtain and safety when his next words pulled me about.

'I do hope you sort it out. I bumped into your tutor yesterday, the lady I met during the call-out, the one who spoke up for you – I forget her name...'

'Maisie,' I said.

'Yes, that's right,' he said, 'she's very familiar – I think I've seen her on TV or something, is she famous? Anyway, she mentioned you'd had a tough time.' I felt the tips of my fingers dig into my palms.

'Did she, now?' What exactly did she say?' Murgatroyd was stone faced.

'Only that you'd been a little, well – up and down, since your friend died. She thought that maybe that was why you'd des—'

'She's confused; I haven't lost anyone.' Murgatroyd stuck out his bottom lip.

'You didn't know the lad who drowned a while ago? Who fell from the bridge? Wye Stammers.' The aura from Petra's gaze was clouding my peripheral vision.

'I knew of him, I didn't know him, we weren't friends. He was acquainted with some of the people I see socially, that's all. It was awful, but if Maisie thought it had some far reaching effect on me, well, she wasn't really paying attention. People project all sorts, don't they? Everyone's an amateur shrink nowadays.'

'Everyone but the pros,' said Murgatroyd. 'Well good luck anyway.'

Ignoring Petra's quizzical stare and retreating to the back office, I found a glum-looking Ragesh seated by the desk.

'Ah young man,' he said, 'glad I caught you – I've got an appointment this morning but need a quick word.' He frowned. 'Are you all right, you're nearly the same colour as the curtain?'

'I'm fine,' I said, 'I just ran here. What's up?'

'It's nothing to worry about,' said Ragesh, 'I was just going to suggest you cool it with the tickets for a bit.' Radge had just rolled a stone over, unaware it was plugging a hole in the universe.

'Cool it, why?'

'Well I think just be careful, because we've had a few complaints.'

'What? When?'

'That doesn't matter. The point is I like your stuff, you know that, it's a lot of fun, but let's just keep an eye on it; if the owner gets wind there's a problem we'll both be in a lot of trouble, OK?'

I weighed my words carefully, like compounds for an explosive.

'Sure, no problem,' I said.

'Great,' said Ragesh, his familiar smile returning, 'well I'll leave it with you then, just remember they're a sensitive lot round here.'

'Oh, I know,' I said, 'I think of little else.'

★★★

I liked Ragesh, I liked him immensely, but what he was proposing, that I shelve an idea better, purer, than any I'd had at the school, had to be crushed. He was asking me to strangle my newborn because the locals didn't like the smell of talc. Was that how art worked? If people didn't like it, you didn't do it? What better formula was there for rigid, suffocating, sterile conformity? Such thoughts made for productive anger.

'Are you writing one of your funny reviews?' asked Brain Haemorrhage Guy, arresting my flow, just as I'd got down to business. He was typically cheery; a shop mascot with his beanbag belly and large glasses. 'I'll have a bottle of your very cheapest please!' he said, unsteady at the counter, straining to drop his only joke.

'They're sketches,' I told him, 'and we're all out of that Emperor's new wine you like. Spend another pound, perhaps we can trouble your palate.'

'Is this gentleman a joy to work with?' he asked Petra.

'He's all right,' she said, and they enjoyed the moment together as I enjoyed mine, the first ticket in the new series. You'd be amazed how much text you can squeeze on to a small card if you're careful. I thought of Mr Rainstorm.

Lakewater Special Reserve: Lakewater are the undisputed *provocateurs* of the sparkling wine fraternity. As a producer they excel in making fizz that marinates soft minds, producing pure, animal-like aggression. That's right, quaffets, if you're a puffed up ridiculant who expects the world to snap to fit your wholly unrealistic and self-centred expectations, and you've had the worst day imaginable; a rejection from a lady you've groomed for months; a letter from your ex-wife, demanding you leave both her and the children she's conditioned to despise you alone; a car that wouldn't start; a bus that never came; and to top it all, a biblical rainstorm that makes the skin hang from your head as though it had been boiled; you'll go nuts when you see the legend, 'because you're special, and not in a mentally retarded sense either' improving this economy bubbly. Buy a few bottles today, but remember: your wife's gone; there'll be no one to hold the old chap

when you urinate into an airing cupboard now. You
may have to use the empty bottle instead.

Petra watched as I replaced the old, incendiary ticket with
its pacifying replacement. The pep of the previous day had
also been replaced. In its stead there was tension, thicker
than our pungent resin. I looked at Zealot and saw her eyes
drop. Her foot tapped on her stool's rest.

'Did Radge tell you we've had some complaints about
those?' she said.

'Yes, he mentioned something.'

'Then should you be putting more up?'

'He said to keep an eye on it,' I said, 'so I will. Nothing
for you to worry about.'

She raised one hand to her mouth and took small bites
from her nail.

'Is something wrong?' I said.

I anticipated a 'no', content I'd shown due concern, but
to my surprise she replied, 'What did I say to you last night?'

'About what?' I said.

'That's what I'm asking.'

'Nothing really. Work, home, that sort of thing.'

'Did I talk about Ian?'

'I think you mentioned him, yes.'

'He's coming in,' said Petra, she was staring at me now,
'he's dropping in to see me later, so don't say anything,
OK?'

Petra, usually brash and unflappable, was pleasingly
timid.

'What would I talk to him about?' I said.

'I don't know,' she snapped, 'but if he asks – he won't,

but if he does – just don't say we talked about him, get it?'

I got it all right and started to look forward to the visit from that moment on. When he came, hours later, I'd just finished serving Obnoxious Katherine, who'd bounced me all the way from Australia to South Africa, hunting for obscure labels to impress her awful friends.

I watched the hulking figure Fabian had described letch at her thinly veiled front as she signed off with a glib, 'back soon', and then at Petra who glared at both the departing and the arrived. Seemingly oblivious, he reached out to his wife and wrapped his bulk around her slender frame. My imagination added the sound of cracking bones. Petra, released, stiffened. My cultivated nose registered shame, like a teenager abashed by their parent's intrusion on a bedroom fumble. Before I could shake his hand, she'd moved between us. I wanted to touch it, weigh the lumpen mass.

'You all right?' said Petra to Ian, shifting from side to side. 'Do you want to sit down out back, get a drink?'

'I'm Keir,' I announced, pushing Petra to one side and extending a hand, which, following a brief pause, was enveloped with some force, 'great to meet you.'

Ian Zeller eyed me suspiciously, then smirked. I dropped his ape-like mitt.

'Ah yeah,' he said, his voice meat and fish, 'you're the artist.'

Petra chortled. He chortled in kind. I hadn't seen it happen, but they'd conjoined to become a single, simple monster.

'That's right,' I said, 'and what are you?'

'I do very well,' he said, answering a question I hadn't asked, 'I make furniture; cabinets, tables, chairs.' He radiated pride the way a toddler congratulates themselves on their faeces.

'Thanks for clarifying what furniture is,' I said.

Ian Zeller's smirk dissolved. Petra noticed a half second before I did.

'Shall we go out back then?' she said, grabbing his arm, 'Keir you don't mind if we disappear for a bit, do you?'

'Oh no,' I said, 'I'd be delighted.'

With that she dragged him to the back office. He looked at me as they went.

'Take your time,' I shouted after them, 'it's dead this afternoon.' The next wine ticket was a doddle to compose.

Mulhorn Syrah: Mulhorn's mysterious and brooding, much like your ideal partner, and like him it improves with age. But you didn't meet that man, did you? Oh no. You met a lunk; a mountain of muscle and libido that saw a vacancy when Daddy died and moved to fill it before you'd had a chance to place the ad in the newspaper. As you contemplate your life with a large glass of this dark berry and pepper flecked reverie maker, will you regret being one of those women? The kind that couldn't let go of Papa, despite him ignoring you all those years, so looked for a surrogate? And how's that working out for you now you're stuck with your opportunistic ape? You've nothing to say to each other, if you ever did, and the days when you could walk into a pub and flirt with ten would-be suitors is long gone. Now it's just you and him… for ever. At least you've got this wine. It's a pity you can't marry it.

The new ticket, neatly written if I say so myself, was sheathed in a plastic jacket, pulled over the neck of the bottle, then returned to its proud position in the centre shelf. The second sketch was on the wall.

'The perfect accompaniment to a bit of marital discord,' I said to an empty shop floor.

Petra and Ian were gone a while. Sometime during their grumbled conversation, a sound like gas working its way through guts, I was joined by Drunken Lawyer who'd stumbled on the step, then, noticing I was distracted, started to interrogate me.

'Who are you listening to?' he said, rubbing a rash on his neck.

'A cross section of the public's in there with the bar association – they're debating whether the law would be improved if more people from ordinary backgrounds made and practised it.' He was still swaying gently, his thin lips pursed in preparation for a reply, when the happy couple finally emerged.

Ian Zeller burst through the curtain, as though coming on stage to a packed theatre, and walked to the door, giving me a disdainful glance as he went. Petra watched him go, miserable, then returned to the office. I didn't see her again until early afternoon when she cameoed to say, 'Thanks for not saying anything earlier – he'd just be pissed off if he knew we'd talked about him, that's all.' I nodded, saying I understood, while looking through Petra to the Mulhorn ticket over her left shoulder.

That evening, Petra was morose, unwilling to offer even her brand of caustic small talk. The shift was dead, the shop deserted. Tired of propping up the counter and listening to one of Radge's outré compilations, I went in search of the colleague I hadn't seen since the middle of the day. I found her hunched over the back office desk, a full glass within easy reach.

'You've abandoned me,' I said. 'Is everything OK?'

'You don't need to check up on me,' she said, 'I'm fine thanks.' Next to her glass stood the bottle she'd opened. It was two-thirds empty.

'Normally you'd compact all your binge drinking into the evening,' I said, 'was hubby's visit really that traumatic? You must be used to his conversation by now.'

'You wouldn't understand,' she said.

'Try me.'

'No, you'll just take the piss.' I pulled out the spare chair and sat down.

'I might,' I said, 'but if you don't tell me I'll report to Radge that you're drinking the stock.' She looked up at me.

'I'm not sure about you,' said Petra, 'not sure at all.'

'What aren't you sure about?' I said. She took a sip of wine.

'Oh nothing really, just whether you're a good guy or evil incarnate; silly stuff like that.'

I reached for her glass and filled it. We watched each other in silence.

***

Fuelled by the new project's promise, the weekend that followed was one of the most productive of my life. By bulb, and when that blew by candlelight, I spent long nights and ambient mornings writing out ticket after ticket, using

77

a printed inventory of the shop's last delivery order as my reference. It was so easy and so enjoyable that I had to stop many times, wondering if something this simple could be construed as work at all, but the shop's customers, with all their archetypal ugliness, made it work; they were the perfect muse.

The punters spoke to you often, or you heard them speak to each other, and from this biographical residue came the set-ups for card upon card.

'This wine's like coming home to find your husband in bed with your younger sister, but then you realise she's not looking her best.'; 'Are you desperate for attention? Do you crave a media profile and a legion of bespectacled acolytes? Being bedevilled by a lack of charm, personality and talent needn't be a break on your ambitions. Here's a Prosecco that makes befriending those with the right connections a doddle.'; 'At last, the wine that says "put me in your fridge sized cooler so I can ogle all the other high-end goods you've purchased to fill the void in a life without children". Babies: they'd only ruin your stuff, right?'; 'Mask your uncultivated understanding of the arts with this bluffer's sherry. Everyone's an expert at 2 a.m.'; 'Why take the family to live in Australia, a cultural necropolis, when you can sample the very best of the climate in this bottle?'; 'Calling all weekend dads: why not offer the older kids a glass of this sumptuous, full-bodied Northern Rhône, and maybe they'll tell you what (or who) their mother's being doing during the week.' And so on, for three days and two nights.

By the third night, the Sunday, I had a hundred new cards ready to go; the exhibition was ready to open. Cooped up, restless, eager to get them on the shelves, I resolved to walk by the shop and, should the coast be clear, should Petra be meandering around, should Fabian be out back, should Radge be off duty, I'd slip in and start replacing the old with the new. Maybe a third at first, the rest as the week unfolded. The shop would open on Monday but it wouldn't be a business any more, but an interactive artwork.

I approached the shop, my head writhing like a wasps' nest. I felt happier than I had in months. I knew it was going to be tough. Radge wouldn't like it at first, but I'd talk him round. I'd manage him; contain him until the school had sight of what was happening and April Zucarro's curiosity was piqued. With Maisie looking on they'd talk of New Shockley, the artist they'd turned away on a whim, who transformed a thankless summer job into the most exciting exhibit in town. He's unstoppable, they'd say. The school should be associated with it. I clutched the cards a little tighter.

I don't remember what I saw first: the lights perhaps, the blue and yellow livery, the legend 'POLICE' – I can't be sure, but there was Fabian, talking to an officer, gesticulating wildly, as though conducting the air. Beyond, through the window, I saw Petra. She was blurred around the eyes. When she saw me her mouth twisted. My walk broke into a run, past Fabian, past an alarmed police officer. I heard the panther say, 'It's all right, he works here,' then I was in, on the shop floor.

Something primal had taken place. There were flecks of blood on the counter, a treacle-like smear on the floor, and in the corner, brushed to one side, a tower of shards, perhaps a few bottles' worth. In the pile I saw little pieces of card with soaked borders, one of my cards. *One of my cards!*

Petra was on the shop floor, her hand to the counter. Her fingertips, once stained by cigarettes, were now carmine.

'What the hell happened?' I said. She didn't answer. 'Petra, did you hear me? Are you hurt?' She was rigid, but her sore eyes slowly rolled upward to meet mine, as though attached to a Lilliputian winch.

'He came back,' she said quietly.

'Who?' I said.

'The moron,' she said, 'Mr Rainstorm.'

I looked at the torn card and knew the rest before she told me.

'He found out Radge was the manager,' she went on, 'he must have called the shop. Anyway, he came back to complain about you, and…' her voice trailed off. The winch broke and her eyes dropped. 'He was looking for that ticket. The one about being special. But you'd replaced it. He said the new one was about him, that it talked about his wife. He just blew up; I've never seen someone so angry. He tore it up, smashed the bottle, he kept smashing them, and when Radge moved to stop him, Rainstorm went crazy – he just attacked him.'

I felt light-headed; an invisible hand had bunched my optic nerves. It began to twist.

'Is Radge OK?' I said.

Petra took a step back from me, her boot imprinting on the bloody smear.

'No,' she said – scornful, rasping. 'No, he's not OK, Keir. Look around you. Look at what you've done. Jesus, poor Radge. The guy didn't give him a chance. I couldn't stop it. I couldn't help him.' Petra began to cry.

I clutched the cards tighter still.

Dinner at Boondoggle

The effort employed in getting Petra to Boondoggle, a restaurant that made good on its promise of a doomed project by serving ox tongue in pig cheek, was back-breaking. It required delicate preparation, commitment and, as Robin noted, whose suggestion it was, going against one's nature: extending a hand in friendship to a turned back when all one wanted to do was shove it and let the stairs to the cellar do their work.

Petra, though quick to say Ragesh wouldn't blame me for the damage to his body, mind, and the likely destruction of his confidence and gregarious character, made no secret of feeling the opposite. A brief moment of elation aside, when news broke from Rosa, our leader's heartbroken wife, that Radge would live – his right eye, chest and kidney a cliffhanger for another day – she'd greeted my every approach with animal-like aggression; 'fuck off'; 'I don't want to talk to you, understand?'; feigning revulsion when I answered customers' questions about what happened with a shrug and a 'who knows what sets people off, the guy was mentally ill', and most seriously, scrutinising everything I did, everything I wrote.

I had 200 cards ready to display now, 200 portraits, but I was forced to keep them under lock and key, the atmosphere in-shop being viscous, like clotting blood. When Petra appeared to insert her hand into Obnoxious Katherine's neck and operate her mouth, a moment of torturous silence following the contention that, 'the bloke was probably wound up by those cards', I knew I had to do something. Such thoughts weren't just diseased, they were contagious and the project was a corpse for the pyre while those fleas of discontent jumped from person to person.

Fabian, who mercifully hadn't seen the attack, so couldn't act as a reserve sanctimonious witness, saw the incident as the inevitable consequence of having an open door to the zoo outside. His attitude, that the mass always stood ready to puncture civilisation's bubble with their inner beast and crudity, came as no surprise.

I'd once seen Fabian recoil when a vagrant, caked in muck and bad choices, had limped into the shop, with a beer bought from a day's takings from begging his moral inferiors, and extended a wretched hand to shake the panther's paw. He took it as though picking up a used condom, holding on to the tips of the man's fingers with unmitigated disgust, trying not to contemplate their toxicity, desperate to reconcile the need to be polite, inculcated into all those of Fabian's class, with the noxious leper, before rushing out back to wash his hands. I stood in the doorway, watching him rub them, working in the antiseptic goo, wondering where else those hands had been.

Petra was the problem. She was tough but not so tough that she didn't shudder at the memory of a limp Ragesh, his hands raised in futility, the dull thud of fist on moist flesh; that crunch sound, a broken bough, skin splitting like a perforated piecrust, the filling oozing out. That she couldn't forget and that it would take more than time to neutralise its corrosive effects was clear. As Robin had immediately understood with Kerry bringing up the rear, Petra now stood between me and the project's realisation, just as she'd once stood between me and Mr Rainstorm. She had to be managed.

I set out my stall by offering to answer the only question she'd asked, why wouldn't I see him? Why hadn't I gone to the hospital with a plastic smile and a bag of unfermented grapes?

I told her it was complicated, that I couldn't explain at the shop; it was too raw, too difficult. I knew I hadn't given a great account of myself and I understood why she was angry. The whole thing had been awful, I said. I lied and told her I couldn't imagine what she'd seen, that I felt guilty and craved the chance to at least, in part, make amends. If she'd let me take her to dinner I'd fill her in, I'd open up. She'd realise that she'd got me all wrong, and besides, wasn't the still-roaming monster who'd beaten Ragesh the real enemy? Shouldn't we be holding hands at a time like this? It's probably what he wanted.

'Fine,' she said, 'but I'll tell Ian I'm working, I don't need the hassle, all right?'

Boondoggle suited my purposes very well. It had been a popular hangout with Maisie, who'd been enamoured by its faux archaisms; the oil lamps, dark wood beams and hand-built furniture. She'd taken us there once, insisting on a secluded alcove, below street level. It was a place made from wattle, daub and romance; the past retooled to accommodate a celebrity chef in a house originally built for the working poor.

I wanted to dazzle Petra, so for the woman used to eating at home, whose nights out were typically scored by the jingle from a fruit machine, this would be a treat. On the evening we closed early, I knew I had a chance when she came cautiously from the back office; hair up, woad applied, draped in a floral dress with matching scent.

At the restaurant we sat in silence for a while, but the arrival of Petra's duck liver pâté, slivers of toast, and accompanying wine, cheered her enough to speak.

'So c'mon, what's the problem?' she said. 'He'd like to see you; fuck knows why, but he would. Don't you think you owe him a visit?'

'Did he say he wanted to see me?' I said.

'He's fond of you, Keir. He wouldn't blame you.'

'But you do,' I said. Petra gulped down some sparkling Shiraz.

'You provoked the bloke; it's only because Radge was defending you he got hurt.' The indictment had been read; the carefully prepared case for the defence now had to be made.

'It's more complicated than you think,' I said, 'what happened to Radge has triggered a lot of bad memories. It's forced me to confront stuff I thought was long buried.' Her eyes widened, Petra was a captive audience.

'What does that mean?' she said. 'What stuff?'

A beat, a long drink of water, a nervous fumble with my serviette, and I told the tale I'd rehearsed with Kerry the night before. I preferred her in the part, her attempts at distracting me with nipple flashes and face pulling trumped this funereal atmosphere.

'When I was eleven, I…'

'It's all right,' said Petra, 'go on. I'm listening.' I was avoiding eye contact now.

'When I was eleven, I – I was involved in an incident and, well, another child died.'

My dinner date dropped her scoop of pâté.

'What? What happened?' she said, affecting to look pained. So I told her the story of a couple of boys who'd bullied me at junior school; a leader and a follower, the alpha and oh my God. I only broke off every now and then to take a sip of water, camouflaging the study of a couple on the adjacent table, photographing their food.

I explained that the follower, the moral coward, who was only brave when the older boy was present – his supple face moisturised with other children's tears – went for me no matter what I did. He never ran out of reasons to find me ridiculous; what I wore, what I said, how I moved, who I spoke to; everything was wrong. So one day, following a particularly punishing session, in which every part of my character had been torn open and soiled, from my parentage to my social class, for kids are such inverted snobs, I knew I had to stop them. I realised that if I didn't, I'd probably kill myself. In fact, the more I brooded, the more I resented feeling that way and the more I despised them. They had to be broken. The key, I decided, was overwhelming both sadists with a simple act of brute force, humiliating the weak in front of the strong and making the strong weak.

I told Petra that following a quick recce of the playground, I chose a spot near a workman's pit. The men, who were building a low wall for a new garden, were gone for the day, but they'd left some bits behind – amongst them a shovel. The work had involved taking down a section of wire fence. This meant we could walk straight into the adjacent woodland. By the part-constructed wall, a few yards from the outlying trees, I waited.

I told her how, when the boys inevitably approached, delighted to find me by myself, I waited for them to start, then hit Anthony, the sheep, with a gush of pleasure, maybe my first sexual experience; the little bastard's nose splitting like a banana skin, blood breaking on his friend's head and neck.

I told her how I watched the shocked Anthony fall to his knees, then ran for the woods, plucking the freestanding shovel from the idle pit as I vaulted past. I told her how I heard them running after me, unable to catch up, screaming, 'Come 'ere, come 'ere!' and that now immersed in thicket, I'd taken refuge behind a wide trunk and waited.

I told her how I heard one set of approaching footsteps on a bed of mud and leaf mulch, that without knowing which boy it was, and caring not a fuck, I swung out with all the force I could, connecting with something, maybe a head, and was already running when I heard the body hit the ground with an inconsequential thud.

I told her how I ran back to school while the other boy looked for his accomplice, waiting it out; frightened, excited, wondering what the survivor would do when he found his friend face down in filth, bleeding and broken. I told her the afternoon dragged on for ever, but by home time neither boy had surfaced.

I told her that the following day I went to school with my stomach in my plimsolls, ready to deny everything, knowing I had to face whatever was waiting.

'You killed him?' asked Petra. Her pâté was now cold.

'Well that's the strange part,' I said, 'he was gone. Anthony, the boy I'd hit, hadn't come home that night, but he hadn't been found in the woods either. He'd vanished. The police came to the school, they interviewed me, I told them about the fight; left the shovel part out, just said I'd run into the woods and they'd chased me and, having waited a while undiscovered, rushed back. Old alpha male, Mr Newly Mateless, admitted he'd run after me with Anthony, but said, truthfully I think, that he had no idea what happened after that. I went back to the woods a few days later, when I was sure no one could see me, and found the spot but he wasn't there. There was no trace of him.'

'Sorry, I don't understand,' said Petra, 'you knocked him out and then what?'

'I don't know,' I said, 'really – I have no idea. The assumption was that he'd been snatched by some pervert waiting in the woods; an opportunistic abduction. I'll tell you this though, I didn't miss him. I stayed quiet, maintained a respectful silence for show, but I was elated. It was as if someone had just plucked this scum from the face of the Earth and saved me from further torment, because I'd had the guts to fight back. The ringleader thought I was responsible though, I know he did, he avoided me like the plague, left rooms when I entered them. He didn't say a word to me from that day onwards. He left soon afterwards.'

'Jesus,' said Petra, 'maybe someone found him laid out and took him?'

'Who knows?' I said.

'But didn't you feel guilty?' she said.

'I felt shock but no guilt, not a shred.'

'Really?' said Petra. I helped myself to her neglected food.

'If a boy kicks a puppy or drowns a kitten, we say they're disturbed and we call a quack,' I said, 'we recognise that the child is psychologically damaged. Proud parents watch little Josh or bedimpled Peter pat the hound or stroke the pussy and they infer their kids have a sweet nature. We're very sentimental when it comes to automatons. What mum and dad *don't* see is their little cherubs torturing some other kid by the caretaker's lodge, unprovoked and apparently without conscience. They don't see them getting off on the cruelty, on dehumanising an intelligent, emotional being, who'll have to carry it their whole lives. That's considered a joke, a bit of character-building knockabout. But these sociopaths are the most sinister of all children. They're degenerate and dangerous, and they become cruel adults, all hidden beneath a convivial veneer, of course. Myra Hindley loved her dog, you know. The only time she cried when being interrogated about the kids she'd buried on the moor, presumably patting the pooch as they were sodomised and strangled, was when the police broke the news her mutt had pegged it.'

'Still, someone died, Keir,' said Petra.

I motioned to the sweets menu. 'Just desserts.' Petra was silent for a time.

'What about the other boy?' she said at last. 'Did you see him again?'

'Incredibly,' I said, 'I did. Years later, months after I'd started at Perrangyre, there he was. I couldn't quite believe it. He was a very different character by then, very meek. Gaunt looking. I didn't recognise him at first. But he soon recognised me.' I smiled.

That was new information, an on the spot flourish; I hadn't rehearsed the last part, perhaps hadn't anticipated the question. Kerry, as Petra's stand-in, had joked around, not realising that the story being told was substantively true or that the identity of the leader, a troubled wretch who'd later, tragically, take his own life, was none other than Robin's allegorical favourite, Wye Stammers.

'We never had the opportunity to catch up,' I said, 'he killed himself before I could say hello. He had a breakdown. Drowned himself.'

'Wait, was he the kid Murgatroyd was talking about at the shop?' said Petra.

'Yes,' I said. 'I didn't really want to go into the history, it's not customer friendly and besides, what I said was true – we weren't friends, and I certainly wasn't traumatised by his passing. Maisie knew I'd known him from before, maybe that's why she thought it had upset me, I don't know.'

Petra's poached salmon had been picked apart and a bottle of wine emptied, by the time I'd explained how the savagery of Ragesh's beating had thrown up long dormant imagery, like a song that reminds you of an old girlfriend. So ingrained was the sense of that difficult time, so vivid, that seeing Ragesh in his current state might be overwhelming. Of course there was also a chance that my end of bed presence might bring the catalyst into focus, that a scorched project order would go out, but I kept that fear to myself.

My dinner companion's pupils were larger now, and the anger she'd brought to the table had disappeared with the half-empty plates.

'I'm sorry for being so teasy recently,' she said, 'I just thought you only cared about those stupid tickets, not Radge.' I poured myself a glass of water and took my time drinking it.

'But now you understand,' I said.

'Yes,' she said, 'I think so.' Her hand was edging towards mine.

'You pretend not to care,' she said, 'but you're quite vulnerable really, aren't you?'

'Are you asking me or telling me?' I said.

'Telling you.' She went on, 'What you were saying about bullies, sometimes I feel like Ian bullies me a bit.' The room seemed to be closing in. The table's candle flickered, making Petra's face look haunted.

'I don't think he means it but he's always dismissing me, shutting me down. I don't think he cares what I think or feel any more. The more I question it, the more defensive he becomes. He feels he has to stick to these stupid ideas because I question them. It's his pride. He can be really aggressive.'

'You should leave him,' I said without thinking. Petra was staring at me.

'I'm sorry for what happened to you as a kid,' she said, 'and about your girlfriend. I think we're two lost souls right now, aren't we?' Her hand, cold from the wine chiller, was on mine.

Something about Petra's declaration of empathy, about the equivalence drawn, and the clumsy romantic overture, cut into me. I'd been misclassified, downgraded. I was the same genus as Ian Zeller. I withdrew my hand.

'I'm sorry,' she began, 'I didn't mean anything—'

'I'm not lost Petra,' I said, 'on the contrary, I know exactly where I'm going and it's not with you.' Her face flushed.

'What?' she said. 'What are you talking about?'

'Maisie thought I was a broken person too,' I said, 'it made me easier to use, but she was wrong and so are you. I pity broken people, I don't set up home with them. Maybe you see a bit of yourself in me. You think I'm like you, yes? A bit hard up? Well you're projecting, not looking. I'm not finished. I'm just getting started. Maybe one day I'll feel ugly and useless and sexless, but unfortunately for you I'm not there yet, not even close. Go home to your substitute dad if you're horny, don't presume I'm happy to fill in. I'll come knocking on your door when I feel that wretched, which will be sometime never.'

Petra didn't stay for dessert. I had the chocolate torte.

XII

Denial

I won't tell you it was a sleepless night. I slept, but I didn't settle. I moved around so much that the covers did a full three-sixty before sun up. Senses, heightened by fatigue, amplified every raindrop that tapped the window like impatient fingers. Some sounded like sparrows hurtling themselves at the glass, Petra's avian revenge drones. I'd meant what I said; her compliment was backward as well as backhanded; but I was unguarded in my response. I couldn't blame childhood trauma. Not twice. Dinner wasn't going to cut it now. It was twelve hours too late for sex. Yet I was sure I could salvage the situation, find the good news story in this man-made disaster. A kid had to be pulled from a collapsed hotel. You'll find pictures of the older survivors on page five.

That afternoon the shop floor was empty. The sun had returned and the air had a glutinous quality as I crossed the threshold. Behind the counter, an open bottle beside him, Fabian stood proud, enjoying the tasting he'd laid on for himself. When he saw me his face rose, his puppeteer yanking hard on those cheek strings. If *schadenfreude* had a look...

'I don't know what you've done but she's not happy,' he said. 'If I were you I'd give it five or six years.'

'What makes you assume it's me?' I said. Fabian raised an eyebrow. I took the point.

'She's in the cellar if you're feeling brave,' he went on, delighted, 'you'll find a hard hat by the chute.' I left Fabian with his stuttering laugh and began my descent.

The basement cellar was every bit as awful as the situation demanded. Weeks before a rat died inside an unreachable hollow; the cavity behind the cellar's back wall. It must have been a portly rodent because the elements couldn't digest it. The summer heat, cameoing every few days, had soured the atmosphere, thus the poor bastards obliged to shuffle stock around the labyrinthine basement were forced to inhale the particulates of death. A storage area for wine cases was now a readymade serial killer's lair. Insect strips hung from the ceiling, decorous with bluebottles. Most were dead, a few twitched, pawing desperately. At the foot of the stairs I glanced at one, terminally stuck but still conscious. We had an affinity, I thought, though I'd be damned if I'd end up a goth's Christmas decorations.

I heard shuffling from the rear of the cellar, a sound too big to be a fly. Wading through the stench, I found Petra, arm raised to a case, marking the box with a lime green pen. She was dressed for a wake. Mine, I thought.

'Look,' I said, 'I wanted to say sorry about last night.' She sighed, the noise my grandfather was alleged to have made when his heart gave out. She didn't look up.

'You've not come to pity me then,' she said.

'I didn't mean any of that,' I said, edging a little closer, 'I'm not thinking straight after what happened to Radge. It's like I told you, it brought back a lot of bad memories.'

'Well thanks to you I have a new one of my own,' she said. 'It's this recollection of a night with some arsehole, who apparently thinks I'm going to cheat on my husband because a man's bought me a bit of toast.'

'I think perhaps there was a misunderstanding,' I said.

'Do you really think I'd want a man like you?' she continued. 'Someone as empty as you? Aw, you got a little stick in the playground, how terrible. Well guess what? So did everyone. You're nothing special. In fact, given what you did they should have locked you up, you sound like a bloody psycho. That poor kid. Christ.' I took a deep breath.

'Poor kid? He was a parasite,' I said. Petra looked up at last.

'Parasite?' she said. 'Is that why you have no remorse? Kids are kids – we were all horrible at some point, that doesn't make us evil. He might have grown up to be sorry. You know, the way you didn't.'

'There's no might about it,' I said, 'you go when you go, that's all there is to it. I don't really expect you to understand.'

'You don't have the right to play God,' she said.

'Bacchus is fine, surely?' Petra's mouth opened a little.

'Keir, do you think I'm stupid?' she said. I paused, probably a half-second too long. 'Because I think you think I am, and that offends me. I think you reckoned on taking me out, giving me a sob story and I'd forget how terrible you can be, and worse, how little you care about Radge.'

'I care,' I said. 'I like him very much. But I'm not to blame for what happened. Mr Rainstorm made those choices. There are people who antagonise and those that respond, and there's all the difference in the world.'

'My God,' said Petra, 'you're really in denial.' I hated this psychobabble, the arrogant messenger even more so.

'I'd been to that restaurant with Maisie,' I said, 'when you touched me the way you did, it just reminded me, that's all.'

'Oh, so now it's about her, is it?' she said. 'Not whatever you think you're doing upstairs?' The reek was overwhelming now.

'What I'm doing upstairs,' I said, 'is none of your business.'

'Is that a fact?'

Now she reached into her pocket and produced one of my wine tickets. It was crumpled. It had been scrunched, flattened out, then stowed. Petra now read from it.

'Mulhorn Syrah: Mulhorn's mysterious and brooding, much like your ideal partner, and like him it improves with age. But you didn't meet that man, did you? Oh no.' She paused. 'Remember this one?' She continued, 'You met a lunk; a mountain of muscle and libido that saw a vacancy when Daddy died and moved to fill it before you'd had a chance to place the ad in the newspaper.'

'Petra,' I started, 'he'd been rude to me, I was just vent—'

'Will you regret being one of those women?', she continued reading, her voice unbearably shrill now. 'The kind that couldn't let go of Papa, despite him ignoring you all those years, so looked for a surrogate? And how's that working out for you now you're stuck with your opportunistic ape? You've nothing to say to each other, if you ever did, and the days when you could walk into a pub and flirt with ten would-be suitors is long gone. Now it's just you and him, for ever.' Petra stopped reading, re-scrunched the card and threw it at my face.

'I'll tell you why I married Ian, shall I?' said Petra. 'I married him because he was kind and he wanted me when I was so miserable, so angry, that I struggled to get up in the morning. He's not perfect, not like you obviously, who could be like you? Just good. Not a man who finds it easy to express his feelings, but someone who has them. Try to imagine. And yes we're having a tough time right now, and no I don't like the way he talks to me these days, but he's still—'

'Twice the man I am?' I said.

'You wouldn't get close to half.' Now she pushed me back, my head perilously close to a strip of dead flies!

'You fucking dare to put my marriage problems on public display,' said Petra rhetorically, 'you think it's funny, something for you to have a laugh over while I go home to apply some hard graft to a real adult relationship, unlike your icky campus shag? Well we'll see who's laughing when Radge comes back.'

'Meaning what?' I said.

'Meaning,' said Petra, 'that I'm going to open his eyes. I'm going to tell him that you don't care about him, or the job, that the shop's just a little outlet for your ego. I see right through you. It's not hard. I'm going to tell him what you wrote, remind him, in case he's forgotten, or is in denial about it, that it's because of you that he got the shit kicked out of him, and I'm going to tell him, in my capacity as his deputy, because I am, you know, that I think you should leave.' A fly twitched.

'Listen Zealot, he won't believe you,' I said, 'Radge and I have an understanding. He sees the real me, not your caricature. He'd much rather have me up there than a yokel like you. He's not going to give a damn what you think. That you think at all will probably astound him.'

I left Petra in the cellar to think about that with the stink and the Goldblums.

★★★

Providence, happily, gave me a couple of days off following my subterranean shakedown, and I used it to get a little counsel on my increasingly precipitous situation. If Petra did give Radge her little speech, if he took it seriously, then I might face the sack and everything would be lost, a fact that Kerry was slow to realise as we sat at Fore Street, chewing on crispy shredded beef and flat wheat tendrils.

'Couldn't you just do it elsewhere?' she said. 'It's a great idea; surely it would work in any shop?'

'No,' I said, 'it's specific to that place, those people. Only a shop like that has such a narrow and self-regarding clientele, that's where the characters go. The subjects of the cards have to grapple with their incongruity in that setting, what they imagine to be a safe space – that's the point.'

'Well can't you just apologise to her and give it some time, you know, let things calm down?'

'I couldn't apologise now even I wanted to and besides, it's too late for that, it's gone too far. And no, it can't wait. The new term at Perrangyre starts in five weeks. It's the height of season, it has to be now. The school has to have the chance to hear about it, see it.' Kerry sucked up a mouthful of noodles and squinted.

'What about this guy Fabian,' she said, 'if you put the

cards up anyway, could he be a bit of an ally, I mean, he's got no love for the girl, has he?'

'Or indeed any girl,' I said, 'but no, it'd be like barricading a door with a wet towel.'

'So what are you going to do?' said Kerry.

'Perhaps,' I said, 'I can get her to quit, make life there so miserable that she dutifully buggers off. I can't believe she's that far away. It would only take a little push.' And with that I began to relax, content that I could see a way out, that it wouldn't be hard if I pressed the right buttons. Petra didn't want to be there; her husband certainly didn't want her to be there. It'd be a mercy killing.

As that comforting notion took hold my phone began to vibrate. I hardly ever got a text; those most likely to send one saw me too often, so I scrambled to look at it with an irrational and all-consuming sense of dread.

'I may need a plan B,' I said, passing the phone to Kerry so she could read the message.

Can you come along to the shop? Rosa's (Radge's wife) is here, she's clearing his stuff from the back office – it looks like he's leaving. Fabian.

By the time I arrived, twenty minutes later, the woman I assumed to be Rosa had finished packing Radge's things into a plastic tub and was chatting with Fabian over the counter. His head dropped as I bounded in.

'Hi,' I said, nearly out of breath, 'I'm Keir. You must be Rosa?'

Rosa broke off from Fabian to look me over. She had dark, accusing eyes. There was an Italian lilt to her voice.

'I know who you are,' she said. 'I thought I'd meet you at the hospital, but I must have missed you.' I let it pass.

'How is he?' I said, 'any better?' Rosa took a moment to answer.

'Well he won't be coming back here,' she said, 'I won't allow it. Not now.'

'He's not coming back?' I said.

'He foiled a robbery once, at the St Ives place, did he tell you that?' she said. 'He chased the guy down the street, grabbed his leg and got his shoe off, that's how they identified him and picked him up. I said to Radge at the time he was lucky, the guy could have had a knife, anything, but this time he wasn't lucky and twice is too often for me, so as I was telling Fabian, he spoke to the owner this morning and that's that. It's not safe any more.'

Fabian, who'd plucked a bottle from the shelf and opened it as Rosa spoke, poured a drop into his glass and nonchalantly swilled it around.

'You've missed Petra,' he said, looking at me, amused, 'the owner spoke to her this afternoon, apparently. It looks like she's been promoted; unofficial deputy to official shop manager. I believe you're on with her this Friday.'

'Petra's a good woman, she'll do well,' said Rosa.

'She'll no doubt want to make a few changes,' cooed Fabian, holding his glass aloft.

'No doubt,' I said.

XIII

Goodbye, Old World

A naked girl and I exchanged glances, she with a bag over her shoulder, me accessorised with clothes. I'd seen many nudes at the art school you understand, just seldom strolling through its corridors, seemingly oblivious to the social conventions that still had some purchase, even here. In the interests of divesting the incident from its sexual thrill, because I wouldn't want you getting off on judging my libido, I'll recall her as she was not, in pieces: wisps of honeyed hair, a freckled arm, poppy red nails, a darkened swell of areola, a bestubbled chink. 'What's your story?' I asked. It seemed like a reasonable question.

'I'm here for an interview,' she said.

'Why are you naked?'

'This is a part of my art,' she replied.

'Do they know you're coming like that?'

'Well, yeah.' And with that I watched her walk to the next door, knock, wait for the 'come in', then enter. I missed this place; how I wish it missed me.

The world was crumbling and I needed to see Maisie. I thought if I could tell her what I was up to, perhaps show her before Petra could tear it down, she'd know what to do, how to save it. Sure, Maisie could be callous, even cruel, but she was an imaginative being first and foremost, a pragmatist second, and she'd find the idea of an artwork being destroyed by a malicious sprite, a blunt intellect and provincial nothing, content in her stick figure world, horrifying. Perhaps she didn't care for me any longer, maybe I was a liability to her now, but she'd always been my creative ally, and I couldn't believe that had changed on account of something as transient and slight as enmity and humiliation.

Many heavy strides still separated me from Maisie's bolthole when a right turn led to the wrong counsel. James Trevenna, a self-parody in tweeds, flanked by Jane, his unfortunate adjutant and reticule on legs, awkwardly plugged the corridor's width. When they saw me they stopped, but didn't give way. Trevenna feigned disgust. His flunky looked on, embarrassed.

'Can I help you, Rothwell?' he said.

'No,' I said. 'I hear you're leaving. When's your last day? I'll send a cake.'

'What are you doing here?' Trevenna demanded. I looked to Jane and she broke eye contact.

'I'd love to catch up,' I said, 'but I'm here to see someone and it's rather important, so…'

'I hope you haven't come expecting to see Maisie,' he said, 'she's not here and in any event it's not appropriate for you to bother her. I think you should leave.'

'That was a great guess, James, what gave it away?' Trevenna moved towards me, threatening in his way.

'You best go,' piped up Jane, finding her voice at last. I harrumphed, motioned the two of them away with a half turn of the hand and took a step back, regarding them wide. With Jane's body cut off by the old man's shoulder, her head looked to be growing from his trunk.

Addressing Jane as a person in her own right, perhaps the first to do so, I said, 'Why do you work for this slobbering pervert? A woman of your experience could get another job; you can't be that lonely, surely? I mean, look at him; it must be like a giant snail travelling across your face.'

Jane began to splutter, as though someone were struggling with the starter in her neck, half turning the key. 'I-I-think you better go right n—'

'Must I call the police?' interrupted Trevenna.

'Only,' I said, 'if you intend to confess.'

★★★

Friday morning had been a disaster. It's funny to write that now, thinking about Friday evening, but I'm trying to tell you how it was – how it felt at the time. From eleven that morning I was due on with Petra and was unready. I thought about ducking it, taking the weekend to regroup, but considered that leaving my work-to-date in the care of a poisonous femme, enabling her to sack me *in absentia*, was handing an unearned victory to a vindictive also-ran.

Even now, in the shadow of defeat, I wondered if I could charm her, reason with her. Humility, taking a fist up the guts – this was a kind of misdirection. I'd be employing a tactic that might yet buy the weeks I needed. Fabian would have to be brought on side, to keep Petra tied up with managing the place while I attended to the shelves, but in the hour before that shift, the door, however heavy, was still ajar. I briefly toyed with visiting Radge but dismissed it as heavy-handed. I would go later, once I'd reached an accord, then it wouldn't seem theatrical; it would strike the right penitent note.

Enslaving people to their will, making them embarrassed for having the audacity to think for themselves, that's all a sniping conformist like Petra wanted. By the time she realised the truth, that a man like me would never be cowed by a woman like her, the stable door would be hanging off broken hinges.

I was late for my shift. I had to be. There was no sense investing the situation with undue importance. Petra expected me to sidle in around quarter past the hour and that's exactly what I did. Her reaction would be the first normalcy marker. Usually I'd get a lumpen piece of sarcasm, 'up late adding length to your self-portrait?', 'done stalking your ex for the day?' and pitiless so on, but on this morning there was an acknowledging nod and nothing more. It was going to be a long twelve hours.

The day that followed has a particular significance now, for reasons that will soon be apparent, but in the moment it was simply a fascinating exercise in what might be called the art of the proxy conversation. Brain Haemorrhage Guy made his early afternoon appearance, tape affixed to his monstrous, thick-rimmed glasses, and having followed his script, asking for the cheapest thing we had, ignoring my advice, Petra took an uncharacteristic interest in a man she usually ignored from an unsocial distance.

'What happened to your glasses?' she asked him.

'Oh, nothing really,' he chirped, 'I sat on them, I'm going to need new frames. It was so silly of me.'

'Yeah, you best take care,' she said, 'you'll come a cropper if you can't see straight.' The earnestness struck a false note. Confucian throwaways seldom spilled from Petra's mouth. I was sure I was the one being spoken to.

I was certain of it later. Obnoxious Katherine was greeted by Petra like an old friend. The warmth wrongfooted her; she had a crumpled piece of paper in her hand and had clearly come to do battle, rifling through the shelves for some social function or other, but Petra didn't so much as glance in my direction, taking on this most unenviable of tasks with impish glee. Katherine, perhaps feeling obliged to make conversation, such was her victim's enthusiasm, asked after Ragesh.

'So what's the deal, he's not coming back?' she said. Petra feigned solemnity.

'No, I don't think he felt safe any more, not after the attack.'

'Did they ever catch the guy?' said Katherine, as I sat behind the counter, fascinated by this chat between two women, neither of whom were as interested in their conversation as they pretended.

'Well we know who was responsible,' said Petra, 'but no, he hasn't got his comeuppance yet.'

'I hope they get the bastard,' said Katherine, oblivious to the innuendo, 'I liked Ragesh, he was a good bloke.'

'He still is,' said Petra.

I hoped that would be the last of it, but of course it wasn't. Later a glaze-eyed Drunken Lawyer, desperate to make sense of his surroundings, made the astute observation that the shop had seemed less busy since Radge had been pulped. Were the punters frightened? Petra beat me to an answer.

'We've had a bad period of late,' she said, 'but I'm

planning to make a few changes, get the place back to what it was.'

'I'm so glad,' slurred Drunken Lawyer, 'this is a wonderful little place, you mustn't let some lunatic ruin it for everyone.'

'I won't,' she said.

***

Throughout the afternoon I struggled with how to puncture this atmosphere of animosity. I couldn't congratulate Petra on her promotion. In the first instance I didn't mean it, it was a disaster, and in the second she knew I thought so, consequently breaking the wine bottle this way would hand her the sliver of power her hungry ego craved.

The air was thick with things unsaid, but as the hours passed I began to fool myself into thinking that I could ride it out – endure a set of shifts like this one that would, eventually, segue into something more comfortable. Sitting on my stool, making small talk with a couple of casual browsers, I contemplated a masochism strategy, looking guilty, building to an apology of sorts, perhaps volunteering to do more on the floor (to keep Petra away from the cards). I wasn't sure how it would work in the long run. Still, in the absence of out and out confrontation, an escape felt possible. Then Maisie came.

It didn't take Petra long to work out who she was. Maisie gave a cheery 'hello there' to her fellow woman, then headed for the New World section. I'm sure I was checked by her peripheral vision, but perhaps her brain didn't make the connection right away, just as a horse on a seesaw would require a double take. When she finally saw me, perched on my stool, she made a sound, someway between a laugh and a splutter. 'Keir? I was told you might be working here – never thought I'd see you behind a shop counter.'

'Told by whom?'

Petra studied the scene with great interest, noting the change in atmosphere. This was no casual acquaintance and she knew it; things were too stifled. She was already working it out when I made an unfortunate slip.

'Listen, Maisie – I have to talk to you, about this, it's not what it lo—'

'So you're the famous Maisie!' piped Petra, and before I'd got halfway around the counter she was already toe-to-toe with her. Alert to my beeline, she motioned for me to stop.

'Keir, Australia and New Zealand are looking a little bare, can you bring up a couple of cases please?' Awful, palpable tension.

'Now!' said Petra.

Maisie looked embarrassed for me, but she was just collecting the excess. I couldn't have a blow-up; not here, not now. I moved quickly, listening to Petra complete her introduction with, 'Don't worry, Keir's only had good things to say about you.' I'd begun my rapid descent to the cellar by the time Maisie responded. I could hardly bear to imagine the rest.

When I emerged a minute later, breaking a sweat, cases stuck to my chest, Petra stood alone on the shop floor. 'Thanks,' she said, 'I'm going to take a break, so if you wouldn't mind doing a bit of shelving?'

'Listen,' I said, 'I need to catch her, it's important.'

'Sorry,' said Petra, 'I'm taking a break like I said, I need you here.'

'What did you say to her?' I demanded. Petra smirked.

'Nothing,' she said, after a long pause, 'she just had to go, apparently. She's pretty; a little old for you but very attractive, I get it. I'm a bit surprised though, a woman like that doesn't need to slum it.'

I affected a laugh. 'Nor did she,' I said.

'Aw, well maybe you'll get her back,' said Petra, 'couples row, don't they? Ian and I had a spat last night over something and nothing. Tonight we'll kiss and make up. Making up's the best part actually, but I don't suppose you'd know about that bit.' And with that she retired to the back office; the beginning of a break that lasted well into the early evening.

***

It was a little after eleven when the last customer left. The door was closed and locked. Petra hit a button under the counter and a sheet of corrugated tin cranked and whined, slowly falling from a slit above the display window. The street, wayward drunk and all, was blocked out. In silence we went through the end of day routine. Bottles were straightened, displays corrected, money counted and logged on a yellow sheet. 'We're a pound and a penny under,' said Petra, avoiding my gaze. Money always went missing in dribs and drabs, but no accusations were made; the politics of mutually assured destruction.

At the close of a difficult and, in bursts, mortifying day, serenity had settled on our scene at last. Twelve hours had passed in the pressure cooker with barely an incident. Maisie's visit had been horrific, premature; it would have to be unpicked, but she and Petra had barely spoken; the ship and the landmine had missed one another. I'd live to fight another day, I thought. The lights on the shop floor were turned off. I plucked my jacket from behind the counter and was about to leave when Petra said, 'Do you need to go or have you got a minute?'

'For you,' I said, encouraged by the conciliatory tone, 'I've got five.'

Without a word she walked to the back office and I followed. The room was cluttered and airless. Little separated the tatty desk and geriatric PC from an opposing wall of damp case boxes; homes for breakages. Petra leaned against the desk, forcing me to stand by the wall of upturned bottles and shards. As I positioned myself I noticed the remnants of the wine I'd seen her break on the day I met her, a day that felt a long time ago now.

I was about to open the window when Petra broke into what sounded like a well-rehearsed bit of spiel.

'Listen,' she said, affecting a sombre tone, 'things have been very difficult of late and neither of us want to work in this atmosphere, so I've made a decision, because I expect you want it to be over as much as I do.' I held my breath. 'This situation, you and I, isn't working,' she continued, 'we both know it, so basically, I think you should move on.'

I stared at her. She'd been restrained all day, and now I knew why. She'd been playing me, keeping the threat on the down-low so I'd relax a little, feel the full force of the words when they finally came. A figurative back foot became a real one. I felt the bulked-out boxes rub against my spine.

'Best for whom?' I said. My heart started to palpate.

'For you, for the shop; best for Radge.'

'Ragesh is gone,' I said, 'and I'm fine as I am.' Dum-dum, dum-dum, dum-dum.

'And why is Radge gone, Keir?'

The adrenaline was surging through me now; there was a tremor in both hands. I was helpless; cornered. I thought of childhood.

'I'm not going anywhere,' I said, 'I have a contract, I have rights.'

'You have no rights,' she said.

'I have rights, I have a contract.'

'You have a zero hours contract and I don't have any more hours for you. Business has been bad. We've lost a lot of customers of late; customers Radge worked hard to build up. *I wonder why that is*. I spoke to the owner about the dip in business. Didn't mention you directly; I'm polite like that. He agreed we had to cut back, balance the books. It's nothing personal, Keir, it's just you're the last one in, so…'

She'd wrapped it up beautifully. She'd even made a business case for getting rid of me. Later, I'd admire her moxie.

'Then I'll talk to the owner,' I said, 'perhaps he's not aware of the facts.'

'What facts?'

'That you've harassed me, that you came on a bit strong, that I rejected you.'

She laughed. I recall it going on for the longest time though in reality it was probably just a few seconds.

'Best of luck with that,' she said. She edged along

the desk as though her back were greased, putting a little distance between us. She was at the end now, perched at the mouth of the cellar staircase.

'In the meantime I'll tell him about your cards, about the offence they've caused, about the customers that have told me, sadly when you weren't around to hear it, that they'd never come back until our experiment with you ended.'

One of the boxes propping me up started to give way and I temporarily lost my footing. The hand I put out to steady myself brushed the contours of Petra's introductory batch of broken bottles.

'You have to leave that stuff,' I said, my voice trembling, 'it's important, there are others that have to go up. They're a set.'

Petra made fists. 'Are you stupid or something?' she said. 'I'm sacking you. All of that crap – whatever you think you're doing – that comes down tomorrow. I'm going to pull the lot personally. I'll be enjoying a little toast while it burns, because then there'll be no trace of you. If it wasn't for the fact that you cost us a boss we liked and respected, then I could forget you were here, but then, if you hadn't done what you did then I wouldn't be manager and wouldn't have the immense pleasure of telling you to fuck off now. Let's hope your inability to hold down a shop job doesn't hurt your chances of getting back artist lady. It would be awful if a catch like you ended up alone.'

The speech was capped with an inane grin, an indulgent display of triumphalism that uglified Petra absolutely. She regarded me with total pity, part tossing her Rapunzel tress; a feminine full stop. I was kissed off, dismissed. Fury, the likes of which I'd never known, had purchase on my soul, and my hand, in turn, gripped the base of the upturned bottle that brushed against it.

'Off you go,' I heard her say, 'feel free to take your tickets on your way out.' I registered a noise, something like a gargled scream, my sound I think; a sound that filled the tiny room and changed that obtuse face. My hand was raised, its jagged extension catching the light as it moved through the air. Petra was drained of colour, statuesque, lifeless. A moment later, contact.

The glass punctured her neck with a dull squelch. I drew back and heard a faint hiss, like air escaping a tyre, then watched as she rolled her eyes, a suffocating fish, and clawed into my chest, twisting the fabric of my T-shirt, trying to tunnel to my heart. I prised the hand free. She was soiling me, my face and chest contaminated by dark jets from her nape. I cried out and pushed her away, watching her stagger back, clumsy and ridiculous. A second later she crumpled, as though demolished. The limp form hit the ground with a violent crunch. Petra had fallen on to a wine case. The contents were crushed. I swayed, shaking, watching the floor turn to liquid. Blood and Syrah eddied in the gloom of that tiny office. The broken mound was face up, looking through me.

It took a moment, but in that awful room, in that charming shop, I realised I'd seen this vaguely feminine mass before. It was *End of Termagant*, my failure.

It was the end of the world.

PART TWO

THE NEW WORLD

I

The Shock of the New

Shock. Anger. Despair. Regret. Had Petra felt any of these in her final moments? As I stood over the remnants, a cocktail of blood and wine that nobody ordered seeping into my loafers, I wondered. The windows to Petra's soul, not that I believed in such specious guff, were broken; her death mask impassive. Her mouth was open ever so slightly, as though a word had been forming on those still moist lips. Of the many possibilities, I felt safe eliminating 'sorry'.

I know what you're thinking: he thought only of himself, but now who else was there? Petra's arterial dump was soaking my socks, dyeing my feet. My hands wouldn't settle. Biting discomfort reigned: the sweat, the damp, my convulsing stomach. Pain radiated down my arms like an iodine shot. The base of my throat blazed. There was half a bottle on the desk, plugged that afternoon. I grabbed it, urgently yanked the stop and guzzled what remained. I caught myself: I was drinking to relax, a cliché. Only now did I feel shame.

The shop toilet was the other side of the office wall. Suddenly overwhelmed by the urge to throw up, I snaked round the partition and fell across the threshold. Whatever else she'd done or tried to do, there was no need to humiliate Petra, making her the unlikely filling of a blood and vomit sandwich.

In seconds I was on my knees. A half second after that, further convulsions brought up khaki-coloured bits. When it was over I shifted my weight on to the back of my legs, only to be confronted by a wall of graffiti, the thought waste from staff past and present. There, a few inches from my face, was the spider handwriting of the late Petra Zealot: 'Nothing matters very much and very few things matter at all.' She was obtuse, even in death.

I returned to the back office, sat and surrendered to a kind of paralysis. On and on it went, the body inert, the mind inchoate. Long into the eerie silence the phone rang. I was startled both by it and the realisation I'd been sitting in that little dark room for the worst part of four hours. Somehow I'd killed the lights, electricity no safer in my hands than integral arteries, and now the only means of orientating one's self was the digital wall clock's faint luminescence. I watched the display tick on to 3.40 a.m. while the phone bleated; it was the loudest sound I'd ever heard.

Who was ringing? It could only be Ian, searching for his spouse. It was quite incredible that it had taken four hours for him to worry, but then I recalled her allusion to an argument, a boorish domestic, and reasoned that he might have cause to think she wouldn't be back that night, or would take some time, though not, it seemed, this much time. Now he fretted. That was my cue to do the same.

The weight of events was bearing down on me now. During my prolonged stasis I'd tried not to look at the mound, the outline of which could just be delineated. I didn't want to see the detail; I didn't dare touch that light switch. By sitting there, finger in mouth, breaking up a nail with jittering teeth, I hoped to slow time down, take a moment. Everything now depended on my ability to think. In hours the shop was due to open. If it didn't it would be obvious that something was amiss. Questions would be asked. I'd have to answer them. Had Petra told anyone else of her plan to get rid of me? The owner was a problem, one that would have to wait for now, but what of Fabian?

A frenzied search now began for the day's rota. In the dark I fumbled for it on the wall-mounted corkboard. Once found, the accompanying elation being equal to a blind man coming to a dirty scene in a piece of braille erotica, I tore it from its pin and held it to the window, allowing the moonlight from the back alley to illuminate the page. There, in the Saturday column was one word written across all twelve hours: 'Petra'. My first piece of good luck. I felt for a pen on the desk close by, nearly tripping on the obstruction I didn't dare contemplate, and once found I crossed out her name and replaced it with my own, doing my best to mimic her manic scribble.

My brain had shut down in those first hours. If there was such a thing as neuro-electrolytes I must have lost my load along with my stomach lining. Slowly coming into focus, the machinery sparking into life, I briefly contemplated picking up the phone and calling the police, but realised, in the next instant, the new rota in my hand, that I'd already decided not to.

I wasn't going to prison for Petra; I couldn't. She'd destroyed herself, she'd picked the wrong fight, but she wasn't going to destroy me; she wasn't invited to be a part of my future. If I confessed now I'd be bound to her for ever. Worse, I'd be her subordinate for ever, just another crude, mentally infirm monster, that's your word not mine, who'd butchered a weak and defenceless woman. There was no seeing past the dead girl. The simpletons in the homes nearby wouldn't care that Petra was malicious. The depth of her hypocrisy would never be known. Who'd listen to the chief witness? A body beached in marinade told its own unreliable tale. The truth was a ruin.

Any thoughts of injustice, of judgement, were broken by a dull thumping sound from the front of the shop. The hairs on my arms stood as I listened to ever more persistent hammering. Slowly I moved to the top of the cellar staircase and angled my head around the nearby doorframe, cautiously peering into the short corridor that separated the back office from our library of lacquer. Another bang and I saw the corrugated wall shimmer. Then, a moment later, a shadow appeared at the door, the wire mesh against the glass rustled. A face was pressed against it. I didn't dare move to get a better look but registered a change of shadows, the sudden imposition of detail. The silhouette became impastoed. There was a squashed nose, tiny eyes; Ian Zeller's face.

I pulled back to the safety of the wall. There was more thumping on glass. From the street I heard his grumble, 'Petra? You in there?' and the question hung as I held my breath, my chest burning, until at last the noise stopped.

When I tell you I was lucky you may doubt me, after all being trapped in a shop with a corpse doesn't read like the bedfellow of inherited wealth and good genes, but what happened next confirmed it. In the panic over my unexpected guest I'd forgotten everything; the layout of the office, the good view of its interior from the window facing the back walkway; and had I been a free-floating daydreamer, instead of one rooted to the spot, I might have walked back into that office and retaken the chair. Had I done so I'd have been facing the husband directly when, a minute later, his hulking frame loomed at that window, his hand held over his brow like a visor, his piggy eyes feverishly darting, looking for movement.

I watched, safely obscured by the dark interstice between the office and cellar staircase, struck by the horror of the scene, for as Ian looked, thankfully lacking the nous to glance down, Petra's husk lay a few feet below. As Ian scanned the room's horizon in vain, I crouched slowly and found myself in the body's line of sight. I couldn't make out her eyes, but I felt them on me; burrowing, judging.

When I was sure he was gone, when I couldn't detect so much as a sound, bar the ambient nothingness that accompanies the early hours, I set about buying time. A plan would come later; for now it was enough to make the shop hospitable for visitors. Petra had to be moved out of sight; even our wholesale customers would baulk at a dead body.

I grabbed her feet and dragged her to the top of the cellar stairs. The way she slid, with the sound of a wet towel pulled across a bathroom floor, made nerves go off like flashbulbs. The thought of pulling her down the cellar stairs to a subterranean morgue stuck in the brain like a glob of food in the windpipe. With each drag her head would clobber the steps – thud, thud, thud – and that, in my sensitive state, was too much. But now my luck returned. I was the man who'd leapt from a sinking ocean liner only to land in the life ring hole. The staircase was lined on its left side by the upturned chute used to funnel wine cases downstairs. The width was perfect for a thin woman, and she slid down in stops and starts, my feet giving encouragement.

No one's born to be murdered, but sometimes those who are befit the unique circumstances of their deaths. At the foot of the chute stood the shop's long rectangular freezer, our repository of ice bags. It took a few minutes to decant it, making a hill close by, but once empty I found it was more than adequate as a makeshift coffin. Petra's body hung from the chute, her legs touching the floor, her head and torso lying flat on the slide. With great reluctance I picked up her limp arms and dragged the body forward, heaving it up and over my shoulder. The journey to the freezer was six feet but it felt like a steep mile. The thud that accompanied her contact with the naked base of the rectangle was stark; it was a mallet hammering on your conscience. She fitted beautifully, as if the makers had a morbid streak and had plotted the dimensions with her in mind.

With Petra laid out I could look at her properly for the first time. She looked wistful in death, the least animated and aggressive she'd ever been. I stared at that face a long time. Turning away felt final. Eventually I had to plough on, my heartbeat aligned with the seconds, making each felt. One by one the ice bags were replaced, Petra vanishing from view bit by bit. The lid was shut and a couple of heavy cases placed on top. I was in a different gear now; so much so that confronted with a strip of dead bluebottles on turning, I didn't wince. There are worse things than poisoned flies.

One had to be grateful for spilt wine, it masked any

trace of blood in the air. Fruit and alcohol was a stench a man could live with, if you'll pardon the expression. As the sun came up it became possible to get a good look at the dark pool that had collected on the office floor. It was a congealed mess and it took a lifetime to soak up using paper towels from the neighbouring slasher. I flushed them away in batches, the occasional blockage catalysing spikes of anxiety and violent stabbing with a frayed toilet brush. Carefully, patiently, I did the same with the soiled water from the mopped nooks and corners. It had to be done twice, it was hard work, but by 5.30 a.m. the office looked normal. It wasn't pristine, but it never had been, it never would be. There was nothing to alert the eye to the scene's closet notoriety.

Now I was bold: I took the sodden box crushed by Petra and stacked it with the rest of the breakages. Any bits of glass, any fragments, were deposited in the bottle graveyard. One accident looked much like another, nothing stood out. I washed the broken bottle end that had slain Petra – I had to. Evidence in plain sight was one thing, being brazen another. I realised I'd have to make little calculations like that all the time now, walking the tightrope between business as usual and being overexposed. It was a new world.

I looked at the wall clock. It was nearly 6 a.m. Now reality flooded in with the smell of rotting berries. The shop was due to open in exactly five hours. A worried husband was contemplating reporting a missing person and I was standing where she fell; the slaughterman who'd forgotten his apron.

II

Over, Under and Through

The distance from the shop to my home on Fore Street was a quarter of a mile, but successive town planners, lacking a sense of the macabre, hadn't imagined a situation where a man stained by morbid ejaculate would be forced to navigate the route unseen.

The path for the unblemished man was a simple one. He turned into Teetotal Street, walked briskly to the mouth of Carlyon's Yard, followed its curve until he saw the intersecting thoroughfare of Causeway Head, then, presumably with a spring in his step, vaulted up the incline until a lime plaster corner signalled a line of cottages and the beginning of Fore Street. From there it was thirty paces to my front door and safety; a ten-minute journey for the fleet of foot, fifteen to twenty for the plum obese.

Audaciousness beckoned. It was a little after six and there wouldn't be many people around; the odd fitness fetishist, a dog walker, a street sweeper; but docile though they were, perpetually self-involved, they'd surely remember a hurrying man caked in crimson, stress etched on his face.

In the moment I could explain away my appearance, assuming they didn't get too close; I could say I was from the wine shop and I'd had an accident, though the quick witted may wonder why I'd waited so many hours to head home and change, or I could spin a yarn about being attacked after a long night out – anything in fact, and given the abstract and fantastical element to murder, divorced as it is from the average Joe's experience, I'd get away with it. But later, when news of Petra's disappearance bled into the community, someone, somewhere would make the connection. I worked in a shop in the heart of town, people who knew me as a sketch, an unnamed bit of background, gave me an acknowledging nod in the street. They knew my face. They'd seen me standing behind a counter with the newly disappeared a hundred times. I couldn't risk an amateur sleuth with a complete collection of ornate Agatha Christie hardbacks putting it together over their Cornish cream tea.

My only option was to risk a route strewn with hazards, the roof tops and everything in between. Commercial premises had CCTV, though of course I had no idea which did or didn't, so the only way to be sure was to try to avoid them all. The topography I had in mind was uncharted; I couldn't be sure I'd get where I needed to go, and if I couldn't I was sunk, but thinking of a spectral Petra writhing in pleasure as I was hauled away, my life destroyed, hardened my resolve. Fear of discovery fine-tuned my focus. I'd make it because I had to make it.

I left the shop by the back door. It opened out on to a small courtyard flanked by garages. Opposite, a thin alley led to the main street. In my agitated state I imagined every scenario, no matter how unlikely, including a patient Ian standing in that courtyard, waiting to see if Petra would emerge following an unlikely sleepover. In the event, he wasn't there, no one was, and I was free to get a foot to one of the elongated garage door handles and make a grab for the metal ducting that lined the flat roof, using a tenuous hold to haul myself up. The tunnel-like tubing wasn't built to take the stress and I felt it buckle and dip as I scrambled for a grip on the concrete edge above. I was forced to pull on it further as my fingers hooked, a few more seconds and it would give way, but as the tethers began to twist, I was able to get a firm hold and let go of the duct, dragging myself up and over on to the roof.

From my new vantage point I could orientate myself. I could see the top of the church to my left and felt the sea breeze behind me, and knew that my direction of travel was north-easterly. The first part was plain sailing, some easy strides over a flat surface, but beyond there was no good news. I could jump to the next building, its steep slanted, grey tiled, algae infested roof making further progress impossible, or I could risk breaking both legs with a tumble to one of three private gardens, walled on both sides, that backed on to the thin parapet running the length of both edifices.

For a moment I thought about handing myself in, thinking my luck had run out, but a mental snapshot of the confession to come cured my defeatism. The police had a pretty narrow definition of accident; one might say it lacked nuance; and whereas cleaning up after yourself was usually considered praiseworthy, conscientious even, following that instinct when the misadventure centred on the death of a failed human provoked indignation and judicial revenge. No, if these judgemental grubs wanted me, they'd have to work for it.

Carefully I lowered myself on to the parapet and followed it for as long as I could, looking for a good place to jump, terrified I'd slip at any moment and break my back. Then, at the summit of the middle garden with space to tread running out, a half chance; salvation in tree form. The furthermost branches were strong, not thick enough to use as a high wire or rope to shuffle along, but robust enough to act as a break on my fall, if how little they moved in the bracing wind was anything to go by. I'd jump to the branch, swing, hoping to stagger my descent, then drop to the grass.

I previsioned the jump and it looked graceful, but reality bit hard. I vaulted from the roof but knew, a second later, I was badly aligned, like a ski jumper, mid-leap, granted Cassandra-like powers, able to envision their forthcoming accident with ominous clarity. I reached for the branch with the only arm capable of getting there, just connecting, but the weight distribution was all wrong, the wrench greater than expected, and I let out a yell as my shoulder buckled and my palm was frayed. I had a grip but soon lost it and, conscious I was now falling, tried to right myself, tumbling on contact with the turf. I was now a heap with an aching arm and a searing pain in my foot.

There wasn't a spare thought for the owner of the house; if they'd heard me I hardly cared. I was winded and taking a breath took an eternity; it felt like my diaphragm had snapped.

When the breath came I was a half second from dying. I guzzled the air, supplying greedy lungs. Now I could think straight, I rolled on to my back and wondered what I'd broken and what it meant for my prospects. My arm wasn't right. I took a silent bet on a pulled muscle rather than a shattered bone. My foot was different. I reluctantly peeled back my damp sock and was alarmed by how red it was. I caught myself; the foot was stained with Petra and Syrah. The skin wasn't broken. It was tender to the touch. I'd fractured a metatarsal a couple of years back and this didn't feel any worse than that. I'd be able to walk on it if I let the other foot do the work. The extremities were down but the body wasn't out.

I looked up at the tree and saw the branch was half off its trunk, hanging low but still attached. With the building behind me and walls either side, I was now boxed in. I was able to get to my feet and hobble to the back of the house. Through the back window I could see a kitchen and adjacent lounge; another local had discovered open plan. Looking through to the front window and the street beyond, I caught the unmistakeable red on black 'HEN' of The Fudge Kitchen. I was a home's length from the mouth of Causeway Head, twenty yards from my street at most.

The time for scaling building façades and climbing up and over walls was over, my arm and foot had made that decision. The only way out of this garden was through that house. Hunched at the back window I realised I'd have to go in. Thirty feet separated me from that front door. If I could make it there'd be nothing but a few brisk steps to the cottages, then ten doors to my threshold.

I ducked under the windowsill and inspected the back door. It was old-fashioned, there was a perfectly round knob, the kind I used to see at my grandmother's house, and below it a keyhole. I pulled my sleeve over my hand and gave the knob a twist. The door was locked. Of course it was.

Could I force it? I peered through the keyhole. It was a thin wedge, maybe half as thick as a modern front door. I thought a sharp, full-bodied shove would do it. If that failed I had one good foot. I stood up and prepared to break through. If I were lucky I'd be in and out before the dozing owner-occupier knew anything about it. A break in so close to the shop was a loose end, but who could make the connection? If I could deal with Petra it'd be a key without a lock. I took a step back and angled my good shoulder. I anticipated pain. I readied myself but an abrupt noise on the other side of the thin wall had me stuck fast like a spider alert to a vibration on his web. It was a clank; an arresting, metallic clank.

Moving to the wall, I edged alongside it and glanced into the house. There, by the sink, was a man, the occupier, taking a spoon from a drawer, hitting the switch on a kettle. He was young, sturdy and fashionably bald. His dressing gown looked fresh, like the kind you'd swipe from a good hotel. He was an energetic milk pourer. He was in my way.

III

Thirty Feet

The situation was appalling. I'd written myself into a corner. There was no time to be reasonable, no time to be human; the clock didn't stop and wait for a propitious circumstance. I had to get through that house. If it flatters your inner righteous head shaker, I'll tell you that I considered every alternative. I ran my hands against the left garden wall, then the right, looking for a foothold. Neither offered one and each was too high to scale. My arm throbbed and my foot stung; I couldn't have made either climb. You neither. The façade of this house was flat. There was nothing to clamber on to, no route to the roof. The only way through was inside.

Why not wait for the occupant to leave, you ask? Why not find a secluded corner and listen for the slam of a front door? I glanced at my now scratched wristwatch. 6.35 a.m. I couldn't wait for this man. If his life was as prim and organised as it looked from the rear then he was up a couple of hours before he had to be anywhere, a practice he double downed on at weekends. He was the type of fellow who enjoyed a leisurely breakfast, who read a freshly delivered newspaper over granola. Later he'd retreat to the bedroom, gently kiss the spilt breasts of his groggy girlfriend, then saunter to the en-suite bathroom, where a full half hour of narcissism would commence. He was a shoe buffer, a tie straightener, a zip checker and shirt tucker. By the time he was ready to get out of my life I'd be lucky to have one. Residents a couple of streets away would be noting In Vino Veritas was closed. They'd make a mental note. The owner would get a phone call; he had to know people locally. He'd ring Petra and when that didn't work, Fabian, and it only took one unsupervised trip to the cellar…

Overpowering this man would be tough. With two good arms and legs there was half a chance. Anyone can be lucky in a scuffle, especially with surprise in your corner, but wounded he'd likely flatten me with a strong word. I considered tricking my way in, hammering the door and telling him a story about being chased by a pack of savages across the buildings that backed on to his home, but once he'd seen me, spoken to me, registered every detail of my character and appearance in such memorable circumstances, he'd be a witness in waiting, a man with a story to tell to an interested plod. I thought of Murgatroyd.

Even if I could convince him not to call the police or ring for an ambulance, and he let me go, how long would it take for news of Petra's vanishing to appear in the local rag he thumbed over cinnamon porridge and cranberry juice? And when he saw where she worked, a shop just a few streets away, and walked past one day and saw me through the window, even the dullest mind would have to make the connection. He could have no tale to tell and that was that.

Now I considered my only benign option; the win-win gambit. I'd wait until he went upstairs, then break through and run as best I could to that front door, letting myself out and on to the street, taking refuge before he knew what happened. If I were lucky he'd hear nothing. If I were very lucky the sound of an electric razor or the coital moaning of an unseen and thus far wholly imaginary woman would muffle the activity below. If he took a shower I was saved. He was saved. It's what I wanted. Believe that.

A testing twenty minutes now followed, punctuated by frequent glances through that rear window. As feared my man had taken his early morning pick-me-up to a table, most of which was out of my eyeline thanks to a separating half wall. I watched slippered feet, crossed and swaying from side to side. I saw an occasional hand reach out to the mug at the table's edge. As the dull spectacle continued my good foot became restless and my chest started to warm. There was a sharp pain in my right eye; a burst blood vessel, I thought. The window of opportunity was closing, the seconds ticking relentlessly on. Despite myself I let out a long bellowing sigh. Was this going to be the morning he savoured every sip, studied every column inch? Taking his time was dangerous; it was time neither of us had.

Now he rose. Finally! I took cover and listened to the muted creaks of a man mulling around; a man oblivious to the importance of his every move. The creaking was close; his tell-tale floor was going to be a problem. The impress of each foot was inches from my ear. I heard the muffled clunk of ceramic on steel basin, the chink of cutlery. I held my breath and closed my eyes. Seconds passed. Silence. Then a subtle change in pitch, a brushing sound from further away; he'd left that part of the room. I swung round and peered through the southernmost pane of glass. The room looked empty. The half wall, behind which I supposed was either the entrance to a set of stairs or the stairs themselves, made it impossible to be sure. Was he sitting behind that divide or had he ascended? I didn't dare back out and look to the bedroom window. I was going to have to pull the trigger in this game of domestic roulette and hope the chamber was empty. This was it.

I took a moment, ear glued to the back door, and satisfied I could hear nothing, retreated a few steps and braced myself for an inevitable new injury. I ran at that wedge, my good shoulder angled to form a buttress, my bad foot throbbing with each kiss of the grass. When I hit the door there was a crumpling, as if someone had strangled the neck of a paper bag. It had buckled, but not given way. My good shoulder was good in name only. I let out a cry, the kind that's baked in your stomach, then drew back, realising I'd have to go again. There was no time to think about being heard, whether it was too late; the past's a relic whether it's one second or a million years old. I lurched forward and hit it again. The door now gave way and I was on my stomach, stretched out on this young professional's wood panel floor. Head up, I saw the exit and vaulted. I didn't look back. I didn't turn, just pulled my own weight, my arms filled with slag, my legs brittle. I was collapsing the distance, twenty feet, fifteen; I was ten seconds from freedom. Then I was falling; the floor rose to my chin; I was flat on my face. I looked to my feet and realised with horror that the heel of my loafer had clipped the corner of a redundant, ornamental fireplace.

I dragged myself to my knees; I was still going to get out of there. I raised one foot, the other wasn't far behind. I stood, but as I did so the shadows changed and there was another presence in the room. There he was, standing at the foot of the staircase I'd rightly supposed was hidden behind that half wall, his face a cut and shut of concern and spooked lion. He regarded me like an impossible object.

'What are you doing here?' he said. 'What do you want?' He didn't wait for an answer. 'Get out!'

I backed away, regarding the front door, but knew I couldn't leave, not now. This man's promise was to be upstairs and he'd broken it.

'Listen,' I said, 'I'm being chased by a gang; they ran me across the roof back there, into your garden. I was just trying to get somewhere safe.'

'What?' he said. 'Where are they?'

'I don't know. I'm not sure if they followed me down.' He moved to the broken door.

'There's no one there. Are you hurt?'

'Yeah, they busted my arm and I hurt my foot jumping down. I'm sorry about your door. I just wanted to get away.'

He was looking me over. I saw his face drop.

'You're bleeding,' he said. I now recalled my appearance.

'Yes, they slashed me, I think.' I began to walk towards him. I went slow, imagining I was extending a hand to a rescue kitten. He was studying me now, no longer looking. I realised he'd noticed the blood was dry and was maybe already wondering why I hadn't mentioned my knife wound without a prompt. What had I said, 'busted'? It never pays to be ambiguous when you're lying. I was going to need a few more seconds.

'Look,' I said, the adrenaline adding a useful tremor to my voice, 'I'm terribly sorry about all this, I just didn't know what to do. Could you call the police and an ambulance? Can I wait here until they arrive, do you mind?' His brow unruffled. He nodded.

I scanned the room, hungry for a weapon. It was him or me, and knowing it, feeling it in every joint, damaged muscle, skin flake and follicle, made the choice easy. He could have stayed upstairs; he didn't. There was nothing to talk about.

He was scrambling around, looking for his phone; any second he'd find it, punch in '999' and there'd be a clue on the record, a pin on a crime map. I rushed him; there wasn't time for anything more dignified. He half turned, but I was on him before he knew it. His smooth head connected with the table edge and he was down, a bug on its back, temporarily stunned. There was a mug on that table, the kind that looked like a vintage paperback cover, and now it became part of a new story, the tale of a man hit in the face. I must have struck him hard, I was left holding an amputated handle, but it wasn't going to be enough. He had his fingers to his forehead; any second he was going to get up, hit back, and when he did I knew it'd be all over. Fatigue had its hands all over me; there wasn't a place on my body that didn't ache.

Now I saw it. On a cabinet, feet from where I stood and my homeowner groaned, there was a chessboard. This wasn't the kind you'd pick up for kids; it was handmade, solid, ornately finished with incused script along its edge and it looked heavy. In a second I had my hands on it. The tossed pieces scattered across the floor. As my opponent raised his head I hit the bulb squarely with the board's full width. The accompanying cry of effort muted the sound of the impact. My man was down, he wasn't moving.

Exhausted I dropped the leaden board and collapsed into the nearby armchair. My opponent lay still. Leaning back, I felt

133

something hard dig into my backside. Reaching underneath, I retrieved it and held it up. It was one of his chess pieces; fine carved, highly detailed. The head of the piece was unusual; a wizened face, a pointed hat. It took a moment to register that it was a character from *The Lord of the Rings*. I'd bludgeoned a Tolkienite. The world could have no complaints.

I didn't stick around to check my man's condition. I was probably OK. I'd have to be; I could do no more. If the occupant's quest had come to an end, then he wouldn't have anything to say. If he recovered, perhaps the sense I'd knocked into him had forced the memories out. He didn't know me, I'd never seen him before, it happened fast. I'm not callous. I could have made sure, but I didn't. There's what we're prepared to do in the moment and what we'll do when we've caught our breath and the intellect takes hold, and there's all the difference in the world.

I now moved as quickly as I could. I hobbled to the kitchen, grabbed a tablecloth and wiped the mug pieces and chessboard, just as they do on TV. It was absurd in an age when they can identify you from a bead of sweat, but it was a crutch and it got me out of that room. I finally reached the threshold, carefully opening the front door with my sleeve once again pulled over my hand. Tentatively stepping into Causeway Head, I saw a woman meander down the opposite side, her back to me. There was no one else.

I didn't look back. I closed that door and ran as best I could to the corner of Fore Street, almost too tired to care about a chance sighting, desperate to get home. A minute later I was there, safely sealed inside. I staggered to my favourite chair and embraced it like an old friend. I was home. It was 6.50 a.m.

I closed my eyes and tried to wish away the morning. I had an ephemeral waking dream of the night before, of grabbing my jacket and ignoring Petra's request to stay; walking on, coming home, planning the next move. Perhaps I'd open my eyes and it would be midnight and all would be well, and the morning that followed would be glad and confident, but when I did there was only the sight of my bloody sleeve and a cascade of pain from my shoulder to my fingertips. Now the eyes were closed tighter. Every blotch of morning was shut out, and the dream began again.

IV

The Puss and the Plan

Sunk and aching it took a while for the weight on my back to register. When I could bear to let waking life impress on my optic nerves, Petra was still dead and the memory of that house call, vivid. Half-dazed and impossibly tired, I arched my head and saw a dark tail with grey flecks touching my arm then bouncing off as though repelled by the morning's stain. I recognised the cat – a neighbourhood stray with a penchant for following you home, climbing through open windows and settling on amateur killers.

As I flipped over he pounced to the armrest, taking position like a lion flanking the entrance to a country pile. I managed to raise myself and his eyes followed the spectacle to the kitchen.

'I don't want to talk about it, Puss,' I said, but he stretched out a paw and relaxed into a smile, as if to say, 'Go on, I'm listening – it'd do you good to talk it through, after all you've only got a short time.' I checked the wall clock. It was nearly half seven. In Vino Veritas had to open in three and a half hours. It had to be business as usual, a hollow proposition yesterday, a ludicrous one today. I turned to the cat.

'All of this counts for nothing if I can't get back into the art school,' I said, 'it'll be meaningless.' The cat nuzzled his chest and licked his nose. He understood very well.

Robbed of the luxury of doing one task at a time I was forced to double, sometimes triple up. All my clothes were peeled off, black bagged and scheduled for sea burial as I thought about how to secure my tenure at the shop. Puss had seen me naked before, strutting around in happier times; he was indifferent to the grazed and the pendulous as I took to the shower.

With the water soaking in, cleansing, rolling back the hours, I realised I'd have to gamble on meeting the mysterious owner and somehow getting myself elevated to the now vacant manager's position. Seldom had so much rested on soft power. Fabian would be a problem. He was a shop veteran with a lot of centilitres under his belt and a crude sense of entitlement. He'd have to go. He was guileless, had no ambitions to take over that he'd ever cared to vocalise; sweeping him aside shouldn't be a problem. Towelling down I was horrified at the purple hue down my arm, the blemishes on my chest and legs, the island of red at the centre of my foot. The cat was purring; I was incandescent.

'Getting off on seeing me like this, are you?' I said. The cat blinked. His dreamy gaze seemed to say, 'Don't take it out on me, everything was fine until you let her get to you; until you fucked up.'

I ignored the bait and pulled on a fresh set of clothes, grunting and grimacing as I went. If I could get through the next shift, I thought, just get to the end without giving myself away, without the would-be drunks, Sunday dinner brigade (the organised ones came on Saturday) and casual browsers realising anything was wrong, then I'd be OK. I was playing a part now, the role of a lifetime; a fine young buck who knew nothing about a sub-zero corpse, a break in and a senseless attack on an upstanding character, beloved of friends and family, who didn't have an enemy in the world. The consequence of a poor turn wasn't embarrassment at awards season or whispering on press night, it was a new voice silenced, art denied; the breaking of the creative covenant.

The cat regarded me with a stretch.

'I'm going to need help, Puss,' I said. 'I'll need new people; I've got to have that place running, so I have time to heal. I can't fill those shelves every day or bring up boxes, look at me! That'll be part of my pitch to the owner. I'll tell him I need to take people on.' The cat stuck his tongue out.

'Oh, that's right,' I said, 'sorry, I didn't tell you did I, I'm going to request a meeting and tell him… well, I'm not sure, maybe that Petra ran away, that Fabian's on the take, has told me he's bored, the details will come to me. I have to control that space; upstairs, obviously, but also the cellar, no one can go down there until I can work out what to do about – *the problem.*' The cat yawned, then licked his lips, or whatever passed for his lips. I heard, 'Is that what you're calling her now?' and felt embarrassed, then angry.

'Don't judge me,' I said, 'she was in that room because she wanted to be. I didn't invite her. She didn't know about the project but she knew I needed money. She knew I had nowhere else to go. She knew I was trying to sort things out. She had a simple choice. Be compassionate or be cruel and she chose to be cruel. Well she vested that cruelty on the wrong man.'

The cat glanced up, as if to say, 'And Mr Morning Person, the home occupier, what about him?'

'What the war fetishists called collateral damage,' I said. The cat looked at the floor.

'OK, look,' I said, 'I have to get Petra out of there. People will be looking for her. In fact, some imbecile already is. So she has to come out of there somehow and everything has to continue as normal.' The cat's impassive stare suggested nothing would be normal from now on.

'It's a figure of speech,' I said, 'obviously nothing is normal now, but I refuse to be beaten by these people, do you understand? I'm not going to be sunk by a glut of affected oenophiles, if that's not too generous a term, which it is. I just have to think. When I think I win. Now how do I get her out of there?'

The cat slipped down to the seat of the chair, plying it for comfort. Once again I read his expressions. A lap of the tongue, 'It's not between you and them, it's between you and you, now,' a retraction of claws, 'Who are you? Meek Keir Rothwell, a victim, or New Shockley, the iconoclast, sent to shake people out of their insufferable complacency?' I like an easy one, first thing.

'I'm New Shockley,' I said, 'always New Shockley,' and I went to the set of drawers that underlined the part-open window, pulling open the top compartment and withdrawing a bundle containing hundreds of handwritten cards, bound by an elastic band.

'It's all or nothing, Puss,' I said, 'there's no way back. The future's all that matters now. Morality's transient, just fashion. In thirty years, fifty years, critics won't care what happened here if I can make my mark, if I get that chance. They'll just say I was flawed, tortured, all that nonsense; whatever the day's opinion formers need to get noticed. If the work stands up, they'll forgive me. They forgave Eric Gill.' The cat was purring again.

I hobbled over to the chair, my muscles still stiff. I plucked the cat from his seat, sat down and laid him on my lap. His claws settled on the surface on my trousers but went no further. On the adjoining table was a stack of old books. The journal I'd written to accompany the wasted year's work lay nested underneath.

'I'm going to have to write it all down,' I said, aloud I'm sure. 'If anything goes wrong people will need to know what happened, what I meant to do, should those spoiling forces out there get lucky.' The cat meowed.

'Yes, it's a risk,' I said, 'but I'll keep handwritten notes – keep them safe; no one will see them unless the worst happens.' I decided to write it as a memoir when time allowed, unedited and immutable; an account that would trump all subsequent attempts at reducing what had happened to the inexplicable mental gyrations of a copper-bottomed lunatic: the journalist's reassuring lie. I'd be catching up with myself from now on, documenting a story, the end of which was unknown to me. I'd find the right ending if need be.

The cat was rubbing his head against me now, rapturously thrumming. I knew what he wanted.

'I've got no cat food, Puss, you'll have to wait.' He licked his lips and I sank my fingers into his fur and half-remembered what comfort felt like. He looked at me. There was adoration in his eyes.

'Now c'mon Puss, help me. How do I get Petra out of that place? I can't carry her out of there; I daren't risk it, not even after hours, there's always some nightwalker or bunch of brain-mulched idiots from the school meandering around, it only takes one person to see me, just one.' The cat's claws started to dig into my leg. 'I can't leave her at the shop. Sure, I could take apart that back wall after hours, put her behind it with the rat remains and God knows what else, but what happens when someone finally comes to treat it, what am I going to say? That she bricked herself in?' The cat was testing the integrity of my skin now, incrementally extending his talons. 'I can't bring her here, there's no way I could keep her out of sight, in fact I can't take her anywhere, because if the body's found then it will be examined and they'll reverse engineer what happened. What do I do, Puss? How do I get her out and make her go away?'

The cat's claws penetrated my leg.

I recoiled, jumped up and watched the cat instantly assume my place on the seat cover. He looked up at me and wailed.

'I know you're hungry,' I said, 'but believe it or not there are more important things than feeding you.' He whined again. It was louder, more persistent.

'What do you want of me?' I demanded. 'What do you want me to do? Can't I have a moment to think?' There was more mewling, a desperate look in his eyes.

I took a moment. Staring at him I realised I understood.

'What? Oh God, there must be another way, surely?' The cat stood and arched its back and I felt tethered to its discomfort. My brain felt as broken as my body, I was losing purchase on the world around me. I no longer felt a part of it, it was an expressionist nightmare now, an Auerbach, and I was just observing it, drinking it in. The cat was speaking to me again: 'Don't be cruel,' I heard, 'don't let me starve.'

I was now beholden to gory pragmatism. I knew how I was going to get Petra out of the shop.

V

Murgatroyd

There's no manual to help you prepare human flesh. It struck me as odd that in an age of information the only materials anyone could get their hands on provided tacit moral instruction. You could find a thousand and one pages in doorstop volumes on dissecting chicken but not a single pamphlet on slaughtering a dog. Butchering lambs was fine, shredding a horse's brain with a bolt and carrying a chunk of it home over your shoulder was not. The internet, that abyssal trench, was there, of course, but one couldn't look at it. The cat had reminded me, or I'd reminded myself, I can't be sure, that imbeciles could always be relied upon to leave an electronic footprint; a page on dissolving a corpse sitting on your bookmark list between a burlesque bar and a piece on Hunter S Thompson's nocturnal telephone calls.

Petra's corpse had a crystal seasoning. By Saturday evening, twenty hours dead, she looked like a sugared strudel. It was a superhuman effort to avoid her iced face; I found my eyes darting, hungry for anything else; her blotched skin, her hardened shawl, the wedding ring I had to knead from her stiff finger. I'd have to revisit it eventually, that snapshot of horror, but for now, for the first time, I contrived to be narrow-minded, the peripheral was expunged. In death, Petra and I were closer than ever before. There was nothing now but my hand, the whetted knife and a limp arm. When I needed it, the bowl I'd nested on a stack of wine cases would be there too, and the cuts would be added to the freshly poured marinade; a well-regarded Trapiche Malbec. We had a good set of utensils at the shop and they were now employed in service to gourmet cat chow.

It was difficult at first. Slicing frozen meat, wherever it comes from and however complicit one is in its lifelessness, is hard work. The blade's wheedled in, then the sawing motion begins, revealing glacé tissue. Each strip is an effort; it's cutting wet leather. It took some guile. *End of Termagant* had been a doddle by comparison. I hadn't spent the day prior to that great work watching the regulars engaged in frivolous small talk with the cows and pigs.

Reticence became satisfaction when I thought of Ian and the events directly preceding this grisly carvery. I'd anticipated a difficult shift that Saturday, it could be nothing else, but I'd hoped for a little time to gather myself, to practise standing behind the counter and looking sturdy, allying with the day's rhythms, having whatever passed for normal conversation with someone whose greatest concern was procuring opulent mouthwash. The first customer had caught me sitting, but was too self-absorbed to notice me wince as I got to my feet. The second man through the door was the husband of the wine seller in the wine cellar.

'Is Petra here?' demanded Ian Zeller. He'd marched to the back office before I could stop him. 'Petra? You back here?' There was panic in his voice, but reassuringly, anger too. I limped after him.

'Ian, she's not here,' I said, 'what do you want?'

'She was supposed to be working today,' he said, 'is she down there?' He motioned to the cellar. I tried not to flinch. This was it.

'Ian,' I said calmly, 'it's just me. When did Petra tell you she was working, this morning? Because I'm the only one down to work today, look.' I unhooked the clipboard from the wall with my good hand and folded my bad arm behind my back. Ian studied it. His eyes danced. 'She was on,' he said, 'you can see it – who's changed this, you?'

'No,' I said, quick as a flash; it was important to keep the tempo now, 'Petra amended it, last night. She told me I'd be working alone today, and she wouldn't be coming in.' I walked, best I could, out into the shop and Ian skulked behind me, his voice redolent of suspicion.

'What did she say to you?' he said.

'I've told you,' I said. I was sounding teasy. That was Petra's word. Petra's words on my mind.

'That doesn't make sense,' he said, 'she was going to fire you.' My muscles tensed and my leg began to throb. I'd been afraid of this, that pillow talk would complicate this clusterfuck. I had to stamp on it, and quickly.

'Yet here I am, and here she isn't,' I said. 'Odd that she should want me to work if she was planning to give me the push. Are you sure you've got your facts straight, friend?' His mouth fell open; an attractive nook for the shop's flies.

'They're straight,' he said. 'She didn't come home last night; did you know that?' I took a half second to consider my answer, a half second too long.

'You do know, don't you?' he said. 'Where is she? Did she say something?'

'She said you had a row, some domestic.'

145

'And?'

'And that she wouldn't be working today.' Ian studied me. The counter separated us now.

'Petra's never stayed out the whole night without me knowing where she is,' he said, 'not once. If she wasn't coming home last night, I'd know about it. I called round this morning, no one's seen her, none of her friends. We had a blow up over a bit of cash, nothing serious, she wouldn't stay away for that. When she didn't come back I thought maybe she'd decided to kip here, she did it once before after we—anyway I had a look last night and there was nobody here.'

'Perhaps it was a tipping point,' I said.

'What does that mean?' said Ian. This was the age of quick thinking and there could be no mistakes.

'I think when she told you she was going to hand me my P45 she was perhaps covering for the fact that she was anxious about something else.'

'What?' he said. 'What are you talking about?'

'Maybe about leaving you, Ian. *About leaving you*.' He hardly moved. His Adam's apple rose, the least practical lift in the world.

'What are you talking about?' he said.

'She has looked unhappy recently.'

'She wouldn't tell you if she was thinking about that, she hated the sight of you,' he said. I felt such a natural high now; the pain in my arm and leg seeped away.

'Petra and I like a tussle but I think she's hyped it a bit, as is her wont, but then you're the kind of guy a wife can't be honest with, aren't you?' A flicker of recognition; a moment of nakedness.

'What?' he said.

'Oh, she told me all about it,' I said, 'she talked about the insufferable boredom and the lack of affection, about your insensitivity, the way you poke her insecurities and get off on it, about how you take the decisions then bully her into living with them.' These were educated guesses, but Ian's face, knotting with each clause, told me they were safe. 'You're a bit of a despot, aren't you?' He reached across the counter and grabbed my T-shirt, dragging me forward.

'You're saying that, not her,' he said, 'she'd never say that.'

'Why,' I said, 'because it's not allowed?'

'Where is she? Why are you doing this?' I prised his fingers from my chest with my good hand. I was stronger than I felt.

'I'm sorry you had to find out this way,' I said, 'but she was talking of getting out and it looks like she has. It looks like she's finally had enough.'

'Enough of what?!' he bellowed. Ian looked stunned, like a man who'd learned he was made of piss and concrete.

'You, Ian. *You*. The woman I've been working with for the past few weeks has been miserable, mooching around like an old carthorse, desperate for a bit of kindness. She invited me out to dinner last week, did you know that?'

His eyes widened.

'She didn't tell you, huh? I don't blame her. She was probably frightened of your reaction. You didn't knock her about, did you pal? I hope you didn't do that, because if you did, no wonder...'

'What did you say?' he said. 'What did you accuse me of?'

147

'Nothing,' I said, 'I was asking a question. She didn't say you did, she just looked scared whenever your name was mentioned. Why would she look scared? That's not a healthy reaction for a wife to have, is it?'

Now he came for me. He was round the counter before I could move and a moment later he'd knocked me to the ground. He kicked out and into my bad leg. I cried out, part in pain, part in joy. I couldn't believe my luck.

'Where is she?' he demanded. He raised his fist.

'She's gone,' I said, 'I don't know where, why would she tell me? I'm nothing, right? She was here last night, so maybe she took the sleeper. Maybe she's in London now. I think you've been cut loose, my friend.' He swung at me and I twisted my torso, guaranteeing the punch would land on my bad arm. My eyes watered. I made a sound; a groan cut with a laugh.

'You know nothing about my marriage,' he said, 'and nothing about her. You're a joke to her.'

'Th- then where is she?'

He moved closer. I couldn't take another hit. I thought of ruptures, bleeds, the need for medical probing. These wounds couldn't be scrutinised. I tensed, anticipating the blow, then saw a hand on the counter and looked up. Brain Haemorrhage Guy, the boorish tightarse, was hunched over, looking from Ian to me, mouth open.

'What's going on here?' he said. I'd never been so happy to see him. Then, to me, 'Young man, are you OK?'

'I've been better,' I said. 'Ian, here, is having a bit of wife trouble. We were bonding over it, like a couple of blokes, when I tripped and fell.' I got to my feet, brushing shop sawdust from my clothes, and heard the shop door slam. Ian was gone.

'You look hurt,' said Brain Haemorrhage Guy, temporarily distracted from the shop's bargain basement grog, 'did he attack you? Shall I call the police?' I steadied myself.

'No no,' I said, 'it's nothing; we just had a bit of a tussle. I'm fine. Between you and I, it looks like his wife's left him. He didn't take it too well.'

'Petra's left?' he said.

'It's none of my business,' I said and shot him a look to say, 'and none of yours'.

'If he hurt you, you really must call the police,' he said. This was Brain Haemorrhage Guy, propriety in all things.

'No police,' I said, firmer than before. 'All is well.'

All was well in that moment. The memory of the attack sustained me in the hours that followed, each burrow into Petra's meat a minor act of vengeance.

★★★

The official story was now in place. It wasn't my job to tell it, rather suggest bits and let the imaginations of others fill in the blanks. When that long Saturday was over I took home the concealed spoils from a day's sporadic carving and gave a grateful feline the meal of his life.

As Petra's meat sizzled in a hot pan, oil spitting on to my hands like a thousand pin pricks, I stowed my discomfort and tried to imagine it as simple food for a simple animal. Once the intellect's been extinguished, assuming it was ever there, what's left is just protein. Petra had no sentimental feelings for me so there was symmetry in my indifference. It felt strangely appropriate, warming even.

With the cat's head buried in a dish, I rang the owner, whose number I'd eventually found in a back office folder. He was in Truro and we agreed to meet there on Monday afternoon. I'd have to close the shop, I said, because Fabian was unwell and wouldn't be able to cover for me. I then rang Fabian to tell him that the stench from the rotting rodent in the cellar had risen to fill the shop floor, and that consequently the owner wanted the place closed while I arranged for someone to come and treat it. This was high risk stuff. Perhaps I would have to call somebody and let them forage around in the cellar, but appearances were everything now. Pest controllers, long overdue if the bodies on fly strips were anything to go by, were unlikely to take an interest in a freezer.

'That's fine,' chirped Fabian, 'I can do the second half of the week. How did you and the woman get on the other night?'

'OK,' I said, 'her head was somewhere else, and I think she's left her husband, but I'll fill you in when I see you,' then hung up to the sound of a deep breath. If all went to plan, there would be no follow-up chat.

***

When Monday morning came I checked on the shop, opening up for the half day as planned. My wrists ached from the marathon food preparation of the previous day. My whole body felt wretched, as though the serrated blade had penetrated my flesh, not the strudel downstairs. I was stooped, hand on the counter, leg hooked under the stool, not thinking, not paying attention, not noticing the man who'd entered through the open shop door like a particle of sawdust on the wind.

Murgatroyd was holding a bottle at arm's length, just as Mr Rainstorm had done, except his expression was warm and lively. He regarded the label with great curiosity and the attached ticket with a wry grin.

'You have a dark sense of humour, Mr Rothwell,' he said. 'I'm assuming this is your handiwork?'

I stood.

'Mr Murgatroyd, nice to see you.' Several seconds passed and I realised I hadn't answered him.

'I assure you, the questions do get easier,' he said, smiling. I forced a complimentary grin.

'Yes, I wrote that one. Can I help you?' I said.

'I hope so,' he said, 'I'm afraid I'm not a customer today. It's the dreaded day job. I'm sure you know, but I'm a detective inspector with the local force.' He started to fondle his top pocket, then gave up and felt around the inside of his coat. A weathered wallet and ID card were presented. In his photo he looked amused. The moment I'd half-expected had arrived. I tried to seize the initiative, pre-empting the thought gestating in his head.

'If this is about the rough and tumble the other day, I'm fine,' I said, 'I don't want to press any charges. He was upset because his wife had left him.' Murgatroyd didn't blink.

'You're referring to Mr Zeller?' he said. I nodded. 'I'm not here about that, though I'm aware there was a scrap.' He was still holding the wine. 'I'm sorry you were hurt, we can certainly talk about that if you'd like, no it was about Petra Zeller, your colleague. As you alluded, her whereabouts is currently unknown and Mr Zeller's reported her missing. You have to wait a certain number of hours before we can look into things, hence we've lost a weekend, I'm afraid.'

'Missing?' I said. 'I thought she'd left him.'

'Did you?'

'Yes, that's the impression I got.'

'From whom?'

'From her.'

'She told you she was leaving her husband?'

'Not in so many words,' I said. 'When we were working together on Friday she seemed agitated, she mentioned they'd had a row and—'

'Yes,' he said, cutting in, 'Mr Zeller said you knew all about it. You were very sure she'd left him, apparently. I just wondered how you knew that?'

'Well I don't, it just wasn't a surprise to learn she'd taken off.' Murgatroyd placed the bottle of wine on the counter.

'I'll take this while I'm here,' he said. He brushed his bottom lip with the edge of his long finger. 'There's nothing quite like a nice glass of Syrah, don't you think?'

'I don't drink really,' I said. Murgatroyd affected to look startled.

'Are you sure you're working in the right place?' he said. 'Would you mind wrapping it for me? I always worry I'm going to trip and break these things.' I wrapped the bottle.

'It's a job,' I said.

'Quite right, and a fine one at that,' said Murgatroyd, hitting the counter. 'Your wine descriptions are very colourful,' he said.

'Yes,' I said. 'Not to everyone's taste.'

'Was Mrs Zeller a fan?' I caught myself, just in time.

'Was?' I said.

'Sorry?'

'You said "was", why did you use the past tense?' Murgatroyd's grin returned. He looked like a farmer's son who'd been caught riding the pigs. 'Force of habit, I do apologise. I was just thinking aloud. Sorry, I can be somewhat tangential sometimes. I was thinking about her working environment, whether it suits her. Whether she's happy. It's odd for someone with a secure job, who's done it a long time, so has ties to people, the community, to just up sticks and leave without a word. How are things at work for her?'

'Fine, best I know,' I said. 'If she was planning to quit she didn't tell me.'

'I see,' said Murgatroyd, 'but, to reassure you, I doubt she's left her husband either.'

'What? Why?'

'Well,' he said, stroking the counter, 'I can't discuss it in great detail, and I'm trusting you to respect a confidence here, but as Mr Zeller may have mentioned, or maybe not, as he's a little agitated, all her clothes are accounted for, all her things. Her wallet's here, her passport's in her dressing table drawer, where she kept – sorry, keeps it, and if she was planning to go somewhere she didn't share those plans with a single friend, at least no one we've identified yet.'

'But she mentioned she wasn't happy to me,' I said. My arm was throbbing.

'Yes,' said Murgatroyd, his eyes snapping to mine, as though woken from a reverie, 'you took Mrs Zeller to dinner, is that true?'

153

'The other week, yes. How did you know that?'

'You mentioned it to her husband, during your recent spat. Where did you go?'

'Boondoggle.'

'Very nice,' said Murgatroyd, 'I assume this was a platonic meal, was it?'

'Socratic, actually,' I said. Murgatroyd smiled.

'Yes, very good. I must remember that. Still, Boondoggle's expensive, no?'

'There's been a bit of tension of late, since the attack on Ragesh, she was shaken up by it. She was an eyewitness. I wanted to do something nice for her.'

'Oh yes, poor Radge. A lovely man. We've yet to find the attacker, but we will, I promise you. I don't think there was a person in the town who wasn't shocked and disgusted by what happened.' He inclined his head slightly, as though a pulse had been delivered to his brain. 'Mrs Zeller's husband said you and she don't get on, though.' Murgatroyd glanced over my shoulder, running a hand through his thick dark hair. 'He said, she found you, and I hope you won't mind me repeating it, hard work. I'll take a packet of those peanuts too, please. Nice to see someone round here stocking Mason's.'

'They're a little sideline,' I said, trying not to look irritated by the digression. 'As I say, there was tension, so I asked her to go for a meal with me, clear the air.'

'Tension over the attack?'

'Yes.'

'Because she was upset by it?'

'Yes.'

'And did the meal help matters?'

'A little, yeah.'

'And at dinner she told you she was thinking of leaving her husband?'

'She said she was lost.' This had the force of truth and Murgatroyd's eyes narrowed, apparently sensing as much.

'Still,' he said, 'odd that she should confide in you and not her closest friends, but it can be that way sometimes, particularly when the friends and husband are close themselves.' It took me a moment to realise that Murgatroyd's gaze had fallen.

'I'm not entirely unapproachable, Mr Murgatroyd,' I said.

'Please sit down if you've having trouble standing,' he said.

'Sorry?'

'I just note you're having a little trouble putting weight on that leg. That was some scrape with Mr Zeller, huh?'

'I'm fine,' I said firmly.

Murgatroyd brushed the display with his spindly fingers. I recalled doing the same on entering the shop for the first time.

'Right,' he said, 'well if she gets in touch, I'd be grateful if you'd let me know.' He passed me a card, it read: 'Detective Inspector Howell Murgatroyd, Devon and Cornwall Police'. A number was handwritten below.

'They printed a thousand of them without the numbers, can you believe it?' he said. 'Taxpayers' money on the pyre. I'm embarrassed every time I hand one out.'

'I doubt she'll call me,' I said, 'but if she does, no problem.'

'Well, let's hope so. I like old Petra, so would like to

know she's safe as soon as possible. You've had rotten luck here of late, haven't you?'

'It's been a testing time,' I said.

'That's about it,' said Murgatroyd. 'Oh, yes,' he snapped his fingers, the sharp sound making me jump, 'what time did you last see Mrs Zeller on Friday?'

'I left at closing, she stayed behind; I'd say, 11.15 p.m., something like that?'

'You're sure of the time?' said Murgatroyd.

'When the shop closes it usually takes about a quarter of an hour to cash up, so yes,' I said. Murgatroyd gently pulled the bag containing his bottle and nuts off the counter and swung it gently from side to side suspended from two talons.

'Oh dear,' he said, 'then I'm afraid your theory may be disproved.' I felt my teeth grind.

'What theory?' I said quickly. Teasy teasy teasy.

'You thought she might be in London on Saturday morning,' he said.

'What?'

'You said so, to Mr Zeller, do you recall?'

'I was baiting him, Mr Murgatroyd, he was being obnoxious.'

'I see,' he said, 'it's just that the last shuttle train to the mainline goes at five past eleven. If you wanted to get the sleeper from Truro, I mean. You'd have to make that connecting train or you'd miss it. You'd be stuck here until morning.'

'Perhaps she drove?' I said.

'Not without her car, I think,' said Murgatroyd, 'both it and the keys remain in town.'

'OK, so she took a taxi.'

'None of the local firms took a booking from her,' he said, 'and thus far her face hasn't jogged the memories of any drivers. In any event, nobody took a cab to Truro on Friday night. It's a bit far I suppose. Twenty-five pounds, easy.'

'Considering you had to wait until you could look into it, you seem to have investigated quite a bit already,' I said.

'When someone vanishes, officially or no, there's no time to lose,' said Murgatroyd, 'you'd be amazed how quickly a trail gets raked over.' His grin returned. 'I wouldn't worry, we don't always know everyone a person's acquainted with first hand, she could be staying with someone, or have spent the night somewhere we've yet to identify, then took off. Maybe that mystery person gave her a lift somewhere. We'll get the picture, then hopefully I'll be able to put your mind at rest.'

'Yes,' I said, realising only then that the sentiment he was fishing for was spilling from my mouth a little late, 'I hope she's OK, thanks for coming by.'

'Thank you,' said Murgatroyd. He signalled he was ready to pay and I was punching in the prices when he reached across and covered my hand. 'Actually,' he said, 'I'm not really supposed to buy alcohol on duty, and those nuts are a little expensive, so I better leave it for now. I may come back for them.' He put the bag on the counter. 'I'd have that arm looked at though. You flinched a little when wrapping the bottle. Don't leave it if you're hurt. Often things look all right, but beneath the surface, who knows?'

And with that he was gone.

VI

Good Housekeeping

The owner's name was Fred Spoor. Surprisingly, for a man who owned a chain of wine shops, he rejected the waiter's list and ordered a cloudy beer; the filtrate from bad kidneys. He was nonchalant to the point of distraction, seemingly incurious as to why he'd been summoned to talk shop with an employee he'd never met. Indeed, there was no thank you for my diligent service, no questions about me, just a quick pat on the arm, a motion to sit down, then small talk.

Given his mellifluous voice and enterprising bent, I'd anticipated a cock of the walk; the kind of man who centred his junk in the mirror each morning and carried business cards in a leather and brushed steel wallet. Yet Spoor was ramshackle, late of someone's couch. I imagined him caught between two families, each ignorant of the other; a man too preoccupied with keeping all his lies in a row to think about much else.

His finger tapped the table as I told him there was a staffing crisis at the Perrangyre shop, but he only started paying full attention when I offered up the fiction that Petra had mysteriously disappeared, maybe overwhelmed by her new responsibilities, likely desperate to flee from her controlling husband. Spoor was sorry to hear that and surprised, not least because she'd been one of his best employees (which was absurd), and someone he knew personally from the old days; a veteran from the team that once ran his flagship store.

'I'd have made her manager years ago, but she didn't want it, she loved working with Ragesh,' he said, and I smiled sweetly, only relaxing the fist made beneath the table's horizon when the jagged edge of my one good nail nicked my palm.

I reluctantly took a swig of the wine I'd ordered, imagining the owner would polish it off; a carafe I now had to guzzle alone with seething annoyance; and pressed my story, that Petra, in the run-up to being appointed new manager, grew distant and apprehensive. It was as though it were 'a burden too far'. She barely spoke during our last shift together, shunning the customers, nibbling her fingers, alluding to her marital troubles. She was not herself at all; a haunted figure whose mind was elsewhere, just as mine turned to Murgatroyd as the story spilled out.

I looked through Spoor and recalled the morning's conversation; Murgatroyd's jovial manner, his playful innuendos. The owner was looking concerned now; I'd moved on to Ragesh's attack, how it had changed Petra, made her irritable and anxious, but in doing so I described my own state of mind. My arm throbbed and I thought of Murgatroyd's feigned concern, wondering how much he already knew and whether my unfortunate home occupier, battered and broken, had been discovered or was still lying there, a swollen, encrusted lump.

'The shop's not doing so well of late,' said Spoor, 'I suppose that's not too surprising. First poor Radge, now this. I can hardly believe it. I wish Petra had told me how she was feeling, I could have got someone in to help out, ease the pressure a little.' This was my chance and I leapt on it. I was here for just that reason, I said, because the shop needed fresh impetus and I wanted to be the one to lead it back to profitability. He didn't stop me so I continued. Fabian, I told him, was a problem, not the kind of guy fit for the consumer experience I wished to create.

Profitability, experience, what a bastard set of words. Spoor was ogling me now. I was offended, not yet mortally, that anyone could think, or will themselves to believe, that another human being could give two fucks about whether or not a wine shop made money, but for once the offensive, intellect-atrophying priorities of the creatively inert were my friends. Spoor took me at my word, unable to conceive that his barter hole would soon be a vehicle for an artwork he couldn't hope to understand. I almost thanked him for handing me the foundations, but instead layered my disinformation with bristling confidence.

Fabian, Spoor learned, repelled the customers with his pomposity. He was more interested in grandstanding, boring patient customers with tangential gush about the mistral wind and the vineyards of northern France, than selling them the contents of the bottle. At one stage I thought I'd gone too far, for Spoor valued that level of wine appreciation, but I recovered, noting that it wasn't the knowledge but its conflation with imperiousness and condescension that was toxic. Ordinary customers were intimidated not delighted, repelled not seduced, and the sales spoke for themselves. Those passing by in the street, carrying the weight of a Fabian encounter, were less inclined to return. Spoor's confidence in Fabian's abilities ebbed away as I spoke. He was slouching in his seat. It was a narrative that partnered perfectly with his bottom line figures.

Now I pressed home my advantage. It was time to kill off Fabian once and for all. He was drinking the stock. Not discreetly, as we understood to be fine, opening the occasional bottle for a weekend tasting, but habitually. It was possible, I said, that he could have a problem, such was his tendency to go one further and swig from opened returns. I ventriloquised Ragesh, imagining him in my place, 'it's taking the piss', not to mention generating it, and I realised I was parroting Spoor's thoughts too, his head shaking, his cheeks flushed, his inner monologue tapped out in Morse on the tablecloth.

'Ragesh and Petra never said anything,' he recalled, looking betrayed. I hypothesised they were protecting him, hoping to manage him, or perhaps they didn't know. I'd studied him at close quarters and had worked a great many shifts with the inebriate in recent weeks. It was possible, I said, that his behaviour had weighed heavily on Petra's mind in the period following Ragesh's attack, and that she couldn't cope. Given how much Spoor professed to know her, I was amazed how easily he was convinced by this yarn of fragility, but then we don't really know anyone, do we?

'I'm happy for you to take over, if you'd like to,' said Spoor, 'and if you need to get of rid of Fabian, do it – I can't have the guy intimidating the customers. It'll be good having someone grounded running a shop, if you know what I mean. Not being funny, but there's a lot of haughty bastards in the wine trade at shop level. Half of them have personality disorders. Believe it, I see it all the time. They love wine but they hate people. I try not to hire them, but they're typically the only ones that apply. They tend to be living on family money – lost in their own little world. It'll be good to have someone normal behind the counter for a change.'

I was grateful, I said, and very excited, grafting this affirmation of retail values on to a daydream of a shop stocked with deconstructing epigrams and well-chosen barbs. I'd turn it around, I said, sloshing the wine around my glass like a human turbine, and I knew a perfect pair to help out in the short term, a couple of friends I was sure would be glad of the extra money and were great with people.

Of course people, whoever they were, meant very little to Robin and Kerry – well, a little more to Kerry – but having them on that counter, soaking up the vitriol (not to mention the stock), would secure the scene and complete the artwork. The Circle was coming to In Vino Veritas.

They'd be styled as no wine shop employees had ever been, a universe removed from the customer service ethic Spoor revered and talked up. Six months from now, I promised, we'd be making double whatever the transient and meaningless figure was today, and I laughed, ostensibly at some feeble joke that dribbled from his mouth, while reflecting that I'd be out of there in four weeks or less, just as soon as the school brass learned of the project and saw the shop, rebranded as a working installation. Oh, I said, I had so many ideas, so much I wanted to do with the place, and pushing a vision of Petra's mutilated husk to one side, trying not to let the mental impress of Murgatroyd's smirk darken my mood, Spoor and I shook hands as a waiter poured the last of the carafe on to the sediment lining my glass. The shop was mine.

★★★

Inevitably not every break with the recent past could be clean. Spoor insisted that as a consequence of my new role, surely the hardest anyone had worked to become the manager of a wine franchise, it fell to me to break Fabian's maddening grip on employment. From the shop's back office, fresh from the cellar and a check on our refrigerated goods, I dialled the number, unsure what to say. Fortunately, Fabian's supercilious bent acted like a whetstone, sharpening the words.

'This is outrageous,' he said, 'I'm going to speak to the owner, you're not doing this.'

'This was his idea, Fabian. He's had reports.'

'Reports?'

'Yes, about your attitude. Customers have complained; they're not too keen on your… tone.'

'This is fucking outrageous,' said Fabian, paraphrasing himself, 'I haven't had a single run-in with a customer. My God, you've had more than me, and I've been there six years!'

'Look Fabian, I know it's rotten, but the truth is you're a bit of a snob.'

'What? How dare you!'

'You're a bit of a snob and our customers don't like it,' I said, 'they don't appreciate being condescended to, patronised, made to feel like uncultured morons, true or not. People come here to buy wine, not suffer your conspicuous intellect.'

'There is no way I'm putting up with this; I'll sue the bloody company!'

'That's up to you, of course, but I've been asked to remind you that the flexible nature of your contract means your employment here is pegged to need, and right now I just don't need you. Takings are down, perhaps because of these issues.'

'Your tickets have driven people away, it's nothing whatsoever to do with me!'

'Perhaps,' I said, 'if you'd taken a full-time contract you'd have a case, but unfortunately it was more important to you to have time out to… well, who knows? Go on picnics, take long holidays, stay in bed to the early afternoon? It's not for me to judge, but some would see that as self-indulgence and this is a business. We're not here to prop up leisure time.'

With that the phone was hung up. I sat back, amused, feeling powerful. This was my office now, my canvas. Only the sticky residue from the previous week, still visible around the base of the desk leg, sullied the atmosphere. I was staring at it when I heard a tap on the window.

Murgatroyd was standing outside, in the back alley, giving me a friendly wave. Seconds passed and I became conscious that I was looking blankly, not moving, dumbstruck and incapable of reaching for the friendly response the hand gesture demanded. He was motioning to the back door, miming its opening. I'd have to let him in. As I walked to the office threshold, I glanced down the cellar chute to the freezer. I hadn't yet placed wine cases atop, sealing the tomb. It was bare and easily opened.

Letting Murgatroyd in, a judicial vampire, I turned,

expecting him to follow me, only to hear him say, 'Mr Rothwell, come out here please, I just want to check something.'

A moment later we were standing in the back alley.

'I'm sorry,' he said, 'I could see the light was on from the front, as the curtain wasn't drawn, so I came round the side. The street door was locked.'

'We're not open,' I said, 'I was just doing some business on behalf of the owner.'

'I see.' Murgatroyd turned to the garages behind. 'Have you had any trouble round here of late? You know, apart from the obvious.'

'Like what?'

'Ooh, I don't know – kids, vandals, that sort of thing?'

'I don't think so, why?'

Murgatroyd walked to one of the garages. 'The ducting above this garage is broken, it's been pulled down; it looks like someone's used it to clamber over.'

'Why bother?' I said.

'Well,' said Murgatroyd, 'who can say? But they've done a lot of damage here. Look,' he pointed to the door handle, 'you can see the scuff mark where some fool stood on it.' He bent down, glowering at the dark scratches. 'A foot caked in filth, ugh. If the owner rents one of these, you may want to let him know.'

I tried to stay calm, remain placid, as I had with Spoor, but he was there for the taking. Murgatroyd was a different animal.

'I just wanted to ask you about CCTV,' he said finally.

'You want it for last Friday?'

'I'd be interested to know if there was any,' he said,

rubbing the underside of his chin with one of his elongated digits, 'perhaps out back, as the shop camera's not working.' The conversation we weren't having was starting to rankle.

'How do you know it's not working?'

'The light was off this morning,' he said. 'Is there a system out back?'

'No,' I said, 'I'm afraid it's been neglected. I think Petra was supposed to get a new set of tapes. It's an ancient system. Perhaps she forgot, what with her personal stresses and all.' Murgatroyd looked despondent, though in a funny sort of way. Had he expected this answer?

'That's a shame,' he said, 'I was hoping that perhaps she'd left the back way last Friday.' His eyes fixed on mine. 'Which way did you go when that shift ended?'

'The usual.'

'From the front?'

I'd committed myself, I had to follow through. 'That's right.'

Murgatroyd took a theatrical step back, like a man with a cockroach on his shoe. His eyes glistened.

'In that case, I may need your help in solving a bit of a mystery,' he said.

'As long as you're happy to share your pay packet.' Careful, Keir. Teasy does it. Teasy. That word again.

Murgatroyd rubbed the lobe of his ear between the thumb and forefinger of his free hand and his eyes danced, as though the ultimate imponderable had seized his mind. 'The question,' he said, 'is this: one day a couple of people go to work in a wine shop. They enter but neither comes out. What happened? How do two people disappear?'

VII

Missing Seconds, Lost Days

Call it pressure, call it creeping, all-consuming anxiety, but the days that followed, be they three, five or seven – I can't be sure – are, as I try to recall them, choppy, tapering in detail. It's time that fails to cohere, refusing to snap to a clear and complementary chronology. I've tried to reconstruct it but each event was subordinate to the only thing that now mattered: the project. That was the golden thread, and everything hung from it, events caught in its wake, like the poisoned flies ensnared on strips in the basement.

Events had an unstoppable momentum now. The shop was filling up with new cards, new ideas, and Robin and Kerry, who'd been cajoled into shoring me up, on the pretext that they were both at loose ends and it would be fun to take over the place for a few weeks and enjoy a free hand, did their bit.

They faithfully reported for duty, buoyed by the relatively generous hourly rate Spoor had acquiesced to on my recommendation. We quickly conceived of a scheme to supplement it; a 'save the shop' fighting fund to appeal against Cornwall Council's imaginary decision to purchase it and open an interfaith centre. Such a scheme was sure to be a hit with the locals.

Robin, amused at the possibilities inherent in baiting

the public, inelegantly sauntered around the place, his long black coat sweeping behind him. Kerry, mischievous, charming, sybaritic, comely and colourful, like a fertile rainbow, built bridges with the regulars who were initially discombobulated by the new faces.

She was fleshy when required; the part of her that luxuriated in flirting turned on by the tease, gregarious at other times and somehow able to take the temperature of each head and mix her personality accordingly. When she spoke to people there were moments of kindness, glints of sex, and a strange call, filling the shop like sweet incense, a sound I hadn't heard in a long time. I later recognised it as laughter.

They were understanding and a little relieved when I told them I'd be dealing with the cellar on my own. 'You must stay up here,' I told them, and on the rare days they'd be working without me, they could concentrate on the shop floor as I'd bring up fresh stock the night before. The reason, I said, were the noxious pest control chemicals, thick in the subterranean atmosphere. As manager I'd minimise the risk by looking after the area alone; owner's orders. The freezer lid was broken and jammed, I said, so I'd used shop funds to buy a back office replacement, which we'd use to store our ice bags until the large one was repaired. The lid to Petra's tomb was covered in wine cases at all times and an 'out of order' notice was promptly affixed to its side in case my new employees got curious and made the journey down the stairs, despite my health warning.

As a support act, my enablers were better than I could have dreamed. They bought me time. The time to write out back, time away from the hordes and their questions about Petra's whereabouts, and crucially, time away from Murgatroyd. His was a constant presence, as though he'd tethered himself to my shadow, and I grew to despise his uninvited sojourns. He bit like a mosquito. He had lots of little questions, discriminate jabs, but by spending each and every night anticipating them, rehearsing my answers with the cat, who purred his approval or spat with incredulity when the replies were cloddish, thin or catalytic – fuelling further questions – I grew in confidence.

Robin and Kerry, my gatekeepers, kept Murgatroyd tied up, just for a moment or two, and those were the moments I needed to compose myself, straighten my clothes, tighten my expression. I'd explained to my unwitting partners that I was being harassed, due to the circumstantial timing of Petra's disappearance and the vulgar picture that had been painted by Ian Zeller. I had no doubt that our loyal customers were also cultivating Murgatroyd's suspicions, signalling a shift from mutual disrespect to attrition. God love Robin and Kerry; a bastard and a beautiful slut that trusted me completely, or enough – it was all the same at this point.

Vigilance was required because I'd come so very close, brought to the point where a wrong word or dropped gaze might have jammed a glass shard into the neck of my ambitions. Having posed his question, the mystery of the disappearing wine advisors, Murgatroyd had led me to the street adjacent to the shop front and motioned to the jewellery shop not quite opposite, but on a diagonal to our front door. He was beguiled by it, as though the place were encrusted with diamonds. He knew something and he was ready to share it.

'There's a camera above the door there, can you see it?' he asked, and he'd pointed to the jeweller's doorframe, where I now noticed a tiny lens with a red light above it. 'You see it?'

'Yes, what of it?'

'That camera,' he said, 'faces on to the street, right way on – it's a static angle and it only just covers your shop's front door, there's no image of anything east of the entrance, no view of the side alley, but you can see the door, that's the important thing.' I said nothing. 'Now,' he went on, 'obviously we've been trying to ascertain what time Mrs Zeller, Petra, left the shop on that Friday – which direction she went and so on. We couldn't find out from inside the shop. There's no functioning camera and, curiously, no time stamp from the security system.'

'What's curious about that?' I said, realising my mistake as the defensive sentence flopped out.

'Well, Petra's very habitual,' said Murgatroyd, 'I was able to cross reference the log of the shop's alarm system with her shifts, going back six weeks – that's as long as the paper rota records – and guess what?' He waited for an answer. I didn't indulge him. 'Every time she was on duty the alarm was set. Usually fifteen to twenty minutes after closing. Never earlier than fifteen minutes, never later than twenty-two. It seems, you could almost set your watch by her.'

I thought back and realised that Murgatroyd was right. I could see Petra telling me to stand by the front door as she prepped the alarm, gallivanting across the floor to make it out before the pips became a long tone – the tinnitus-type ring that gave notice that the alarm was setting and that we had ten seconds to close the door or hear it bleat. I couldn't remember a time she hadn't done it. The blood drained from my genitals. Had it drained from my face too?

'She didn't set it on that Friday?' I said, wanting to choke myself.

'She did not,' said Murgatroyd, face alight, 'and that's the kind of incidental finding we sometimes get in these sorts of cases, that gets the blood pumping. It's highly curious.'

'She was under a lot of stress,' I said, realising the line sounded weaker every time I regurgitated it, 'maybe she forgot. God knows I've forgotten the little things when up against it.' This was dangerous talk, but I couldn't help myself. There was a certain excitement being this close to the precipice, feeling the ground crumble, turning giddy.

'No doubt,' said Murgatroyd, 'and it could be that simple, but it doesn't help us with the time she left. More importantly it doesn't help us discover where she went.'

Time to feign ignorance. 'That camera over there doesn't help?'

Murgatroyd grabbed my shoulder and pain cascaded through my arm. 'Oh, I'm sorry, I forgot,' he said, reading my discomfort, 'no this is the mystery. That camera records the street at twelve frames per second, so it's not a fluid record of the scene, but we were able to requisition the tape, and something interesting came up.'

'Oh, what?'

'There's no record of you or Petra leaving the shop on Friday night. If I forward on to Saturday morning, I see you return to work. You're in two frames – one at the top of the camera's view, coming west to east, as I'd expect to see from a man who lives up in Fore Street, and one at the shop door, letting yourself in, but there's no image of you leaving on the Friday night and none of Petra following you a little while later. Two go in, none come out. Odd, no?'

Think fast or lose your life; when the choice is that stark, chemical forces, synaptic lightning rods, they fuse, fire, the brain hosts a hundred thousand fireworks parties and a lot of kids get disfigured when a rocket goes off in their faces.

'Twelve frames per second, you said?' I'd worked a lot with video; I was a visual practitioner, after all. Murgatroyd nodded. 'Then it's an unfortunate case of the camera blinking at the wrong moment, you follow?'

'Do go on,' said Murgatroyd. He looked genuinely fascinated.

'Well I didn't go home directly on Friday, I'm sorry if I didn't mention that – I had a bit of a headache, it can get stuffy in that place sometimes, so I took a walk down to the seafront, the scenic route by the gardens, so banked right when leaving the shop,' I gestured to the mouth of the alley that snaked round the jewellers, 'and wound my way down from that side street. It's a shortcut. As I did a right when I walked out, then cut directly across, I suppose I'd be out of frame pretty quickly. I was in a bit of a hurry to get out of there, it had been a long day. I suppose it's just bad luck that I left between frames as it were, else you'd have seen me leave after eleven as I said. At least you saw me return, right? If I hadn't left, I don't suppose I could come back.' I laughed but Murgatroyd held his gaze. He let a few uncomfortable seconds pass.

'New information always helps,' he said, his tone harder than before. 'Curious that the camera didn't pick up Petra either though, no?'

'Not really,' I said, temporarily enjoying myself, 'Petra headed that way too most nights. I think she enjoyed a drink at the London Inn. We went there once. I wouldn't know when it closes, it's not really my sort of place, and she did live in that direction, but if you're asking me to speculate I'd rather not. The only one who knows where she went that night is her, and if she was in a hurry to get somewhere or bolted for whatever reason, then she too might have inadvertently beaten the camera over there. If she was in a hurry, that probably explains why she forgot to set the alarm. I hope you work it out, Mr Murgatroyd, you've really piqued my interest.'

I was set to break off when the plod, having lost some of his sparkle, became more erect.

'Why were you early to work on Saturday?'

'I'm sorry?'

'Having reviewed the footage, I took it back a couple of weeks, just to get a sense of Petra's working habits, and I noticed that you, well – I hope I'm not being indelicate – you're generally quite late for work.' It was true. The thought of reporting for duty during those dark, powerless days, hadn't topped me up with pep. It couldn't have mattered less to me whether I was there to greet the first customer of the day. I'd made exceptions for shifts with Ragesh. Sometimes.

'Guilty as charged,' I said breezily, 'I'm a heavy sleeper most nights. My brain still thinks I'm a student.' The cliché was a sop to the plod's likely prejudices.

'But you were twenty-five minutes early on that Saturday,' pushed Murgatroyd.

'I was up early, knew I'd be on my own, so didn't see a reason not to make my way in. There's no point hanging around at home for the sake of it,' I said.

'Would it surprise you to learn it's the only such instance of you being on time in the two-week period recorded by the camera across the road?'

I felt the cold, as though hunched over Petra's corpse.

'Gotta reform sometime,' I said, as though about to launch into an Irving Berlin number, and we parted in the shadow of the shop that was fast resembling a giant headstone.

That, I vowed to myself, was the last time Murgatroyd would catch me short. He was circling the truth, but if I kept moving it would be harder to swoop. So Robin and Kerry kept him busy, bogging him down with inane and frivolous questions about the missing woman their customers were so curious about, and I'd wait behind the red curtain, picking my moment to bestride the shop floor, confident, anxious to help, regretting he'd been kept waiting.

One afternoon, with my lieutenants preoccupied with customers, Murgatroyd made it to the back office, a spike in Kerry's voice providing the only warning, and I had moments to adjust, feigning to be caught writing a ticket as the inspector's shadow filled the pokey enclave.

This, it transpired, was a moment of maximum danger: another brush with justice, however ill-defined, that made the case for pushing on with the project that much more urgent. Murgatroyd had noted the odour, the atmosphere of decay, billowing like mist from the shop's dank cellar. I explained what was down there: a rat behind the wall, a corpse resisting its passage to dust with a vitality and energy worthy of life, but predictably, inevitably, he wanted to take a look. Murgatroyd was polite but insistent and my neck pulsed when he paused at the bottom of the stairs, just feet from Petra's husk, taking a moment to eye the fly strips that were now almost as plentiful as the wine cases stacked on all sides.

'You weren't kidding when you said it'd been dead for a while, were you?' he joked, and I relaxed, content that the multiple strips backed up my story. Yet he didn't move from that interstice between stair and freezer. He lingered, like the stench that eddied around him.

'Where's the body?' he said, studying my reaction. His face was locked in a configuration that looked like mock inquisition – a look out of step with his urgent tone.

'It's further out back,' I said, 'shall we...?' But Murgatroyd stayed put. He looked up at the fly strips lining the cellar's doorframe.

'Why is there such a lot of these at this end?' he asked. I looked and realised he was right. I hadn't noticed before but several had been mounted there, a foot from Petra's body. I'd missed it, but could now see nothing else.

'It's just the easiest place to put them,' I said, weakly. 'Look around you, there aren't many great hanging options.'

Now, to my horror, Murgatroyd sat on the freezer. He was sitting on Petra. My weak hand began to shake slightly. I put it in my pocket and tried to look calm – or normal, whatever that meant.

'Still,' he said, 'there are, what, ten here? Are you sure

there's no rat behind one of these boxes, maybe a relative that died of heartbreak?'

'Believe me,' I said, 'if you think it reeks over here, wait until you get to the back wall. No, there's nothing. We occasionally have the odd wine spillage down at the foot of the stairs as you can imagine,' quick thinking Keir, 'and, well, the flies like the rotten fruit I suppose.'

Murgatroyd was staring at me now. 'Indeed,' he said. He got up, taking just a moment to look at the wine cases weighing down the freezer lid. He seemed to look at them for ever. I was compelled to complete what I hoped was his thought in limbo.

'We have rather more wine than space at the moment,' I said, 'but we'll sell it – it's the right time of year.' There was something folksy about that, I sounded like a genuine retailer. Embarrassment threatened to trump fear of arrest in that dreadful, debasing moment.

The thickening atmosphere, as one approached the back wall, a safe distance from Petra's crystallised remains, acted as a necessary and heaven-sent diversion. Murgatroyd took his time examining the wall, but the hole therein and what appeared to be a tiny hollow beyond was plain to see. No human body could have been hidden there and it was clear that no one had touched this grubby partition in some time. There was nothing around it but dust and damp.

'Mr Rothwell,' he said finally, 'I hope you won't mind me saying, but it's vile down here. It's like a nineteenth-century morgue.'

'I know it,' I said.

He started to walk back towards the freezer, as though Petra were beckoning him. I stayed put and held my breath.

He took another look at the area by the stairs, looking up to the flies and down to the stained floor. After an eternity of contemplation, he straightened up and swung round.

'Little point laying poison now,' he said, 'I think your friend's been dead a long time, but it's not a police matter.' I allowed myself to laugh at that. 'I'd have this place treated, though' – he poked a fly strip with his feminine nail. 'There's enough chemicals down here to kill half the town.'

VIII

Art Unbound

In Vino Veritas was a special place now. It was alive. The tickets were part of it; their uncanny ability to flip moods and stoke brains, the owners expecting nothing more than a little passive shopping, was a joyful thing. Real magic. But it would be cruel to excise Robin and Kerry from the record. They were magnificent, at the peak of the freedom afforded by the will to challenge that now gripped the place. I'd told them to enjoy themselves, insisted that we use the little time we had to best effect, and whereas they understood that the ultimate aim was to displace the consumer and arrest their sense of being somewhere safe and comforting, on a frivolous level there was scope to cut loose and experiment with the regulars' sensibilities.

It was Robin's idea to add a gratuity to the price of a bottle, arguing that the act of tipping was so nonsensical and offensive that the point had to be made in the most vivid terms. I watched with begrudging admiration as he took the normally formidable Obnoxious Katherine to task for refusing to pay the additional pound for wrapping and bagging.

'Is this not service?' said Robin. 'Did I not smile and give you minutes of my time, helping you to decide what to buy?' There was no difference, he told her, between that and the arbitrary cash hike for services rendered in the restaurants across the way. 'This is a minimum wage job,' he lied, 'I'm low paid, how I am supposed to live? Do you really expect the owner to stump up? Get that money out!'

Laughter's a wonderful sound but the pointed, indelicate laughter of a haughty customer, fizzling out as they realise they're being seriously reprimanded, is even better. Punter after punter begrudgingly paid the levy, stuffing notes and coins into a jar while an expectant and impatient Robin looked on, arms folded. In a few days we had well over £60. I added the expected extra (15 per cent) to each new ticket, adding calligraphic finesse to each half loop and swirl, a proxy for glee.

Kerry, who'd taken to wearing a necklace with a card that read 'available for tasting', hated the shop's music, which she was quick to label 'unadulterated guff'. In the days that followed I found she'd brought in a collection of political speeches, recut at home to produce long and passionate montages of ultra-left wing oratory, set to ambient beats, meditative chimes and malevolent violins.

Drunken Lawyer, wearing the misery and deference of others beneath a suit jacket with a faded but conspicuous mustard stain, was quick to stumble to the counter and check that we too heard Tony Benn berating the emptiness of the entrepreneurial society. Later, Brain Haemorrhage Guy's lonely joke, 'I'll have the cheapest wine you have,' was pleasingly drowned out by a different speaker's vitriolic tub-thumping; rabble rousing rhetoric suffused with rolling r's.

I floated around, enraptured, as the BHG tried to prosecute his shtick, the air burning with archived indignation at society's best understood but least remedied injustices. He couldn't think straight, if he ever had, and his uneasy shifting between feet, his grip tight on a bottle of carbonated urine, was rather wonderful.

Kerry's ability to tune it out and speak normally, in contrast to the customers' inability to do the same, was a masterclass in calculated incongruity. I looked on and remembered the tension and tedium that defined Petra and Fabian's spell behind the same counter, and it felt like a shift as significant as any I'd ever experienced. It was a hot bath after trudging through stupidity's bile-like residue. Sometimes I could close my eyes and forget the old guard had been there at all. Only a hungry cat and the necessary after-hours trips to the cellar freezer ruined it.

Every evening we broke new ideas and every day, as I mounted new cards, we implemented them. Nation categories were torn up. In their place, wines were reordered into a pompous hierarchy. The producers that had barely tried, content to furnish their labels with little more than an abstract logo and gaudy font, stayed closest to the door. The journey from front to back became a trip up the ladder of ostentation. Coats of arms, nineteenth-century throwbacks and musical and literary references designed to exclude Joe and Jacinda Public could be found as one approached the red curtain. Kerry had suggested inverting the prices to further undermine the producer's intent, so we did just that. The vulgar wine of Keller Beach, a purple label wrapped around a bottle of bland syrup, was repriced at £25. Our vintage Beaune Grèves, Vigne de L'Enfant Jesus, Bouchard Père et Fils, formally our most expensive swill at £50 a liquid portion, was yours for a mere £3.95.

But it was the new tickets that gave the shop its edge, transforming it from a place of barter and exchange to a hall of mirrors. When I looked at them, and watched customers looking at them, each and every one a potential Mr Rainstorm – time bombs in drag – senses lit up and my troubles turned to dust. This shop was not the world, it was independent and free, and whatever social capital the customers brought to the place was worthless once they'd stepped inside. The punters were part of the work now, nothing more.

Long descriptions were written on old 'Staff Choice' cards. We crossed out 'Staff', replaced it with 'Life' and pluralised 'Choice'. Each member of the new In Vino Veritas crew had their favourite sketch. This was mine:

Violet Lane, Grenache

Tonight's the night you're invited to Sally's for a meal with her family. This doesn't happen often, and you're not sure why, but you're flattered by the invitation and you won't want to come without a gift. Well what about this? It looks nice enough; it should flatter Sally's cultural pretensions. You don't want to palm her off with insipid gut rot. She's saving you from another night alone – another evening in front of the television with your memories and regrets. If you're lucky you'll get to drink most of it. Sure, there's a danger you'll ramble on, the embittered, bigoted monster within, punching through the tits and breaking out, ready to speak her mind after decades of pent-up resentment, but so what? It's about time she found her voice, no? Why did Sally get a nice house, husband and kids, anyway? They may be degenerate kids and, yes, her husband's a gorilla in a shirt, but you were the prettier of the two when you were teenagers, you got all the attention. How the hell did Sally – boring, tight-lipped Sally, with her strange self-regard and flat sense of humour – end up fulfilled, smug and secure, when you have nothing and nobody? It's a mystery that only those who've heard you pontificate on politics and men, understand. Anyway, have a good evening.

Robin liked:

Parker and Hulme Chardonnay – New Zealand

Behold, the perfect partner for young arrogance. You're fresh, you're optimistic; you're still naïve enough to believe your opinion matters. That's why you're going to want to supplement these, the last years of your life that show any promise, with this oak and citrus soak. It gilds opinions, facilitates sex and sugar-coats memories, but it's not a brand for life. In the years to come you'll associate it with now – before the love of your life chose someone else, before you realised your dream job was unobtainable, before your friends changed beyond recognition (becoming people you despise), before you became self-aware and mortified at the repellent and loathsome bilge you spouted when you thought you were being clever during these, your golden years. Still, that's tomorrow. Today it's £10 and highly drinkable.

Kerry's pick was based on customer reaction alone. When anyone approached the bottle she'd tug on Robin's arm like an excited child at a theme park.

Yearbook Riesling

How dare you. How dare you saunter over here and read this. Can't you see this wine wants to be left alone? Don't you understand that it has no interest in being fingered by a passing miscreant? What gives you the right to intrude on its space, huh? What gives you the right to *presume* that it would want your grubby digits around its cork, your lips on its neck? You ooze in here like a polluting fog, your sense of entitlement palpable, and you come over, determined to pluck. Well this is the wine that says, sod off and stay away. Your money's no good here. You can't buy this kind of pleasure and even if you could, you haven't earned it. Now leave, before the good people behind you call the police.

This was the shop now, a working work of art, and it was perfect. Knowing it was ready, feeling the throbbing in my sinuses like a caffeine high, my old confidence returned. I sat out back and wrote a letter to the art school, inviting them to inspect New Shockley's new installation *In Vino Veritas: A Shop Story*. By contacting April Zuccaro, the new

Dean, I was showing I was serious; this was no prank. The guy they'd kicked out had created new, exciting and challenging art on their doorstep. Could they really afford to keep their backs turned?

When I was thinking I was winning, that was the rule, and I'd thought so very hard. I'd kept Murgatroyd at bay and a hungry cat satisfied. I'd swept away discontents and installed my own people. Everyone who'd stood in the way – Ragesh, Fabian, Petra – were gone, gone, gone. Who'd have thought a gang of delinquent proles would ruin it?

IX

A Trip to the Cellar

'I feel like I'm becoming a nuisance, Mr Rothwell.' In Murgatroyd I'd found the last great practitioner of understatement. I waved the taunt away.

'Oh no,' I said, 'I'm delighted to help in any way I can, I just hope Petra's OK.' One couldn't be certain if the words had left the mouth fully formed, or if the intonation betrayed their insincerity. I heard what I wanted to hear and delighted in not being able to see myself. The mind's eye saw a solid, unflappable visage – eyes narrow, lips moist, concern oozing from every pore. What Murgatroyd saw, from his presumptuous perch on the end of my desk, only he knew.

'I wanted to check if you'd seen anyone suspicious on the Saturday following Petra's disappearance,' he said, and on asking why, I found myself ensnared by a conversation I'd role-played many times with the cat as Murgatroyd's understudy. The words, 'there was an attack not far from here, in the early hours of Saturday morning'; I'd heard them many times, but when they left the plod's mouth they had more weight. I reached into my pocket, pinched the skin on my thigh and twisted; anything to keep me sharp, stop the drift into terminal incognisance. Perhaps the look of discomfort aped empathy. There was no way to know.

I listened as Murgatroyd laid the whole thing out. A man had broken into a guy's house, smashed his back door, overpowered him, beat him up. It was a strange, seemingly motiveless attack, just a few streets from the shop. I knew the sequence of events, of course, but hearing them repeated cold, shorn of context, made me uneasy. It sounded terrible. It was inexplicable. It took everything I had not to jump in and explain.

'It's curious in many ways,' said Murgatroyd, 'one of the strangest attacks I've dealt with.' He leaned towards me. 'There's an obvious and terrible parallel with what happened to Ragesh. I can't remember two incidents like it in such close proximity, and I don't believe in coincidences.'

'You think it's Mr Rainstorm?' I said, trying not to sound hopeful. 'Because you haven't found the guy.' A flash of anger lit Murgatroyd's eyes.

'It could be him,' he said sharply, 'but it's far from certain.'

'I don't understand,' I said, 'a man comes in here, beats our manager half to death and now you say it's happened again up the way, it's obviously the same person.'

'What makes you think it was up the way?' said Murgatroyd. 'I didn't say where it was.'

'I presumed,' I said, 'there's not much down the way bar shops and the ocean.'

Murgatroyd smiled. 'There are a few things that don't make it being the same man a given,' he said, hopping off the desk. We were almost toe to toe now. I could smell his citrus breath. 'The man who attacked your manager had been involved in an altercation with you and Petra. He had a grievance with the staff in this shop. It's possible to see why he'd return, why he might want to hurt someone here. I refer to his internal logic not mine, I'm not condoning it, he was obviously temperamentally subnormal.'

'Sure,' I said tonelessly.

'But this attack,' Murgatroyd paused and drew breath, 'this attack was seemingly random. For a start, the victim had only been in town twelve hours. He was renting a holiday cottage. He's a Londoner. No one, bar his girlfriend, who was due to join him later, and his friends at home, knew he'd taken up residence. Here I assume the owner of the cottage didn't decide to show up unannounced, first thing, and brutally beat their tenant. That's a welcome unbecoming of our friendly town.' He paused, studying my reaction, and when there was none, continued.

'He hadn't, best we can determine, seen or spoken to anyone. Second, the intruder broke in at the back. Now this is odd – unlikely, you might say – because the house backs on to a perimeter wall and is terraced, and there are equally imposing walls either side. There's no way in to that garden bar the front. So either this man got in from an adjoining property and climbed over, and there's no sign of that – those homes appear unbreached, as it were, and we've spoken to the residents of each – or he jumped down from the perimeter wall that lines the gardens.'

'OK,' I said, 'so what?'

Murgatroyd was staring at me now. 'The back wall to this place is high, Mr Rothwell. I'm talking twenty feet. I wouldn't be brave enough to jump it. You could easily break your legs doing it. Yet, someone did it seems. I think they must have been pretty desperate to get down there, don't you?'

'Someone high perhaps?' I said. 'No pun intended.'

'Perhaps,' said Murgatroyd, 'high but not cavalier. They tried to break their fall using an oak tree in the garden. They part-snapped a fairly thick branch doing it. It's not the kind that could be broken any other way, I don't think. The tree's healthy, the weather's been mild the last couple of weeks; there have been no reported mass migration of birds to a single branch that we know of.' I laughed, as I thought I was being prompted to, but Murgatroyd remained stone faced. 'It certainly begs the question, where did the intruder come from? Where was he going? Why? I reverse engineered his route, so to speak, and it's likely he started close by, actually, perhaps by the garages out back. He may even have been the man who broke your ducting.'

'Really?' I said. 'You sure about that?'

'We can't be sure just yet,' said Murgatroyd, 'but I'd bet my life on it.'

I fought the temptation to look down to the cellar and won.

'Let's hope it doesn't come to that,' I said. There was more ice in my voice than I'd have liked.

'Do you want to know the curious part?' he said. 'There's no motive. The intruder broke in, surprised the victim – we can infer that because he was still in his dressing gown, and a fight ensued, but the intruder didn't take anything, not even food; he just beat the poor bugger and left.'

'Drug addicts,' I said, 'there's no mystery there. He was probably searching for gear, panicked when he saw he wasn't alone, ran out.'

'Yes, that could be it,' said Murgatroyd, 'or perhaps

he was just anxious to get to the street beyond and our holidaymaker was in his way.'

'What was his hurry?' I said.

'That,' said Murgatroyd, 'is an excellent question.'

'How can you be sure it was a he, anyway?' I said.

'Well the victim's over six feet, was in good condition. A woman could have overpowered him but it's less likely. His injuries suggest he put up quite a fight. His attacker was strong, determined,' said Murgatroyd.

'Hmm, well apart from Ian Zeller storming in here and beating me unprovoked that morning, no I saw nothing out of the ordinary.' The statement was allowed to diffuse in the air like cigarette smoke. 'In fact,' I said, seeing an opening, 'why don't you speak to him? A man's beaten, then I'm beaten; there can't be too many men on the rampage round here, can there?'

'Well he had no reason whatsoever to visit this man,' said Murgatroyd, 'nothing connects them, but we'll look into it, of course. The good news is that we'll soon be able to ask the victim about his attacker.'

'What?'

'Oh, he's alive. Sorry, I should have said. He was very badly hurt – I mean, beaten around the head, so he's been in a medically induced coma for nigh on two weeks now. They had to reduce the swelling on his brain, poor chap. The news this morning was that he's showing real signs of recovery. I may be able to speak to him in a few days. If his attack is linked to Petra going missing, it could be a breakthrough.'

'Why should they be linked?' I said. Murgatroyd stood at the top of the cellar stairs, leaning into the gloom.

'Mr Rothwell, this is a small town, the clichés are by and large true – nothing much happens. I love my job, but I can go for weeks, sometimes months, with little to trouble the faculties, beyond incidents that amount to petty crime, or, following inquiries, are innocently explained. So when, in the space of a few hours, I have a woman disappear and a man brutally beaten first thing in the morning, inside a house not more than 200 yards from where the missing lady was last seen, I say the chances that it's a coincidence, though possible, are teeny tiny.'

'Life's arbitrary and meaningless, Mr Murgatroyd,' I said, 'we love to make connections, impose a scheme on events, but sometimes bad things just happen. That's life.'

Murgatroyd spun round and made his way to the door. 'You're a Londoner, true?' he said, glaring at me.

'Originally,' I said, 'why?'

'Well,' he said, 'there's quite a bit of crime where you come from, but, and you'll correct me if I'm wrong, perhaps less community, fewer lives overlapping, yes?'

'On the contrary,' I said, 'millions of lives overlap, we just don't bother each other. The longer I've been here, the more I've grown to appreciate that.'

Murgatroyd took a moment to look me over. 'I'll tell you the main difference between me and my colleagues up country,' he said, 'those officers, and I have great respect for them and the environment in which they have to operate, will often be removed from the victims on their patch. They're unlikely to feel the threat on their doorstep. They're permitted a certain level of abstraction. But when I think about what's happened here these past few weeks and the man responsible, I think he's walking around my town, rubbing shoulders with the people I've known all my life – people I went to school with, who married my friends, whose kids play with my kids. I think that Petra could easily have been my wife, that the poor wretch fighting for his life in the hospital half a mile from here could have been my neighbour, and I shudder at the realisation that if this man, this chest of bad pennies, isn't caught soon, it may yet be someone I went to school with, someone I drink with, someone I love. That makes me very determined to find the man responsible, can you understand that Mr Rothwell?' I nodded.

'I know you'll find him,' I said, 'it's just a pity that given the, shall we say, vulnerable types that are born and raised in a town like Perrangyre, you'll have so many suspects.'

'I'll tell you what I know,' said Murgatroyd, 'there's a real psychotic out there, someone I believe to be a threat to everyone he knows. He could be one of the usual suspects, a drug addict as you say, or just a man with mental health difficulties, some unfortunate on the street perhaps. But in all likelihood he's a seemingly ordinary man, perfectly affable but a nest of snakes underneath. Either way, I don't think he's passing through. I think he's right here with us. Be assured, though, I'll find him. Every day I get a little closer.' He took a step towards me. 'You know, forgive me for saying this, but it's fortunate Mr Zeller attacked you that morning. The man I'm looking for would have been hurt jumping into that garden; he might have sustained a scrape or two in his tussle with our holidaymaker. If Mr Zeller hadn't hurt you, I might have suspected your injuries.' He smiled.

'Lucky me,' I said.

'Well be careful,' said Murgatroyd, his face falling, 'luck runs out.'

★★★

They were words, nothing more. Just barbs. Murgatroyd had his sequence of events, but he didn't have me. He didn't know why and he never would. He'd walked through the shop without giving the displays a second glance. His brain had filtered out the motive. That's why I'd win, I realised, because the bridge between these seemingly inexplicable events required the one thing he didn't possess: imagination.

This was the thought that sustained me as I vaulted along the cliffside pathway, bounding towards the granite stone protrusion on its periphery. I'd get to the school, find new broom April Zuccaro and follow up on my letter. The invitation to the shop had been made, now I'd reintroduce the artist. I'd charm her, manage her; I'd pique her curiosity and tell her the institution she now headed had made it all possible. I'd kneel at her altar and say my Hail Marys. The exhibition was open, she only needed to come and look.

I was close to making it. On the approaching pathway and twenty feet from the double door entrance, with its magnificent tinted windows and decorative stonework frame, my legs hit an invisible wall of sludge and my head split five ways. Just inside, shored up against a noticeboard, and clearly visible through the hued glass, was Maisie. She was flush, exquisite and draped in flowing, figure-coating fabric. It hung from her with gratitude. A hand touched her hair. It wasn't hers.

I didn't know him, but I knew where he'd come from

and where he was going. He was bulk and easy charm. Everything about him was pointed and confident, as though he was dotted with a hundred thousand miniature pricks. He was warm and inviting. He was a eugenics experiment. He transfixed her. He couldn't have been a day over twenty.

It was just a touch – a brush of the hair – but I knew what it meant. Once I'd done the brushing. Hers was brazen sexuality, without shame, without conscience; the animal yearnings of a monstrous, unprincipled, inhuman delivery system for male ruin. I didn't invite hate, I'd buried it as deep as I could, but it rose to the top now. It was in my head and my chest. It made hands tremulous and guts spasm. Her smile and his cut me down where I stood. I scrambled for something on the ground – a stone, anything. I'm not sure what I found. It was jagged and hard and had left my hand before I'd given it a second thought. It hit the sheet of glass that separated me from them and the resulting crack radiated out like a spider's web with the gormless pair caught in the centre. I didn't hang around to note reactions. I was back on the path in an instant, spit thickening on my tongue, a fog on my brain.

I got to the shop, half-aware, my head boiling. Kerry was behind the counter studying a couple of conspicuous idiots. I recognised the pedigree. They were from the art school. They reeked of style. Everything about them was thin and self-congratulatory. There were no personalities, just pins affixed to jackets, sack bags from local museums and proudly displayed esotery. Their amused faces offended me. Now they turned, a boy and a girl. They saw Kerry look at me and read the recognition in her eyes.

'Did you write this?' said one. 'It's hilarious.'

'We really love it,' said the other, 'this place is amazing.'
Intense loathing shot through me.

'Go and be amused somewhere else, this isn't the place
to get your quota of irony for the day, got it?' They were
looking at each other now. 'What? Are you trying to sync
the thought you share between you? Get out.' The male of
the outfit was moving towards me.

'Look mate, I don't know—'

'No, you don't,' I said, 'and if you don't leave now
you'll never get the chance to find out.' Kerry was now on
the scene, looking apologetic. She was mediating, placating,
ushering the offending backsides to the door, but as she did
another group entered, the worst people at the worst time.

There were four of them. Girls. Young. Fourteen
maybe? It's not important. What mattered was their attitude.
They were prancing around, shouting over one another,
touching the champagne. Kerry, busy being affable outside,
making promises of compensatory quaff, no doubt, hadn't
even noticed them, but for me there was nothing but. They
were pulling out bottles and now, the most obnoxious of
the quad, the leader of this ridiculous group, was pressing
my flesh with the tip of a pink umbrella. It was fluff covered
and touching my ribs.

'Mate, how much for the bubbly?' said the halfwit. Her
friends choked on their own mirth. 'How much?'

I snatched the umbrella from her hand. She looked
taken aback by the force. A moment later it was bent and
tossed towards the door.

'How much for a new umbrella?' I said. Kerry was
back in the shop now. The girls, who'd stopped laughing,
noticed her. I saw the leader snatch a bottle and hand it to

her friend who quickly moved to hide it under her coat. 'Kerry, call the police, tell them we've got a gang of thieves here, trying to steal our champagne.' Now I felt a sharp pain on the side of my head. The leader had picked up her twisted umbrella and thrown it at me.

'Fuck off, you stuck-up cunt!' Once I heard the words my hands were on her. I pincered her arm. Her friends ran; the stolen bottle dropped from the coat and rolled to the counter. The leader tried to follow them, but I wrenched her back.

'Oh no,' I said, 'not you.' I ordered Kerry to shut the shop door. Surprised but compliant, she did as she was told. 'Stay here,' I said to Kerry, 'make sure no one gets in.' The little bitch was clawing and squirming now, trying to prise my fingers from her blanched limb. In seconds I'd pulled her into the back office. I twisted my grip as she struggled. She began to cry. 'Shut up,' I said, 'don't you dare make a sound.' I hauled her down the stairs – she tried to bite me, but I held her chin with my free hand and squeezed hard. At the bottom of the stairs I released her face and swept a case of wine from the freezer. I prised up the lid and forced my captive to bend over the cavity.

Poor Petra. There wasn't much of her these days. She was part-skeletonised, part clumps of carefully fileted flesh. I didn't recoil when I saw her any more. I was past that. My new companion was just acclimatising.

My captive screamed and I pressed my hand hard over her mouth, forcing her head down with the other until her nose was mere inches from Petra's ghastly, gaping maw. There was snivelling now; awful, pitiful snivelling.

'You see her?' I said. 'Like that, do you? Would you

like to get in there with her?' The girl made a sound – it was whiny and unedifying. 'If you ever come back here I'll kill you, understand? And not just you but your imbecilic friends, yes? Then your family. Nod if you get it.' I felt the tension as she tried to move her head. 'Now let me tell you what else you're not going to do. You're not going to tell anyone what you've seen. If you do, I'll know and I'll be coming. I'll come for you with everything I've got. No one's going to believe a thief, anyway. I'll bet you've stolen from a few places, haven't you? You and the gang. Do you like the idea of prison? Spending your childhood in a detention centre? That'd be a life ruined, wouldn't it? It's not wise to invite the police in when you've got a past. Believe me, I know. So you're going to leave here and keep that ridiculous mouth shut, or I'll make sure you never say another word to anyone, OK?' More snivelling. 'My cat has a taste for this kind of meat now. It won't eat tinned food any more, just this. I couldn't let my puss starve, I'm too fond of it. It'd enjoy you. Remember that when you're thinking of sharing. Maybe you'll get to the right person before I get to you, but maybe you won't. I don't think you're stupid enough to take that risk, are you? Nearly, but not quite.' I angled the girl's head so it directly faced Petra's. 'She thought she could take me on too, she was very full of herself. Now my cat's full of her, and she had a hell of a lot more brains than you.'

I let her go and brought down the freezer lid, listening to the sound of my confidante bolting up the stairs. I followed quickly, getting to the shop floor just in time to see her trying to push past Kerry, whimpering, angling desperately for the door handle.

'It's OK, Kerry, let her go,' I said, and a moment later she was gone. Kerry's face, normally bright, had contoured to form a question mark.

'New, what the fuck?' she said.

'I just gave her a fright,' I said. 'I forced her to look in the hole in the wall downstairs; she got an eye full of dead rat. I don't think we'll be seeing her again.' The adrenaline was draining from me now; the nerves in my stomach began to fire. I walked to the back office, sat in my chair and crumpled. There was no panic, just the merest hint of despair and then, with a speed I still find surprising, numbness. There was nothing. I felt nothing.

X

The Waiting Room

Now I waited. I waited for arrest. I was powerless, beholden to forces beyond my control. When the rest of the shift passed without incident I went home and waited for the reckoning. When would it come? Would I make it to bed or would the door be hammered long before the witching hour?

Collapsed and desolate, splayed on my geriatric armchair, I'm ashamed to say I swigged from a swiped bottle of tannic swill. My father would have been proud of that weakness, for it's so terribly human, isn't it – drinking to forget? 'Good on ya boy,' he'd say, with venom and spittle drowning each syllable, 'it's about time you were a little less sanctimonious and joined the real world.' Ah yes, the real world – the derelict's Narnia. But what was real about this dank room with its peeling honeysuckle wallpaper and judgemental feline, eyes alert to a broken man?

There was nothing natural about this place, nothing congruous in the cat's whines that broke the silence: modulating, changing, coalescing into sounds that aped – no, were – had become human speech, with its trademark rhythms and cadences. 'What do you think you're doing?' That's what I heard. The cat had spoken to me before, on a subliminal level, only intelligible to those attuned to his ticks and innuendos, but now I could see it. He opened his mouth and the words, once heard in a silent otherworld, were sourced from his throat. It sounded like I imagined I sound – authoritative, commanding and lucid.

'I'm waiting for them, Puss,' I said.

'Who's them?'

'Murgatroyd, the law, I don't know – the wrath of the idiots, what do you want me to say?'

'You've given up, how unedifying. It's embarrassing to see you like this.' The cat outstretched his claws, arched his back and settled.

'Like what?' I said.

'Awash with self-pity,' said the cat, 'I can hardly bear to look at you.'

I wanted to get up and sweep him from his cushion, put him out, but I was too tired and he was entrenched – positively burrowed.

'That ingrate's seen Petra now,' I said, brushing the bottle's label with my thumb, 'it's only a matter of time.'

'Why show her?' said the cat. 'Did you want this to happen? Do you want to be caught?'

'Kids like that think they can do anything they want,' I said, 'they're junior fascists – pigs, they don't respect a thing. Everything's frivolous to them. Life is throwaway. I grew up with the likes of her. Well I wanted to show one of these degenerates that some things aren't a joke. I wanted her to know they're not in control, and if they push the wrong person they'll get a full and definitive correction. I wanted her humble before the truth.' A long silence might have been appropriate now but the cat, perhaps anxious to experiment with his new voice, would not be silenced.

'You're an elephant who's been toppled by a fly,' he said, 'you're a fool.' I looked at him, this non-achieving, furry dependant. What the hell did he know about it? 'Your concern is the project,' he went on, 'that's what matters, not some cleft in a puffer jacket.' I wondered how he knew what she'd worn. 'You have to collect yourself, toughen up. Yeah, they're coming, they have to, girl or no girl. They suspect you now and they can't pretend they don't. They'll come and they'll try everything – they'll want to trick you, manipulate you, make you do the work they should have done themselves, had they the stomach for the heavy lifting involved. Maybe they've got a handle on the whole story but they haven't gone into that shop cellar, they haven't opened that freezer. Why not?'

'I don't know,' I said, 'perhaps they're missing something.'

'As long as that freezer remains closed you're still in the game,' said the cat, 'it means they don't have all the answers – you can still win.'

Maybe that was true, perhaps they didn't know everything yet, but they surely would. I thought about the terrified bully I'd dragged to within an inch of Petra's leftovers. I saw her in another place, her place perhaps – inconsolable, withdrawn – unable to engage with the attentive parent who'd noticed she wasn't herself, while the other part-timer languished in the bath, playing with his inseminator. I saw mother shaking daughter, cajoling her to speak – demanding to know what was wrong, until finally the dam burst and the whole, awful story frothed forth, buoyed by sobs, shortness of breath and hysterical gesticulation. I saw Murgatroyd taking the call, motioning for officers to follow him, as he ran out, hungry for an arrest.

When they came what could I say? I wouldn't confess, I couldn't give them that, and I wouldn't run, as that was tantamount to confessing. They'd had it handed to them, the whole story; a testament to the luck of one man and the enfeebled detecting faculty of the rest. I could and should push Ian Zeller front and centre, I thought. Why not implicate the imbecile further? His was a half-life at best. When Petra failed to return, when he understood that he was alone and there'd be no one on hand to give succour to his shortcomings, no patient woman to listen to his self-important preens, no one to satisfy his animal urges, he'd be an insect with its legs pulled off – a nothing creature. He'd be locked in. It's doubtful he'd want to live in such a circumstance, and he'd be too old to get an impressionable girl in the flush of youth and impress his dominance on her, as he had with his late wife.

Older women were more discerning, less tolerant of character flaws; my dad had learned that the hard way with his first wife, many years his senior. He talked about her sometimes, then fell silent for long periods. Such women had one crucial advantage over their pert rivals, they knew whether the men they were dating were on their way to fulfilling their potential or not. They could spot a fabulist. There was no rubbing the blarney stone and making a wish. Ian Zeller didn't know it yet but his luck had run its course. He was yesteryear's fool. Prison, at least, offered the possibility of companionship, introspection – the opportunity to reflect on every injustice he'd vested on his disappointed, unfulfilled, bored wife, before I'd put her down.

The circumstantial case against him was simple and compelling; it was a story that any dunce could understand, particularly the kind who read the tabloids and imagined they were topping up their news. Zeller was an easy score for the police. He'd been threatening, he'd beaten Petra's colleague in front of a witness, and another man had been savagely attacked less than a stone's throw from the shop. Murgatroyd had said it himself – there were no coincidences in this self-involved town. The likelihood that two men were responsible for this run of violence and moral turpitude was slim to none. That it was the case was blind luck, the machinations of an invisible agent, but you couldn't put a pair of handcuffs on that.

I looked at the cat and saw his head turn sharply and his ears pin back. Before I'd registered a thing there was a rustle at the door, a footstep and then knocking.

'Stay calm,' said the cat, 'remember, when you think, you win.' That was right; the cat was correct. Perhaps the girl had talked but even so, even if the body had been discovered and men and women in white plastic suits were poring over it now, all they really knew was the girl had found it. She'd have told them what I said, of course, but that was just her version of events. Who's to say she hadn't run down there while her friends were distracting me with their little show of amateur anarchy, and was now minded to punish me for realising what she was up to, trying to steal stock, and throwing her out?

Yes, I'd say she was covering herself and that I hadn't known a thing about it – that the old freezer had been broken for a while and we'd been using the mini-fridge upstairs, so no one had any reason to open it up. I knew no more than I'd said, that I left work that Friday and had never seen Petra again. She and her spouse were having 'problems'; maybe he'd come after hours to remonstrate and things got out of hand? If he had access to Petra he had access to her shop keys, did he not? He could come and go as he pleased. Couldn't a man responsible for one act of violence in the shop, have attacked his wife in that same spot? After all, a man killing his partner is the oldest story in the world: so old, it writes itself.

The knocking was persistent now and the cat had sprung from the chair opposite, taking sanctuary in the neighbouring kitchen. I took a deep breath, drank the last of the wine and headed to the door, with a face I imagined to be the very model of placidity. When opened, Murgatroyd stood bold and relaxed on the other side. He was alone.

'Mr Rothwell, I'm sorry to bother you, I know it's late,' he said.

'That's no trouble at all,' I said. This was it. It was best to remain dignified. 'What can I do for you?'

'I just need to tie up the odd untidy thread, and I hoped you'd be willing to help.' I waited a moment – just a beat. He wasn't arresting me. Not yet.

'I'm sorry?' It was all I could think of.

'Ah, you're going to make me say it, aren't you?' said Murgatroyd. He grinned. 'How I hate cop show clichés. OK, I need to ask you to come down to the station and answer some questions.'

XI

The Inquisition

Perrangyre Police Station was an unremarkable granite shack with an overhanging premonitory and a surplus of parking spaces for what, one imagined, was a tiny force. Murgatroyd and I had walked there, it being just a few hundred yards from my street. He'd been upbeat and apologetic throughout, explaining that in complicated cases such as these it wasn't always possible to conduct business in civilised hours and that it was nothing to worry about, just a clean-up exercise. Yes, he was terribly sorry for the inconvenience, making theatrical asides about the stillness of the night, the swooshing of waves within earshot, and how settled the town looked, how peaceful, with its streets clear and an unblemished star field visible in the unfathomably vast night's sky.

If I hadn't known better, I'd have thought this treatise on nature and the richness of the local environs was a calculated contrast with the oppressive, clinical white room that succeeded it, once we'd negotiated the station's labyrinthine interiors and nested in its bowels. Freedom was a wonderful thing, he seemed to say, look at this embarrassment of accessories, but now, get used to this pokey, airless pit, with its nervously scratched table, tape machine and glaring female officer in plain clothes – just the kind of environment the guilty must get used to once the world outside is firmly and irrevocably denied.

Murgatroyd offered me tea, which I accepted, and a choice of biscuits from a tatty plastic cracker box, which I declined. I was then asked if I'd consent to answering a few questions and having the answers recorded for evidence, which I agreed to do, only to have to say it all over again when the tape was started and the question repeated for its benefit.

Would I like a solicitor present? I said not. I was happy to help, had no qualms about my legal status or potential threat to my liberty, and I was anxious to do all I could to reunite Petra with her friends and family, even Ian, whom I understood had lashed out in anger under difficult circumstances, and was probably not a violent man in day to day life… though Petra had been wary of him in the days running up to her disappearance. Seed duly planted, Murgatroyd sat straight, both hands flat on his side of the table, and launched his opening salvo, taking great care to fix his gaze so the gap between us felt like an inch at best.

'Keir,' he began, 'I hope you don't mind me calling you Keir – I was chatting to your friend Kerry the other day and she referred to you as "New", why is that?' It seemed like an impossibly trivial opener.

'Oh, well you see that's my handle, if you like,' I said, 'the persona I adopt for my art work, New Shockley.'

'When you were an artist?'

'I still am an artist, Mr Murgatroyd – one doesn't stop being an artist. It's not a trade, it's innate.'

'But you were asked to leave the school, were you not?' I took a sip of tea.

'Well that's still part of an ongoing dispute,' I said.

'Is it?' said Murgatroyd. 'Because I spoke to the new Dean, what's her name...' He consulted his notes, 'April Zuccaro, and she was clear that you were no longer a student there. She said you'd failed to meet the requirements for progression and had, oh dear, slandered a member of staff.' I felt the centre of gravity shift in the room; I was beginning to slip, just ever so slightly – slip away.

'That's not what happened,' I said, 'they're closing ranks, protecting their reputation. I didn't slander anyone, I tried to tell the truth. That's what I do, it's part of my art.'

'Telling the truth?'

'The fundamental truth, yes.'

'So you're quite an honest person, you'd say?'

'Whenever possible.'

'When wouldn't it be possible?'

'Oh, the usual reasons, because if you tell a thug they're a thug you get battered, don't you?' Murgatroyd scratched the back of his head and paused to chew one of his stale-looking biscuits.

'I'm interested,' he said, 'as to why you took the job at the wine shop.'

'Why wouldn't I?'

'Well,' said Murgatroyd, brushing his front teeth with his tongue, 'you don't drink – indeed, it seems to me you judge those that do, and, forgive me, but retail doesn't look like your scene.'

'I'm not sure what any of that has to do with Petra,' I said.

'It's just that when I talk to your regulars, and I've spoken to quite a few, not to mention your old colleague

Fabian Stroud, whom you fired, I understand,' he let the revelation hang in the air, 'they generally say two things – one, that you've never looked happy behind the counter, except when writing your wine descriptions – but we'll come back to those – in fact some have suggested you're, well, a little abrupt with the clientele, and two, that you and Petra didn't seem to get on, that there was an atmosphere between you.'

'An atmosphere?'

'Indeed,' he went on, 'it made many of your customers uncomfortable, did you know that?'

'They're a sensitive bunch,' I said, 'and a lousy group of amateur psychologists.' Murgatroyd's lips part rose – not quite a smile, not quite a sneer.

'Are you sure you won't have a biscuit?' he said, angling the box at me. I shook my head. 'Keir, what I'm seeking to do is to understand the dynamic in the shop in the days before Petra went missing. I can imagine you took the job because you were at a loose end, that perhaps it isn't a great fit for someone who's not comfortable with the public, or imagines himself to be suited for bigger and better things, and that perhaps a personality clash with Petra exacerbated the situation.'

'Petra and I got on fine,' I said.

'Well that's not what your former manager says, nor Mr Stroud, nor, for that matter, Mr Zeller. I'm not sure I drew that inference either, frankly, on the few occasions I visited the shop as a customer. In fact, thus far you're the only one to vouch for your friendship.' His words were booby-trapped and I knew, despite my best efforts, that my brow had sunk and my eyes had narrowed considerably.

'She and I had a sometimes combustible relationship,' I said, 'but it was the kind of fiery clash that people thrive on – we were at odds to the uninitiated, but for people like she and I, the thrill's in the conflict – you know, it's adversarial, combative; it kept us both interested. We were similar in that way.' My God, there was some truth in that.

'She was going to fire you.' Murgatroyd's words brought me back to the room.

'No,' I said.

'No?'

'That's what she told her husband, but she was grandstanding – she'd have never done it. Sometimes the arguments went a little far, I'm sure she said all sorts privately. We all exaggerate, don't we?'

'Though not you, you're a truth teller,' said Murgatroyd, 'is that not so?'

'You overhear people reliving arguments all the time,' I continued, 'the villain's always a beast and the storyteller's always righteous and absolute – it's a second take to improve a dull original.'

'She said the same thing to Mr Stroud.' This was new, potentially devastating information. That woman had apparently been incapable of keeping her bloody mouth shut.

'I'm at a loss,' I said. What else could I say?

'What's interesting,' said Murgatroyd, 'is that she indicated to her husband that she was going to let you go on the Friday she went missing.' The cat's face flashed across my frontal lobe. Claws were extended, lips licked.

'Well, she – she must have had second thoughts,' I said, 'the shift was normal as normal can be. When I went home, leaving her alive and very well, I might add, I was fully employed. If she had a problem with that, she failed to share it.'

Murgatroyd now consulted his notebook. 'You left the shop at 11.15 p.m., approximately?'

'Yes.'

'But you didn't go home, you went for a walk, is that correct?'

'Yes.'

'To the seafront?'

'Right, as I told you.'

Murgatroyd looked up from his spidery doodles, feigning something like amazement. 'Do you know, it's remarkable,' he said, 'but the route you mentioned, it's all back streets, alleyways and coastal paths.'

'What's remarkable about that, the piecemeal town planning?'

'No, Keir,' said Murgatroyd, 'what's remarkable is that it's a route devoid of cameras. There's not one. So there's no record of your journey. In fact, you seem to walk between the raindrops, because there's no footage of you anywhere in the hours immediately following that shift, just a few seconds of you returning to work on the Saturday. What do you think of that?'

'I think that's remarkable,' I said, 'and reassuring.'

'Reassuring?'

'Yes, I'm anti-CCTV. State surveillance is the bane of our age.'

'Helps us catch criminals, though,' said Murgatroyd, 'you wouldn't argue with that, would you?'

'I concede Big Brother's a good snout,' I said. Stay calm,

Keir – I let those words roll over and over. When I think I win. I was sitting opposite a man who was nurturing an inkling. One wrong word and it would be baptised.

'You took a circuitous route home, to clear your head, I understand that,' said Murgatroyd, hands interlaced, 'it's just rotten luck there's no record of it, but that aside for a moment, why do you think we've been unable to find any footage of Petra?'

'What, nothing?' I said. I hoped I wasn't hamming it up at this point. Surprise is hard to fake.

'Not a frame,' said Murgatroyd. This, I felt, was a moment to risk being brazen.

'Perhaps she's still in the shop,' I said – Murgatroyd's expression hardened. 'Perhaps she's crouched under the counter, awaiting her husband's arrest.' I smiled and took another sip of tea.

'Would you consent to a search of the shop?' he said, ushering in the inevitable.

'Mr Murgatroyd, I was making a bad taste joke. Perhaps she'd be able to squeeze under the counter, but she's not known for being quiet, I think we'd have noticed if she was squatting on the premises.'

'Indeed,' he said, 'but nevertheless, in case there's something in there she left behind, something that might help us.'

'It's been weeks and we've come across nothing – there is nothing.'

'Perhaps we can look harder.'

'It's not my decision to make,' I said quickly. 'The owner may not be comfortable. After Ragesh's attack, several customers never returned. We don't want to get a reputation as a crime hotspot; we are a local business, after all. I feel you'd have to ask him.'

'We'd be discreet,' said Murgatroyd.

'Nevertheless.'

Now there was a change in Murgatroyd's demeanour, a drop of the shoulders, a clenching of fists. He was wound, irritated. Had he contacted Spoor already and been refused? No, that wasn't it. Why, I thought, had they not simply gone in? Why weren't they ransacking the place as I sat there? I glanced at the female officer, sitting behind Murgatroyd. She broke eye contact. She was looking at him now. No, not looking, glaring, and in that moment I had a hunch. The case was circumstantial. They needed Spoor's permission to search the shop, but couldn't contact him. Knowing I had no good reason to refuse, had they hoped to bounce me into giving consent? If I was right, I'd find out in seconds.

'So,' I said, 'because of the recent upheaval and the fact it's a small town – fertile ground for gossips, the provincial mentality being what it is – I will need to get the nod from Mr Spoor directly. My job could be on the line otherwise, and I do love it so. I don't know what I'd do if I couldn't sell wine to inebriates.'

The room had turned; any pretence this was a pocket of civilisation had evaporated. This was a bear pit. I'd played my only hand, but now, with Murgatroyd uncharacteristically quiet, I realised it was decisive. Fred Spoor, that beautiful ape, had gone dark. Who knew why? But it meant I had time – it could be hours, it could be days, but time nonetheless – time to walk out of that room and make a last stand.

If there was any doubt it vanished when Murgatroyd said, 'I understand, we'll speak to Mr Spoor and take it up with him.' God bless the elusive Fred Spoor.

'Can I help you with anything else?' I said. I wasn't enjoying this, exactly, but I wasn't under arrest either. Murgatroyd looked to his colleague, then back to me. There was a pause; the longest yet.

'Yes,' said Murgatroyd. He produced a card folder. Once opened, I saw a scrap of paper in a marked-up plastic bag and a second packet, containing what looked like – they were, it was a handful of wine tickets from the shop!

'I just want your help in clarifying a few details before you go,' he said. I was going. This was cause for optimism. 'You'll recall we talked about the damage to the passage behind the shop,' he went on, 'the broken ducting, the scuff on the garage handle?'

'Yes,' I said, 'I vaguely recall.' I teased out the 'vaguely'.

'Well,' said Murgatroyd, 'my feeling is that someone climbed on to the roof and took a journey to one of the houses on Causeway Head, where sadly, they decided to attack the occupant.'

'Yes,' I said, 'I remember you saying – is he awake now?'

'Yes he is,' said Murgatroyd firmly. 'He's not talking yet but it won't be long now.'

'That's great,' I said, 'so your theory is that his attacker used the rooftops near my shop to complete his escape? What a monkey.'

'No,' said Murgatroyd, who hadn't smiled for some time now, 'the reverse – it would be quite impossible for a man to climb on to the roof adjoining the back wall of that property – they dropped down, as I think we discussed.

They started in the passage that wraps round the shop.'

'How can you know that?' I said.

'Well,' said Murgatroyd, 'men typically don't clamber up a high brick wall with no obvious footholds. In any event, the route our man took isn't in doubt thanks to a trail of breadcrumbs.'

'Breadcrumbs?'

'Yes,' he said, 'in this case, breadcrumbs in the form of scrap paper.' He held up the first packet. 'This is a receipt, for a pair of new glasses. Can you read that OK?' I made a point of leaning back.

'Yes.'

'This was found on a rooftop, close to the point where someone would have to drop to get into the garden of the home attack victim. It's in bad shape, as you can see.' He affected to look at it more closely. It was torn and covered in filth. 'I think it was in someone's pocket for a while, probably rubbing up against all sorts, and it's been soaked and subject to the elements, but the very fact it was there, and all alone, suggests that it perhaps fell out, and this wasn't a spot where there'd typically be people. In fact, this was the only bit of rubbish up there. Do you own glasses, Keir?' Murgatroyd knew I did, he'd seen me wearing them.

'I do, mainly for reading, but I've not bought a pair for a while. They sit awkwardly on my face – like a bored prostitute, you might say. And I don't keep receipts.' Neither was true and he'd check that, perhaps was already checking, but that was a problem for tomorrow. I had to survive today.

'I have to ask, you understand,' said Murgatroyd. 'There was another bit of rubbish in the garden, an empty peanut bag – Mason's – a rather fancy brand. Indeed, I bought a bag from your shop, do you recall?'

'I don't eat them,' I said.

'But you wouldn't have to pay for them at the shop, would you?'

'Nevertheless.'

'Do you know who else in town stocks the brand?' said Murgatroyd.

'I wouldn't know,' I said.

'It's not an exclusive, then?'

'I think I just said, I don't know.'

'Well don't worry – we're looking into it. The person who dropped the bag we're interested in used the tree I told you about,' said Murgatroyd, 'he dropped down, breaking the branch as he fell, and the bag slipped from his clothes.'

'Could it not have blown in?' I said. I realised how flippant I sounded but it was hard to take a case against me seriously that hung on a bag of peanuts.

'Unlikely,' said Murgatroyd. 'We had great weather that week, barely a gust, say our friends at the Met office. No wind that morning, certainly.' I knew this wasn't true and felt my jaw drop ever so slightly, ready to undercut his certainty, only to see the trap and skip over it, barely in time. Following a short pause, Murgatroyd, apparently resigned to me not taking the bait, continued.

'The property had only been occupied for one night,' he said, 'it was empty for three months prior to that and the landlord had both the house and gardens attended to in the week prior to the new let. It's also a walled garden, as I told you the other day. They're high walls. Too high to casually chuck a bit of rubbish over. You may be interested to know that both sets of neighbours denied either consuming the product or littering. The latter's not something one would wish to admit to, obviously – no one likes a litter bug – but we're talking about a man who was nearly beaten to death, and I'd struggle to understand why, under those circumstances, anyone would lie about eating a bag of peanuts. To do so would be to introduce a piece of false evidence. I made it clear to them there'd be no arrest for littering, by the way.' He was smiling again – snake like.

'You said there was a second thing?' Moving the conversation on may have come across as impertinent but both Murgatroyd and I knew where we stood now.

'Yes,' he said, perkier than before, 'you said there was no animosity between you and Petra, correct?'

'As I said, yes.' Murgatroyd pulled out the second packet.

'I've taken a great interest in your wine descriptions,' he said, 'they certainly are quirky. Everyone I spoke to agreed they're the one big notable change on the shop floor since you started working there. They're quite polarising, it seems.'

'There's always likely to be a split in opinion when someone tries something new,' I said.

'No doubt,' said Murgatroyd, 'but I noticed, on my first few visits to the place, that some of the descriptions read like, I suppose you could say, commentaries on people. Keir, this really piqued my interest, so, and I hope you don't mind, I had officers in a sort of, well, mystery shopper role, if you like, go in and snap any that might reflect the mood of the author – especially those that, you could say, captured a moment in the life of the shop, because I think you draw inspiration from what goes on in there, am I right?'

I said nothing, which Murgatroyd took as confirmation. He laid out the packet on the table. 'What we have here,' he said, 'are a small selection of those which caught our eye. We've isolated these, because they're less abstract, more specific. You can read them, but I have a typed version here, if you—'

'I know what they say, I wrote them,' I snapped, realising a second later that I'd confirmed ownership on tape, and Murgatroyd had just been given a free hit. He fished out a bit of a paper and began to read aloud.

'Bandstand Shiraz,' he began, 'the wine that says, "Don't be perturbed by that insufferable, incendiary ball of rage and malice blighting your working day, just drink me and forget." Not an off the shelf description of a work colleague, if you don't mind me saying so, pun intended, rather it has the feel of being drawn from life.'

He went on, '"Denver Dell Zinfandel – with its blunt character, tastelessness and bitter finish, this billed-as-sweet-and-easy drinking wine, is in truth, a monster. Similarities between individuals, living or dead, are strictly coincidental." Now who did you have in mind when you wrote that?'

'No one,' I said, 'no one in mind at all – it's a burlesque, a sketch; it's just designed to allude to a type that everyone knows. It's universal.'

'Is this next one universal?' said Murgatroyd, clearing his throat. 'This is Juna Bay Merlot – "A cheap quaffer for the common drinker, as recommended by staff member Petra." Now, I'm going to suggest that you might be speaking for her there, am I right?'

'Mr Murgatroyd, I don't know what you want me to say, I—'

'Ball of rage and malice,' he repeated, 'blunt, tasteless, cheap, common, monster – these are your words, describing the missing woman, Petra Zeller.'

'They're words you've strung together to support a spurious argument.'

'Do I quote them out of context?'

'Mr Murgatr—'

'You tell me,' said Murgatroyd, 'that you and she were friends.'

'We were. We are!'

'But this is how you describe her?'

'She did recommend the last one. That is what she thought of it – the rest is supposition,' I said.

'You hated her, didn't you?'

'No.'

'Did you hurt her, because she was going to sack you?'

'No!'

'You know where she is, don't you?'

'I have no idea; how could I know?'

'Keir, it's only a matter of time now, do you understand? When we find her, and we will, we'll know what happened. And if you haven't told us before that moment comes, then it's going to be a hell of lot worse for you than if you had. Personally, I don't think that's justice, but some do.'

'I've done nothing wrong,' I said, 'arrest me or let me go.'

'I have a man,' Murgatroyd continued, 'lucky to be alive, brutally attacked in his holiday home.' He moved his mug of tea to one side of the table and placed a biscuit on the other. 'The gap between your front door and this man's house,' he motioned between the two, 'is fifty yards. This man was either very unlucky – the victim of some freak home invasion – or was impeding someone's escape route. I believe that someone to be you. I also believe that regrettably we're going to find Petra close by. You were the last person to see her alive. Now take a moment. Think hard. Is there anything you want to tell me?'

It may surprise you, but to hear the words was a relief. I'd waited so long to be named, having been so fatigued by the constant barrage of innuendo, that to have the finger of suspicion poking me openly felt liberating, as if an embargo had been lifted. Murgatroyd had his man, but he hadn't charged him. I knew why, and I was ready to say it.

'I'll tell you what I think,' I said.

'Do,' said Murgatroyd.

'I think that your case against me is circumstantial; it's a lot of nothing. Just talk of wine descriptions, receipts, peanut packets and a few unreliable statements from a woman who's not here to provide the context. I think you've wilfully ignored the fact that her husband's a violent man, who's attacked someone, in broad daylight, at his missing wife's place of work. This is a jealous man, a brutish man, and when most women go missing it's the husband that's to blame nine times in ten. Poor Petra's probably in his loft. Yet you're talking to me, whose only history of violence is the organised kind against complacency and sense-deadening cliché. Ian Zeller was jealous – she said so – a possessive grunt. Check it, because I won't be the only one she confided in. Yes, that's me she confided in, the alleged enemy. Maybe he drove her into the arms of someone else, then found out. I don't know. As for Petra and me, I think the people of this town saw and heard, but as usual didn't understand. We liked a little verbal sparring. That was our game. That's no crime. It's not even the prelude to a crime. I've never hurt anyone in my life and I never could. My weapons are ideas, materials – my only victims are the thoughtless. Now arrest me or let me go.'

Murgatroyd arched his back, took a breath and looked through me. His next words were piggybacked on a sigh. 'Keir,' he said, 'you're free to go.' I thanked him, trying and failing not to sound mocking as I did so, and gave a turn of the hand, distending the moment with a little *coup de théâtre*. The path to the door felt long as Murgatroyd officially terminated the interview and got to his feet. As I reached the threshold he spoke up, the vigour in his voice restored.

'You're certain you've never hurt anyone?' he said. I turned.

'Of course,' I said.

'Anthony Courcier, remember him? He disappeared from your junior school. Eleven years old. His traumatised friend, Wye Stammers, told the investigating officers that you were responsible.' The scale of Murgatroyd's investigation was now laid bare. He'd gone all the way back to the beginning. 'That name, Wye Stammers – so distinctive. But I'd heard it before. So I checked it out. And, would you believe, it was the same boy who drowned locally a while back. Such a small world. Of all the places he could have chosen to study, he picked Perrangyre, only to come face to face with you. That couldn't have been easy. All that childhood fear rising to the surface. All that trauma. I'm surprised you didn't mention your history when I brought him up at the shop. Did you forget about your schoolfriend who died?'

'Man, you must be desperate,' I said. 'We weren't friends. Tony was a monster. Well I whacked that monster, if you'll pardon the expression, and it's one of the proudest moments of my life. It's the moment I stopped being a victim and became someone the bastards, like Stammers, were afraid of. I'd done nothing more than that. But staying silent, letting the myth ferment as it were, kept me safe. Nevertheless, it happened just as I said it did. Tony chased me, I hid, and while he was hunting me, lusting for revenge, some pervert snatched him. Tony was a predator who got taken by the kind of man he'd probably have grown into. If he hadn't died, the degenerate would have become an estate agent or bank manager; a chimp in a suit who reads the *Telegraph* on his way to work – the respectable veneer that hides the brain-damaged sociopath. What happened to him was cruel, it was brutal, but it was justice. And I've never looked back. That's all I know about that, and apparently everyone was convinced I had no case to answer because here I stand.'

'Everyone but Wye,' said Murgatroyd. 'Goodnight, Keir. Sleep well.'

PART III

THE WORLD BEYOND

I

An Evening with Cassandra

Stray waves lapped together, forming white lips, then yawned to nothing, and in the centre of it all, pitched and inanimate, was an object. It was being swept my way. As my eyes followed its course it was furnished with detail. What I'd supposed to be a leathery skin was clothing, a jacket, shawled around a bloated buoy. There was a stump of hair attached to it, froth hugging its outline like scum. I saw a tentacle from the deep, periscope-like on the surface; a finger, two fingers, crooked and pale. This poor creature had been a man and somehow he'd come to rest here, in this familiar, uninviting sprawl of ocean.

Now there was another, bobbing in the slipstream – a woman this time, on her back, face frozen in shock, her flesh grey, her large, pockmarked areola visible through a sodden blouse. And behind her a man, then a child, another child, a woman; God's teeth, a debris field of human remains, animated by the current. It went on and on.

From my divine seat, somewhere above it all, able to take in the scale, I could see these wretches stretching all the way to the coast, washing up on Perrangyre's mustard shore like shipwreck fragments. What had happened to them? I asked the question subliminally, within my own skull, and had the most awful feeling that I knew the answer, that I'd condemned these doomed souls.

From my new vantage point, no longer bound by time or gravity, I had the freedom of the town; I could go anywhere I wanted, instantly – I was everywhere: in the shop, at the police station, in the homes of the regulars, unseen in their bedrooms, stuck to their ceiling, a ghost in their dining rooms, and in each location the same motif, an open bottle of wine. In some places it was on the table, in others the kitchen counter; it stood next to half empty plates of food in the town's restaurants. At Boondoggle an entire case had been opened, the corks close by. Wherever I looked it was decanted, already in someone's glass, someone's stomach.

I could see Murgatroyd, fresh from his interrogation room, looking pleased with himself, perhaps even a little bloodthirsty. His colleagues were equally smug, congratulating him – backs were being patted, hugs exchanged, and there were full wine glasses in most hands. I saw my would-be turnkey take a big, crude gulp, not taking the time to taste what he had, then start to speak, though the words petered out in the ethereal void, and suddenly those around him stopped laughing. Now they looked concerned. He'd lost his composure; he was stumbling; his hands were to his throat. Panic reverberated throughout the room. One could taste it.

He fell to the floor, his colleagues desperately tugging at his collar, trying to remove any constriction. What was wrong? He was spluttering, writhing, convulsing like a beached fish. What an undignified spectacle, how embarrassing. It seems no one knew what to say. His mouth was wide open, his eyes huge; it was likely they'd explode.

I wasn't fond of the man but didn't wish upon him such an undignified finale, but it wasn't my place to intervene. There was more panic, more holding, and finally a gasp, and poor Murgatroyd, who just moments earlier had been in his pomp, was dead. What remained of his wine seeped into the station's carpet, the glass on its side like that first body on the ocean.

I'd barely had time to contemplate what any of this meant for my prospects when the scene shifted, as though someone had shaken the kaleidoscope, and I saw friend of the shop, Obnoxious Katherine, emerge naked from her bathroom, reaching for the open bottle on the bedside and crassly filling a mug with the contents. My attitude to Katherine had soured somewhat; it's likely she'd spoken to Murgatroyd and helped plant the idea that Petra and I were at loggerheads in her final days, but there was an undoubted eroticism to the scene. I felt no guilt about being there, no shame in my voyeurism; Katherine was without self-awareness, it's likely she'd have ignored me even if she'd seen me, which curiously I knew she could not.

Now she was falling, hitting the bed with a dull thud – there was no attempt to break the descent – and she bounced, yes bounced, and hit the ground with unladylike gracelessness. There were flecks of her burgundy quaffer everywhere – on the bed, on her face. She contorted, like a grub flailing underneath a boy's magnifying glass in the summer sun. She gasped, pulling in all the surrounding air, then a sigh – greater than any I'd heard her make when decrying my careful selections on the shop floor, and silence. The morbid milieu signalled the end for the shop's one guaranteed source of social retardation. I'd miss it, I thought.

A hand was reaching for gigantic, ridiculous spectacles. It was a weak hand. Brain Haemorrhage Guy, that poor sap, was in his plain living room with his marine walls and generic family photographs lined neatly above an unremarkable fireplace, and he was drinking – guzzling that cheap, featureless plonk that he insisted on buying week after week, dismissing my better judgement, mocking my informed opinion. He drank straight from the bottle, he cared not a jot about letting whatever he had breathe; he hadn't devoted a single solitary thought to unlocking the simple, though possibly gratifying flavours nested therein, for though the producer had no ambition he may have had pride in his work.

Now, an explosion! The red lubricant, so recently imbibed, was thrown back up with comparable force. It broke out in all directions, over the neck of the bottle, around the lips, and there were rivulets creeping down the fat man's throat; blotches on his podge. His stomach jutted out, as though a claymore was buttressing his back, and he was clawing at his face, his glasses knocked and upended across it, like a raised bridge. Another desperate swipe and they were off and his eyes watered. I felt desperately sorry for the guy, his real name lost amongst other redundant trivia in these trying times, but I couldn't quite rouse myself to help.

Had Brain Haemorrhage Guy felt compelled to contradict me, telling Murgatroyd, as I suspected, that I wasn't comfortable in my shop role, despite my careful attempts at painting a picture to the contrary? What he had told the plod about Petra, that he'd seen us argue? That she didn't care for my attitude? Could he not instead have minded his own business? Here was a man who'd had a glorious second chance at life, an opportunity granted to so few, and he'd wasted it being a busybody. One couldn't respect a man like that, let alone act to stave off his death throes. No, he'd die most surely; whatever was in that bottle was as dark and toxic as the distillate of vengeance itself, and it was beyond my power to reverse that just happenstance.

The entire town seemed subject to a righteous corrective. Wherever one floated or sublimated or eased between walls, there were bodies, late of the shop, but then most of the natives had walked through our door at one time or another. I saw Drunken Lawyer immersed in a bush – a comic scene, undercut by the dogs that tugged on his husk. I saw Fabian, splayed on the floor of his wine cellar. He'd died drunk and unemployed, like the people he pitied. I saw the spoilt, undisciplined brat that had forced me to lower my guard. Her parents were trying to wake her, shaking her violently, years too late, but she was still and rigid. She must have sneaked out a bottle after all. Theft is seldom a victimless crime.

Yet everywhere I looked the one person I wanted to see eluded me. I wanted Maisie. Where was she? Why was she hiding? Then, on the air, I heard the telltale yelp of pleasure, the erotic exclamation I knew so well, and finally I was there, I'd reached her, and I knew that my inability to let her go had cost me again.

The bedroom was familiar but it wasn't Maisie's. The assembled bric-a-brac, an emerald swag lamp, a vinyl record player, browning *Star Trek* novels; I knew them. I knew them well enough to know they weren't quite right, arranged in the wrong places. By the bed, clothes. They were strewn across the floor. Light and dark rags, each from different bodies, yet both familiar, made a hollow in my chest. I took a long, shallow breath.

I couldn't see Maisie at first. She was overlaid by a groaning, sliding form; a thrusting buck that refused to turn his head. Her hands were burrowed into his back and she writhed with him. There was a succinct, urgent rhythm to their vomit-inducing dance, yet she wasn't so involved that she couldn't reach across and grab the wine they'd opened before my arrival. This was the height of decadence – rutting and drinking; hard to pull off but, many would argue, worth a try. She opened her mouth and poured it in, she didn't care if it fell cleanly or not. She pulled his head to hers and invited him to lick away the excess. He obliged.

Now a sound; a gargled scream, an unpleasant and painful surprise. Her bedmate, noting the change in tone, recoiled, as though his member had grown thorns. She was shaking, rocking from side to side, and I reached out to touch her, to steady her, but the limb I'd extended failed to enter the scene; it was a phantom.

The crying continued, accompanied by pawing at the throat, but there was nothing to be done. A second later and this formally proud stag, once virile and arrogant, let out a complementary gasp. There was violent thrashing, wheezing, beautiful futility. Now she was white and fixed on his dark grey bed sheets, like a chiaroscuro photograph. He lay by her side, twitching slightly, then was still. I watched them both with great intensity, feeling a strange sense of release, then harder still, as the man's face gained definition and form, settling on features I knew like my own.

'Robin!' I said aloud. Poor cheating Robin, whose corpse purred in time with the inflating bristles on my cheek.

'Sorry, did I wake you?' The cat was looking at me, pressing his nose to mine. It was wet and unpleasant. My bedroom was dark and the air stale. The night sky was clear in the world beyond the window. I saw the moon and took comfort from it. The scene cut through the fog of my troubled subconscious. The cat was pawing at my face.

'There's no time to sleep, friend,' he said. 'Sleep when it's over. They're hours from walking into the cellar, you know that. You have to do something. It's you or them now. Have you made your choice? Because you tried to leave them out of it, but they wouldn't let you be, would they? So come on, have you made your choice?'

I sat up, throwing the cat off me. I turned on my swag lamp and reached for my notebook, desperate to record my nocturnal impressions before they bled away.

'I've made my choice,' I said, beginning to write, 'I'm going to save us.'

II

Scraps

April Zucarro, the new Dean of the Perrangyre Art School, rose from Trevenna's old chair as I imposed myself on her office. She looked me over, her eyes flicking up to my moist forehead, then down to the hands that doddered, as though diseased. Watching her, watching me, I remembered Maisie's words.

'She likes you, always did, and fortunately for you she was on sabbatical when you put up that misogynist monstrosity of yours, so perhaps she'll be disappointed but she'll only be hearing it second hand.' And the kicker: 'She's a sucker for an artist's breakdown.' I had to hope Maisie had half a clue about Zucarro. Everything depended on it now.

'Keir, what are you doing here?' she said. She was so slight; the vessel hardly seemed robust enough for the awesome responsibility that had been emptied into it.

'April,' I began, 'I don't know what you've been told, but you have to listen to me.'

'Keir,' she said, her voice tuneless, 'I can't help you, I'm sorry.'

'I need my place here, April. I've created something important, something way better than any nonsense end-of-year project I had on the burner. Did you get my letter?

It's all in there. Once you see it, you'll understand.'

'I've had the police here,' she said, 'I've been asked questions about you, about Maisie – they wanted to know about your record, about any history of violence. They asked if last term's problem was the only thing or if there were other incidents. Look, I don't know what's going on here, but the school can't get involved.' My neck pulsed and I found my arm swinging, rogue from my head, catching the lamp on her desk and sending it to the floor. Spooked, April moved for the door, but I grabbed her and held her steady, a hand to each shoulder.

'The school's already involved,' I said, registering her fear, 'don't you understand? It's because of your imbecilic predecessor that I've had to do what I've done. It's because of this school and the perverts you employ that it was necessary. I don't care what they told you, or what Murgatroyd's said; I've created a hell of a piece in town – a vibrant, original, working installation. It's relevant, urgent even. And you need to see it. Once you have, you won't care about Maisie's lies or some mischief-making plod. The shop's the only thing that matters now.' Zucarro wriggled free and tried to move around me. I leapt to the door and blocked the threshold.

'Keir,' she said carefully, 'please get out of my way.'

'Will you at least come to the shop?' I said.

'I'm not interested in your shop,' she said, 'I care that you're holding me prisoner in my own office.' Zuccaro had always enjoyed a bit of hyperbole. She'd once described a misplaced pen as a disaster.

'For God's sake, April, I didn't come to hurt you, I just want you to give me a chance, else nothing I've done will count for anything, don't you understand?' Her face dropped.

'And what have you done?' she said.

'Only what was necessary.'

'Keir,' she said, 'if you're in trouble, talk to the police, not me.' It took a moment, but eventually I caught up with my laughter.

'The police aren't interested in the truth,' I said, 'and they're not interested in art, either. Perhaps you don't care about the first any more than they do, but I thought you might want to look at the second.' I opened the door and stepped out into the corridor. Zucarro deflated as I did so, the anxiety seeping from her part-opened trap.

'I can't help you, I'm sorry,' she said, rooted to the spot. 'Please don't come back here.' My forehead was dry.

'This is no art school,' I said, 'and you – you're less than nothing. You'll be a footnote in my story. Just a bloody footnote.' Moments later I was winding my way through the school's maze of hallways and connecting passages. My heart had gone; anger alone seemed to pump the blood on. Was there anything left in the world worth saving?

★★★

'C'mon Keir, this is getting ridiculous.' Maisie didn't know how right she was, or how deeply I longed to look at her and feel something other than longing and homicidal lust. She'd met my entrance with the kind of eye rolling dismissal that one associates with a sexist joke. She was an illegitimate court of appeal, but she was all that was left. Wrongly, unjustly, her opinion mattered.

The night before, in a fatalist haze, I'd written out little bits of my beneficence – scraps of my manifesto; the guiding principles that had made the shop project a necessity, and worth killing for, and betwixt these, a thought tree and way out for my beleaguered puss and me, but I couldn't get the first to cohere and I baulked at the second. Decapitating Murgatroyd's investigation and making things right with the loose-lipped townsfolk – that may be inevitable, I thought, but perhaps there was still another way – a more humane ending, if there was humanity to shape it. That was my only hope now.

Maisie kept a desk between us and wore her annoyance well. I noted a bottle of Pinotage from the shop stashed by her in tray. I tried to ignore it as I became acutely self-conscious, my speech laboured. I had to try one last time. As she began talking at me, telling me there was nothing left to say and that I was juvenile and deluded, I was struck by the chasm that had opened up between her understanding of the moment and mine.

She thought this was just another jilted lover, wounded and pathetic, clawing at her ankles, begging for withheld affection. But I knew she was locked in a battle for her life. Hers and the obnoxious cattle she'd inadvertently imperilled with a lack of self-control and junk values. I let her jabber on for a while, giving her a chance to work through her exasperation, and thought of my hastily sketched diagram and the line that linked the toxic wine bottles of my subconscious with their many planned delivery points. The art school was marked in capitals.

'Anything to say to me?' I said. 'Anything on your mind?' She had to have this chance.

'What are you talking about?' she said. I moved towards her. She wheeled her chair back a comparable amount.

'Listen,' I said, aping a non-threatening tone, 'think carefully about what you say in the next few seconds. It's important. I don't want us to be enemies. I'd do anything to prevent that. Just tell me the truth. Is there anything you feel I should know? Anything troubling your conscience?' I took a sliver of hope from her dry lips – the only sign she understood, but her face, though flush, was expressionless, like a head made of glass. I'd said my bit and had been met with nothing. My heart began to kick like an unborn baby.

'No, Keir, nothing's troubling me,' she said finally, 'there's nothing I want to tell you. Now please leave.' I leaned across her desk and she backed into the corner. We were both in one now.

'I'm trying to give you a chance here,' I said. There was no reaction, no words, just an awkward tableau, and in that moment something extraordinary happened. The woman in front of me, the woman I loved, disappeared. The shift was almost imperceptible. It was like a brief change in the light or a drop in temperature of a single degree. But one could feel it in the back of the eye and the upright hairs on the arms. Maisie, the fantasy, was gone. All that remained was this thing, this disappointing ghoul, whose vanity and arrogance was so out of keeping with the individual's worth, as to be instantly and ostentatiously absurd. I threw my head back – a grunting laugh. For a moment I thought I saw rage in Maisie's hazel snares.

'OK,' I said, 'just checking.' I backed away. 'Are you sure you don't want to give things another go?' I couldn't stop grinning now. The lunacy of it all had hit me for the first time. 'This is your last chance to redeem yourself, do something meaningful with your life.' Now she laughed, seemingly reassured by my frivolous flip.

'I'm sure,' she said. And now, so was I.

'Oh, that's a shame,' I said, 'I won't be seeing you again.' I noted the raised eyebrows. The certainty in my voice had cut through. 'I did love you, y'know.'

Finally, sympathy. 'I know,' she said.

'But now,' I continued, 'I love me more.'

★★★

I was out of the building in moments, powering on, bursting on to the grounds. There was urgency, yes, because the freedom to act might be measured in hours, but there was purpose too, plaited with the knowledge that each and every being in this redundant little town would now be subordinate to an artistic statement greater than themselves. They'd earned the right; such was their individual contribution to the concentration of perfidy and mediocrity they collectively represented, to be the centrepiece of the ultimate New Shockley work. I thought of sentences from my manifesto – fragments sketched in the dead of night on scraps of paper.

Art's aim is to repurpose the functional and everyday, living or dead, object or subject, and imbue it with meaning. The new 'thing', as we must call it because it initially defies definition, lacking immediate categorisation, has no use in the mechanical or scientific sense, rather it's instructive; it creates a new perspective. It recasts roles, it unsettles reality, it mocks the complacent. It provides a fleeting glimpse of the truth.

As I wound round the path and ogled the coastal precipice that flanked the same, a figure emerged, far in the foreground. I was walking fast, using the adrenaline as a balm to clump ideas together – the constituent parts of the plan to follow – and as I did so the form of a man grew and became defined, finally, inevitably, settling on the shape of Murgatroyd, who was plying the path with equal purpose. Moments later the distance between us had collapsed.

'Mr Murgatroyd,' I said, 'as I live and breathe. Looking for me, perchance?'

'No,' he said, lip upturned, 'I've got all I need from you now. I just had a bit of further business at the school.'

'Are you enrolling?' I asked. There wouldn't be many more of these encounters, so one might as well enjoy them.

'I am not,' he said, 'I'm not sure I understand artists – I don't think I'd be a very good one.'

'I'm inclined to agree,' I said.

'No,' he went on, 'I'm more a student of human nature, really. Envy, self-delusion, intellectual vanity, hubris, fear, jealousy. These things I understand very well.' He was looking through me now. 'Though to understand is not to condone, of course.'

'I'm sorry,' I said, walking round him, 'I have to go – things to do. I'm glad to see you're still at it, though. Now you're not wasting time with me perhaps you've got half a chance of putting this thing to bed, eh?'

'I'd say the chances were excellent,' said Murgatroyd,

'in fact once we've spoken to your boss, Mr Spoor, I don't think I'll need to waste another minute on you. Does that reassure you, Mr Rothwell?' He looked me over, twinkle-eyed, like a boy who'd stumbled on a rotting lamb. 'Don't worry,' he said, 'the end is closer than you think', and I watched as he turned and continued to the school, buoyant with each arrogant step.

'Right you are,' I said, my words following him with the sea breeze and rolling waves.

III

The High Price of Borrowed Time

When I returned home the cat was sitting on a bed dotted with idea fragments; dark fantasies and tangential doodles from a night of propulsive thought. As I grabbed his middle and pulled him off to better survey the scheme that would decapitate the investigation against me and bring the town to book, the animal extended his talons and lacerated the skin on my right hand. A line of crimson duly formed and I threw him to the corner, only to watch him bounce where he landed and spring to the arm of the nearby chair.

'Just checking you're awake,' he said, 'just making sure you're sharp. There's a lot to do now. Are you sure you're up to it, because if not you may as well hand yourself in. You may as well take what they've got for you.'

'I can do it,' I said, 'I just saw Murgatroyd – the man's never going to leave me alone. I have no choice now.'

I grabbed the various bits of paper from the bed and moved them to the living room table. There it was, the grand plan – tangible thought. I wondered if seeing these doodles removed from the fevered tiredness of the previous night would dilute my resolve but it didn't. A red splotch landed on the sheet closest to my hand. I was still bleeding.

The pain brought everything into focus. I needed to visit my doctor's surgery; the plan called for supplies. My nocturnal scribbles suggested calling up and claiming I had wax in my ears, or getting a referral for a same day blood test – anything to get me into the nurse's room. I'd been treated in the past year and noted, amongst the nurse's anatomical wall charts and leaflets on venereal disease, a stack of yellow trays containing bandages, creams and, for the purpose of those aforementioned blood tests, syringes. She had a whole tray of syringes. My throbbing hand was my new excuse.

I rang the surgery and told the daft receptionist with her generic phone voice that my cat had gashed my hand and I needed the wound looked at. Yes, I'd cleaned it and yes I'd applied a bit of dressing but it was deep and I was worried about infection. I didn't want to bother the doctor with it. Would the nurse have a chance to look at it? I'd take a late appointment, but given the risk of infection it would have to be today. Keys were depressed, a patient breath taken, and finally I was offered an audience at 5 p.m.

'Thank you, that's very kind,' I said and noted the wall clock. Three hours separated me from my rendezvous. I glanced again at my prompt sheet.

Robin was working alone at the shop. His voice was heavy and thick with boredom when he answered the phone.

'It's been a pretty dull day,' he said. 'We had yet another visit from your friend Murgatroyd. He wanted to know if the owner had been in touch. He's trying to reach him.'

'What happened?'

'Nothing really. He was only here a few minutes. I did what you said. I told him he'd need permission if he wanted to ransack the place. Keir, what's going on?'

239

'Nothing,' I said, 'he's got it in his head that the shop's a vault of clues that will point the way to Petra. I'm just trying to protect the business for a little while longer. I don't want to scare people away before the school has a chance to see the piece.' That part had been true until this morning.

'Have you heard from them yet?' I consulted my notes. We digressed.

'I'll talk to you about that later. Listen, I need you to run an errand for me. You can close the shop for a short while. If you do it, I'll cover you for a couple of hours from six. What do you say?' Unsurprisingly Robin agreed. I now told him about a little domestic art project I was working on – something to boost my portfolio. It was a work on canvas; a work that would require a lot of clean brushes.

'The bits I have at home are caked in oil-based paint,' I said, 'I have some of that environmental paint cleaner, the chemical-free stuff, but it's pretty useless. I'm going to need the heavy duty solution – the ammonium hydroxide. The lab grade stuff. They have small bottles, so get six.' There was a short silence on the line.

'Do you really want that at home?' said Robin. 'It's not very safe. There's a reason we use the other one; the ammonium's bad for the eyes, it can fuck up your lungs too. Plus, it's expensive.'

'The art supplier on Chapel Street does it,' I said, 'The Emporium. I'll take precautions, don't worry. Can you buy it and bring it to the shop? I have to go out shortly; I'll pick it up from there when I relieve you.'

'Do you really need that much? How many brushes are you cleaning for crying out loud?'

'I'm stocking up,' I said. With Robin's 'OK', I was about to hang up when his voice spiked.

'Oh, Keir – I forgot to say, I might have screwed up with Murgatroyd.' I hurriedly stabilised my grip on the receiver.

'Meaning?'

'Well, he mentioned Petra, and without thinking, I said I liked her – you know, that I knew her a bit from before.' I started to feel giddy.

'From before?'

'Yeah, when I used to shop here from time to time. We'd chat occasionally. I mean, it's not important – but I know he's harassing you, making mischief with your relationship – so anyway, I shouldn't have talked about her.'

'Did he ask about her and me?'

'No,' said Robin, 'he just wanted to know what I thought of her. He said he liked her too. What do you think happened to her?' Robin, whose role in the events to come was central, had now had his part expanded. I could hardly believe my luck. If Robin and Petra had nurtured a rapport, perhaps someone had noticed it – someone who'd be around to tell the tale in the weeks ahead. Ragesh, Fabian; they might yet help me in ways they'd be loath to imagine.

'Don't worry,' I said, 'just go and get me those supplies and we'll say no more about it.' I hung up and checked my bits of paper. Now another call, this time to a local courier's firm. Dirk, the man who often handled big deliveries for the shop, wasn't right for what I had in mind. He knew me very well and I knew him, right down to the watery eyes, old rocker stubble and the broken family chains he carried with him when reticently discussing his estranged wife and daughter. I liked him, he wore his regrets well and tried to make the best of his haunted afterlife, but today wasn't a day for the sort of man who can smell desperation on another, whose quotidian stylings hid a dissecting eye, whose visits could last a full hour. Above all else, I'd be hoping to pass for someone else, so a stranger was a must.

Now, with my heart hammering and skin alive with heat and irritation, I looked at the list I'd drawn up – a roll-call of names, representing the shop's most loyal customers. Each and every person listed had a fast mouth and a taste for other people's business. Each of them had helped Petra mock me while I stood close by, pretending to enjoy it. And each had undoubtedly talked to Murgatroyd with memories of conversations half-remembered, atmospheres sampled – talk that might have buried me. Well now I'd bury them.

Brain Haemorrhage Guy, Drunken Lawyer and Obnoxious Katherine were a given, of course, but to them I'd added the War Veteran that Petra regaled with talk of difficult colleagues, 'we talked about you', on her home delivery visits, and the athletic Thorwald couple, of whom Petra once said, 'I bet they have great sex.' There were many more, too many perhaps, but the point I'd be making had to be made well. At the foot of the list were Maisie, April and other friends at the art school. Last, Murgatroyd and his colleagues at the Perrangyre cop shop. All were due a special delivery from their favourite local wine business.

Now, armed with the information that Robin and Petra had been acquainted, I'd been gifted the opportunity to improvise a motive for the events to come. Implicating others was easy, but there had to be a spur for an individual's actions – something the simple people who sit on juries could understand.

That was the fatal weakness in Murgatroyd's case and the likely reason I was still at liberty; he had a chronology but no concrete motive. His best guess was that a slightly unstable character with an unsavoury history flipped when he lost a shop job. It was pathetic. Who'd kill for that? It was almost worth confessing to counter that insult. But if defending the importance of art was attractive, decapitating the investigation and throwing the police a few alternative scenarios was better still. Robin's aside was a minor miracle; it brought everything into focus. Sitting at my desk, I now started to write a letter.

It was a dark tale of a woman trapped in a loveless and abusive marriage who'd sought comfort with the man who'd showed her a little affection across the shop counter. In this piece of maudlin melodrama – too middling for a soap opera but tedious enough to be ripped from real experience – Petra was a mouse, scared of her brooding, ogre-like bedmate.

He suspected she was playing around and let it be known, as she recorded in this longing missive to Robin, that he'd kill her if his suspicions were confirmed. How she preferred her lover – his tenderness, his empathy, the way he stroked her hair and held her long into the night – something the brutish Ian never did. How she wished they could be together.

This plea for emancipation, for humanity, was so affecting it almost brought a lump to my throat. I toyed with ending on a flourish, something portentous like,

'Every day he tightens his grip and makes me feel less safe. It's only a matter of time before he snaps and hurts me' – obvious to be sure, but people don't write these kind of letters to win prose prizes, they're typically cliché stacks. I was backspacing and changing sentences, intent on getting it right, when the door shook and I heard my name, muffled but urgent through the old wood.

***

Fred Spoor stood at my threshold with cheeks like a brothel's curtains and a brow bleeding drink. He seemed lost, unable to settle, scratching his palm with his thumb. In his right hand I saw a phone, his fingers wrapped round it like a desperate gambler holding on to his betting slip. When he spoke the air thickened and my sinus was treated to a blast of noxious spirit. I was so taken aback by the surprise visit that the significance of it had only just begun to register as he pushed past me and into the flat.

'You with anyone?' he said, apparently unwilling to trust the evidence of his own eyes.

'No,' I said, 'it's just the cat and me. Fred, what are you doing here?' I closed the door quickly and Spoor, reassured, sank into the battered armchair.

'Howell Murgatroyd, you know him?' He held up his phone. 'I have six voicemails and fourteen missed calls from the guy. I got fewer than that on the day my daughter was born.' I took a moment to locate the cat in the panorama. He was stretched on the desk, resembling a draught excluder, covering my scraps of jotted consciousness.

'Did he say what he wanted with you?'

'Never mind that,' said Spoor, 'what's going on?' I took a seat on the sofa opposite.

'Murgatroyd's investigating Petra's disappearance,' I said, certain I was telling Spoor something he already knew.

'So why he's calling me?' said Spoor. 'What's so urgent?' The cat was looking at our guest, wide eyed and fixated. I felt the same. Spoor had been chased, yet he hadn't responded. Instead he was here. It didn't make sense.

'Fred,' I said gently, leaning in, 'is there a reason you don't want to talk to Murgatroyd?'

'I just don't like being pestered,' he said, 'I want to know what's what before I talk to the police about what's happening in one of my shops.' That was a reasonable if incomplete answer. Spoor asked for a drink and had begun to tear into his cuticles when I informed him there was nothing in the place but soda water and flat cola.

'I believe they want to search the shop,' I said. It occurred to me to lie, of course, but I had an instinct that fragments of the truth would be enough.

'What?' said Spoor. 'Why?'

'I'm not sure,' I said, giving the cat a consoling grin, 'perhaps they expect to find Petra half-eaten in the cellar.' Spoor's face flushed anew.

'Son, I'm serious,' he said, 'I need to know what they're looking for.' I had wondered if there was something else to find. Now I knew it.

'It's just about Petra, best I know,' I said, 'though I'm with you, I can't imagine what they expect to find. I told Murgatroyd what happened. She left work on the Friday and we never saw her again. Best I know, all she left behind was the week's rota and a lot of bottles to shelve. Oh yes, and a psychotic husband – you know, the kind that keeps women's refuges in business.' As I'd spoken, Spoor had raised an unconscious hand to his mouth and was now prying the underside of his nail with a bottom layer of crooked teeth.

'Shit,' he said, 'I'll have to call them, I suppose. Shit.' He hadn't yet, then. I was now overcome by a silent panic. There was a chemical taste in my mouth and sudden pain cascaded across my brow, circling my right eye. The cat began to purr. My good optic flicked to the wall clock. It ticked on to 4.15 p.m.

'Fred,' I pressed, 'why don't you want to speak to Murgatroyd?' I could think of a thousand reasons, but knew Fred's to be distinct. Spoor sighed and flopped back into the chair.

'Because,' he said, 'there's more in that cellar than old stock and flies.' He was staring at me expectantly now, in that presumptive way people do when they think you're sharing a thought but aren't.

'I'm down there quite a bit,' I said, 'there's nothing except cases and a dead rat. What are you talking about?'

'Yeah,' said Spoor, 'well there's a reason I insisted Ragesh leave the pest control situation with me, right? Your friend is still there for a reason.' The choice of words was chilling.

'What? There's something else behind that wall?'

'Right.'

'Like what? Drugs?'

'C'mon Keir, do I look like a drug lord?'

'Appearances can be deceptive,' I said. 'What then?' Spoor rested his head in his hand.

'The shop was doing pretty badly a couple of years ago,' he said, 'and I have a lot invested in it, not to mention its brother and sister, so I was contemplating closing the Perrangyre place and shoring up the other two. But, well I suppose you could say, a mate of mine, had access to some bits and pieces – vintage bits, you might say. Worth a lot. Obtained from an anonymous benefactor, if you get my meaning. He suggested I might like to sell them on. Anyway, it was tiding us over but then customers started asking a few questions, so...'

'Ragesh and Petra knew about this?' I said.

'Petra did, yeah. Radge was in the Perranporth shop back then. I told you, she's a good girl; she understood we needed a top up.'

'The stolen stock's behind the wall,' I said, thinking aloud. Spoor nodded.

'I got a man in – we created a cavity, put up a bit of plasterboard, painted it over. There's a lot there, maybe three pallets worth. It was supposed to be temporary, but there's never been a great time to move it. I don't have a buyer. Anyway, it's an old building, vulnerable to pests, there are a million routes into those wall cavities and, well, you know.'

'A rat made residence in the hole and died,' I said.

'Right.'

'Do you think they'd find it?' I said. Spoor's knee was restless.

'That depends what they're looking for, doesn't it?' he said, getting to his feet and pacing. 'Could you keep them out of the cellar?' An irrepressible snort forced its way through my nose and mouth. Poor, spiv-like Fred. He imagined Murgatroyd would be rifling through old papers and lifting wine books. How to tell him that the cellar would be the invading army's first and only port of call? I doubted they'd get to the wall cavity, of course. It'd be a miracle if the search lasted any longer than five minutes.

'Murgatroyd's very thorough,' I said, urgency creeping into my voice, 'I doubt I could keep him away from anything.' Spoor let out a long breath.

'I have to call the guy back,' he said, 'what else can I do?'

'Perhaps wait a couple of days,' I said, 'we can think about getting the stuff out of there?'

'If the police are interested in the shop, then they're going to notice if I send in a man to knock down a wall and take whole pallets out under cover of darkness!' Spoor was agitated and pacing hard.

'We just need time to think it through,' I said. Spoor focused on me. He retook his seat.

'You have nothing to worry about,' he said, 'you've only been there a short time; no one's going to talk to you about it. Just say you knew nothing. I'll work something out.' The cat made a noise – a curdling whine that broke from his gut. His head snapped to face mine. Spoor, who'd never let go of his phone, now looked at the display and swallowed. 'All right,' he said, 'perhaps if I just explain, I don't know – he's trying to find Petra, after all, maybe he won't be bothered over a few dozen cases of knocked off vino.' He looked at his phone.

'Fred, I wouldn't.'

'I can't dodge him for ever, Keir. Just give me a moment. Let me think about what I'm going to say.'

I felt the crushing weight of circumstance on my chest and primal tension in my head and neck. I made a move towards Spoor, crab-like, and a moment later my hand had a skin-whitening grip on his wrist, and a moment after that his phone was on the floor, the former owner coiled and shaken, like a man who'd felt a wasp goosestep through his open fly.

If he said something it was lost in the eliding time that followed. He pulled his arm free and tried to stand, I forced him back into the chair. He pushed me away and alongside the cat. I grabbed the cat, propelling him, like a basketball, into Spoor's face. There was wailing, hissing, a yell – the feline had struck out in panic and mauled his nose and lower eyelid before landing clumsily and running clear.

Now I was on him again, keeping him pressed down, pinning him to that awful chair, compounding his confusion and multiplying his panic. The grip I had on his throat, both hands, hard-pressed and claw-like, made the tips of my fingers deep red, like the ends of lit cigarettes. It didn't falter, it was a chain – bent steel, impossible to break no matter how valiantly and incessantly Spoor tried, thrashing out and arching his back, gripping my wrists, which in turn moved this way and that, the neck in tandem, making it hard for him to retain purchase. I make no excuses – I could have let go, but the integrity of that grip was maintained by the sure and certain knowledge that this man's life would mean the end of mine, that an early word from him would silence me, that I hadn't come this far, hadn't debased myself for my art, to have the footnote eclipse the story – a rural shopkeeper whose only brush with risk had been to acquire a few cases of knocked-off bladder fill.

The thrashing ended, the tension in the muscles dissipated and the room returned to its fragile equilibrium, but now Fred Spoor lay where he'd once sat, dewy-eyed, bloodshot and still. The knee that had held him in place throughout my latest ordeal was damp. I withdrew it and realised that this empire builder, forced back inside his borders, had soiled himself in his defining moment. Fred Spoor would not be giving Murgatroyd permission to search the shop. There would be no search today. This alone made it all seem worthwhile. I got to my feet, brushing my knee, quietly disgusted. The cat, still on edge, followed my movement as I encircled my former patron. Spoor's death had bought me a few hours at best. Now, out of respect for my benefactor, it was essential to make them count.

IV

Decapitation

'It's a nasty gash, no doubt about it,' said Bennett, the surgery nurse, surveying the damage to my hand. 'It is deep, you're right, but I don't think you need a stitch. There's a risk of cat scratch fever, though. Have you had that?'

'I'm not sure,' I said, looking across to a stack of yellow trays; medical supplies that filled an entire open cupboard. She felt my forehead.

'You're a bit warm,' she said, 'and you have a little tremor in your hand there. Are you worried about it?'

'A little,' I said. 'I haven't felt great since it happened.'

'But this was just a few hours ago?'

'That's right.' It was time to get her out of the room. 'Listen,' I said, 'I think I may have been tested for a cat allergy, some time ago. To be honest I can't remember the result. I don't have any pets, you see.' An image of the cat's face, talons extended, dug into my brain. 'You wouldn't mind checking my records, would you?' Bennett's anteroom had no computer, so I knew she'd have to move to the other side of the partition to make her notes or retrieve records.

'Sure,' she said with a warm smile, 'won't be a minute.' A moment later I was alone in this tiny cubicle. I quickly reached over to the trays and began pulling them out. The first had bandages and other dressings, the second what looked like prescription medication – painkillers and the like – but the third, as I'd remembered, had syringes in plastic wrappers, along with directions for use. I grabbed a handful and quickly dropped them into the over-the-shoulder rucksack that lay open on the chair next to mine. Would I be able to get through corks with them? I'd soon know. The rucksack was zipped.

The nurse emerged from the room next door. 'I can't find any test for allergies,' she said, 'so I'm not sure what you're remembering, but I reckon cats are still your friends for the minute.' I smiled at her.

'Good,' I said, 'because I like my stray very much.'

***

'It's like looking at a budget version of myself,' said Robin, as I walked into the shop, the hourly chime of the town church bell just audible on the breeze. It was faintly alarming he'd noticed the imitation straight off, but then the truly narcissistic see themselves in everything. Robin knew something, he just didn't know what.

After a quick change at home I was draped in black from head to toe, complemented by a flapping dark coat I'd ripped out of mothballs and beaten against the bed before leaving. It wasn't a perfect mirror image, but I wasn't looking to pass for a body double in a Hollywood stunt. Robin dressed simply, one might say formulaically, and it was only necessary to appropriate it.

I'd once read a book on the Jack the Ripper case and identification evidence that suggested a typical person, men in particular, could describe a human face with all the precision and talent for verbal reconstruction of a nearsighted racist. Such people, it was alleged, looked for other crutches to help them paint a picture – clothing being the most common. Soon we'd find out.

'Did you get my stuff?' I asked.

'Yes,' said Robin, 'it's in the back office. They only had a couple, though, so you'll have to make do with that. But they're the large ones. You have plenty if you ask me.' I walked to the room and checked his purchase. Ammonium hydroxide, as ordered. The labels were simple, plastered with hazard warnings; pleas to safeguard health. Would two bottles be enough? They'd have to be.

I turned to see Robin standing in the doorway.

'You got a receipt?' I said.

'Yeah.'

'Good. Keep that on you for now. I'll settle up with you tomorrow.'

I now tried to usher Robin out, pushing him to take the break he'd earned, but curiously he was in no hurry. My mood darkened as he swanned about.

'So Murgatroyd, huh?' said Robin. 'He's persistent, isn't he? I wonder if he's got hold of the owner yet.' I looked through him.

'I'm sure he'll find Fred soon enough,' I said. I handed Robin a letter.

'When you go out I need you to post this for me, is that OK?' Robin's eyes flicked to my gloved hand, then to the address written in capitals on the envelope.

'Sure,' he said. 'Are you cold, why are you wearing gloves?'

'I'm cold, as you say,' I said. Robin read the address on the envelope out loud.

'The Editor, The West Country Watchman, Truro, TR1 3PD. You've written to the *Watchman*?'

'I have,' I said.

'Saying?'

'It's a mass murder confession,' I said, 'from you.' Robin smirked.

'Fine, don't tell me,' he said, and turned to leave.

'Take two hours, as agreed,' I said, 'I've got a bit to do, anyway.'

'Yes, sir,' said Robin, on the back of a laugh.

A moment later I stood by the window display and watched him saunter down the street and out of view. Satisfied I was alone for the foreseeable future, I closed the shop, mounted a 'back soon' sign, and got to work. Once in the office, I planted my second letter in the desk drawer, the envelope torn open. This was the note I expected Murgatroyd's successor to discover; a sop to a broken bobby, desperate to close the door on a bleak and personally affecting local tragedy. Computer typed, written in Petra's preferred short sentences, as found in her handwritten notes on shop matters, and the odd, historic wine ticket, and signed with an imitation of her scrawl from old stock order forms, it read:

Dear Robin,

I hope you won't mind a traditional letter. I know it's old-fashioned, but you've made me do a lot of old school things recently. You've made me believe there's something like romance for a start. Oh God, that's corny! I'm sorry. But I know you won't mind.

That's the thing about you, I can embarrass myself and I don't care. Ian would never let me forget it. He'd rip the piss out of me whenever he needed a cheap rise. That's what he does. He gets off on making me feel stupid, it makes him feel clever. You've made me realise that's just one of the ways he controls me and has always controlled me. There are many ways to abuse people, to keep them in line. Some women get battered, others get put down. But you and I know it's all the same. I've known it for a long time, but didn't feel it until you reminded me there was another way. You've made me feel human again, like a real person. I'll never forget that.

I hope you can forgive me for what I have to do. I have to let you go. I have to do it for both of us. I want you to know that ever since you started coming to the shop you've made a difference to my life. I soon began to look forward to your visits. I've never hit it off with a man like that. I've never felt so comfortable with someone. I knew it was different, something special. The problem is that Ian knew it too. We haven't been happy for a long time, but there's no sense going over that. You know the worst of it – the threats, the intimidation, the cold shoulder. I'd been lonely for the longest time before you came along. But, like I said, Ian knew something. He sensed a change. When I realised he'd been leaving work to spy on me, that he'd seen us talking, I tried to tell him it was nothing. But I'm not a good liar and he knows that about me. I didn't tell him anything. I didn't have to.

I had to put up with innuendos and insults. He got really aggressive. I hoped it'd pass; it's not the first time he's been possessive; but this time it didn't, it got worse. I denied it. I kept my promise. I know you don't want to be dragged into 'a domestic'. I get it. So I kept our secret. But Ian's no fool. He can smell the guilt on me. He knows my head is somewhere else. It's with you. Being together is all I want now, but I know that can never happen.

Last night is the reason I'm writing to you now, because I have to say goodbye and beg you to respect my decision. The consequences for me if you don't are something I can't bear to think about. Last night he was drunk, he was angry, he was shaking me and demanding to know who you were. When I didn't tell him he said that if he ever found out I'd been unfaithful he'd kill me. He used those words and he meant them. He was shaking as he said it and I was terrified. I know him and I know what his bluster looks and sounds like, and this was something else. A line was crossed.

Robin, when you said you loved me I hope you meant it. I suppose now I'll find out. If you did, please stay away. I'm protecting us both by doing this. I know what this will do to you. Don't think it won't be the same for me. I wish I was strong enough to leave him, or believed that he'd ever leave us alone if I did, but I don't. That's a fairy tale. In real life people get hurt. Forgive me.

Petra

The awful letter duly stowed – perhaps the tritest, most sentimental insurance policy ever written – I took to the shop floor and began filling empty boxes with mixed cases; our finest wines for our very best customers. A random selection would have been desirable, more plausible perhaps, but I couldn't resist tracing a line with my finger to the most incendiary-ticketed items, the wines that had really inflamed the colons and pinched the arteries of our most sensitive and pious clients.

With the boxes full, and my now crumpled list of names withdrawn and laid out on the back office desk, I filled out the delivery chits for each. The line that went through each name felt decisive, more a throat slash than a strikethrough.

As I neared the bottom, the time ticking relentlessly on, I caught myself and felt surprise at how calm I was. There was no anxiety about what I was doing, no guilt. This was a stepping stone to a crime in the eyes of Murgatroyd and his ilk. Why then did it feel so matter-of-fact, so incidental? One couldn't feel any mawkishness for the people on that list. I felt nothing for them.

It was best to be methodical. Adding the ammonium to screw-capped bottles was easy. I just opened them, poured out a measure, carefully topped up with the odourless fluid, keeping my mouth and nose as far away as possible – holding my breath – then screwing on the cap. I now washed the glass neck in the nearby sink, then shook the new blend, dropping each treated wine into an empty cell in an open box. One bottle of ammonium stretched to thirty-six wine bottles. The lucky customers chosen to receive this special gift, thanking them for their custom, would have to settle for a half case each. One bottle would probably be enough, I thought, but one never knew how many would be present when the boxes were open, or if some bottles would be passed off as presents to third parties. I wouldn't put it past the cheap bastards.

Tearing open a medical syringe, I now got down to the tricky ones – the bottles of champagne, Prosecco and the like. This was for show, really. In order for the delivery to look like a convincing selection, something celebratory had to be included. The more expensive wines would act as an incentive to plough into the rest, and I gambled on the majority of recipients opting to drink the mid-price wines first, saving the good stuff for special occasions. Consequently, the concentration of ammonium in the fizz could be less. It would have to be. There was no means of inconspicuously opening the bottles and reducing the liquid inside. So less but not zero, because who knew? It might be someone's birthday or wedding anniversary or a dinner to celebrate a new baby. One had to cover all the possibilities. Some, I knew, remembering my dad, needed no excuse – they just liked the decadent stuff. Including expensive wine sealed the old-fashioned way, with the snobbery still attached to the method – grossly inefficient so said Ragesh and prone, ironically, to contamination – should persuade any cynics who might have thought this was wine past its best, or unwanted stock, that the gift was sincere.

The syringe was plunged into a succession of Champagne corks, and the clear ammonium pressed through. It was hard work; a few of the needles broke – lucky I had spares – and I soon learned that nothing less than precise penetration would do. I took great care not to make a conspicuous gash that would discourage the sharp-eyed oenophile.

After an hour of shaking, injecting and checking to see I hadn't got any of the noxious stuff on my skin, I proudly stood over the cases, awaiting the man who'd ferry them to their final destination. Lining them against the wall, hidden from street view by the red curtain, I felt powerful again. I felt free.

The weedy-looking courier was early, necessitating the quick swipe of empty ammonium bottles into my open rucksack. His joviality and tactility – he touched my arm twice – made him an unlikely triggerman for this round of magic bullets. He seemed determined to talk, to drag out the loading of the van, and I found my mouth pursing and my strained replies to his inane small talk getting mangled through grinding teeth.

I watched each box go, the shop's eloquent logo on each side, and realised that if I were going to call it off, perhaps give in to the foreboding that became more pronounced with each pick up, the ever shrinking number of boxes acting like a countdown, then I had better do it. Yet ten became five, five became three, then two, and the aborting words would not come. The final case to go had the art school's name on it.

'Is this the last of them?' said the courier, peering round into the office, sweat bleeds under each arm. I took the chance to look at the final box for a few seconds more.

'Yes,' I said, 'that's it now.' Relieved, he presented a clipboard and asked me to sign the client box. Clearly, and with great fidelity to the genuine article, I wrote, 'Robin Eep.'

***

The shop had reopened when a swaggering Robin returned. A moment later he was swinging the back office chair from side to side.

'Did you have a surge while I was away?' he said. 'The shelves look depleted.'

'It's been very busy,' I said, 'Katherine was in – she's having a party.'

'Ah,' said Robin, 'I'm amazed we've anything left then.' His eye settled on a bottle by the sink.

'What's open?' he said, and without waiting for an answer he grabbed the lonely Merlot.

'This is nearly full, Keir,' he said, 'I've been gone a couple of hours, what's wrong with you? I thought for a moment you might have succumbed to alcohol's charms.'

'Not me,' I said, 'not ever,' picking up the cork, which, unseen by Robin, had a pocked glans – a wound caused by much jabbing. The Merlot had been my practice bottle for the champagnes.

'Well,' he said, 'I'll drink anything, as you know, pass me a glass, would you?' It occurred to me to dissuade him, to insist it was spoilt, undrinkable, worse than distilled impotence, but strangely the words would not come. I handed him a Riedel and watched him crudely fill it to the top.

'Your very good health,' he said, and took a couple of gulps in quick succession. His face changed.

'Ugh, that is corked, definitely,' he said, putting the glass down in disgust. 'Sorry I doubted you.' The concentration had been high in Robin's practice bottle. Too much, I'd suspected. It was refined after that, so the taste of the wine would obscure the added ingredient. It was OK if it was a little off. Most pissheads would drink it anyway. But too much and they'd abandon it, which would be a disaster.

I was watching Robin now. I couldn't speak; I was stuck to the floor. There was no moving forward and no going back. He remained slumped, his feet elevated to the desk, brass on wood.

'You didn't ask me what I got up to on my break,' he said, fingering his collar. His expectant glare jabbed me. I forced an answer.

'Tell me,' I said. Robin cleared his throat.

'I bumped into, guess who, your friend, Murgatroyd,' he said, and with those words I felt myself grow limp and unsteady. Robin got up and helped himself to a glass of water from the nearby sink.

'God, that stuff is dreadful,' he continued, 'I feel like I've swallowed iron filings.'

'You saw Murgatroyd,' I said, prompting, 'when? What did you say to him?'

'He wanted to know if I'd seen you,' said Robin, retaking his seat and raising a hand to a now-pallid forehead. 'I told him you were here, covering for me. He thanked me

261

for volunteering that I was acquainted with Petra – said I didn't have to worry. They're close to arresting someone, I reckon.'

'He said that?'

'He didn't have to,' said Robin, 'he had the air of a man who'd just met someone special. So either he's made progress or he's got laid.' Robin was sweating.

'Oh,' he said, trying to get up but defeated by his weight, 'that wine…'

'Are you OK?' I said. My voice was thin. Now he began to cough. I looked on as Robin, soaked through and the colour of stale bread, tipped over. He reached out to me, a hand to his throat.

'Keir – the wine.' I stared.

'Would you like me to call an ambulance?' I said. He was nodding, though badly, as if one side of his neck had collapsed.

'Yes, quickly,' he said, 'there's something wrong. I can't breathe, my… oh God.'

'Well I'm afraid I won't be doing that,' I said. Robin was clawing at his throat now, his normally assured tone reduced to a deep gargle. 'You're right for once,' I went on, 'the wine's bad. Really bad. Poisoned actually. Your bottle's a tester. The others are on their way to every whore, degenerate and Marlowe in town. It's what you might call a decapitation strategy. You were going to be part of it – a scapegoat. Now, I suppose you're just the first.'

Robin's eyes watered, his mouth twisted. No sound came out.

'You want to know why?' I said. 'Why I didn't stop you? Why you were going to take the blame? Because we're friends, right? And I'd never hurt my friends.' He made a fist but it collapsed and became a hand again, just as quickly. 'But fucking Maisie wasn't a friendly thing to do, was it?'

His eyes widened. Only tiny bursts of air were being expelled now.

'Yes, I know all about it. I worked it out. I dreamed it, actually – some of my things were symbolically placed in your bedroom, along with the woman herself. When I woke it tormented me. I couldn't dismiss it. Later, I realised my subconscious had given me a tip, confirming what the heart already knew. I mean, I've never trusted you exactly – I thought you were playing around behind Kerry's back – but still. It was lots of little things. It's all circumstantial. Or it was until I saw your reaction.' Robin began to convulse.

'The way you looked when Kerry suggested Maisie had other lovers, the fact you were there the day I followed her to the shop. You were meeting her, I think. You probably signalled to her while we spoke, ushered her away. I saw your favourite ginger wine when I went in for the first time, the day I met Petra. In Vino Veritas is expensive for you, but not for Maisie – I think she gave you a taste for the good stuff. That's what she does. Then there was the look on her face when she came into the shop the night Petra died. She wasn't surprised to see me. Why? Because she knew I worked there, because you'd told her. Since you've worked here she hasn't returned once, but the other day, when I went to see her, there was a bottle of Pinotage in her office – Cape Longhorn. That's an exclusive line, Robin. I know you can't get it anywhere else. Not in this town. And of course you're her type – the right age, build, and your close relationship with me would have made coordinating your meetings with her easy as pie. And you're a shit, obviously.'

A low groan escaped from Robin, like a distended belch.

'You see Murgatroyd suspects me of killing Petra, but he has no concrete motive. He thinks it's about a shop job. That's weak and he knows it. Whoever picks up the case when he's gone will want an easy answer, something they can sell to a jury. So I gave them Ian Zeller and you. Two hunks of reasonable doubt, pushing me to a distant third on the suspect list. The abusive husband and the jilted lover. I gave them the first chapter of the story, so to speak, letting them imagine the rest. Maybe Ian killed Petra here after hours, you found her and lost your mind. Maybe you couldn't cope with being ditched, suspected her hubby had got rid of her and the guilt addled your brain. You brooded, snapped, then decided to punish this suffocating little town; the provincial shithouse that had trapped her in a loveless marriage. Who can say? I mean, for all I know, you could have been banging Petra. I wouldn't put it past you. No, no one would have understood exactly why you poisoned those wines, but you doing it, on the back of a mental breakdown, in the shadow of an affair, with your lover's body in the cellar, would make more sense to grieving plods, desperate to join the dots and move on, than a man who killed to preserve his art. Who, but a creative, could understand that? Who, but an artist, could imagine it?'

Robin's head rolled back. Half of one eye remained open, looking over my shoulder.

'But wouldn't you know,' I continued, 'you managed

to ruin it with a single conversation. All you had to do was disappear for a couple of hours, go and play with yourself, whatever the hell you do on your own, but no, you talked to Murgatroyd and now he'll know it was me who sent out that delivery and not you. Assuming that is, he's not already tucking in to the complimentary wine sent by you as a thanks for all his hard graft in looking for Petra Zealot.'

Perhaps I'd bored Robin, as he no longer moved. I heard a long sigh followed by a longer silence.

'Petra's downstairs,' I concluded, 'in the freezer. She's been here all the time, so how good is Murgatroyd really? I'd say chances are, he got laid.'

I waited for Robin's rejoinder but there was none.

V

Drinking Alone

A glass of fine wine, redolent of wrongheaded metaphor, with notes that are neither musical nor explanatory in character, must be savoured. But your last glass, your very last, should be studied and respected and feared. Now I'm enjoying mine. I'm comfortable and at peace, basking in the warmth of my burnt orange living room. Nothing can ruin the moment. Fred Spoor's desiccated husk is covered nearby but cannot detract from this beautiful solitude. Time is short, so paradoxically everything must slow down; each action vital to the appreciation of this ignoble rot must be stretched across these final minutes. This time shall not come again.

The stabbed cork is weeded out like an old molar. Then comes that wonderful sound, the pluck; and from the cavity pours the blood. I hold it to the light as Ragesh taught me, and, despite the limitations of an energy saving bulb, the carmine lacquer is well illuminated. Mine's a Burgundy glass with a luxury, airy interior that allows the juice to eddy in full – taking on the air, unleashing the bounty.

Once illuminated, my discriminating eye, acute twice over on account of my duel apprenticeship in art and wine advising, is duly satisfied. At a thirty-degree angle to the lamp, I can see great maturity. How I envy this wine. There's a thin, watery membrane on the periphery, insulating a second layer of arterial red and, finally, like the soft centre of some magnificent bombe, the autumnal nucleus. This is an aged wine, a wine to paint Regency walls, a wine of mystery and facets.

Now it's to my nose. I breathe deeply. My olfactory nerves are fooled, as people are sometimes fooled, into recognising what isn't there: forest fruit and the smoke from a dead campfire. The smell returns me to Banff, Canada, three summers ago, before I began at Perrangyre; before Maisie, Petra, and this carefree walk down a dead end, and then it's gone, supplanted by a scent that's very much of the now; a chemical afterthought, the juice from a bull's eye, an interloper from a foreign bottle.

I hold the glass aloft. One must respect one's adversary. Patience Keir, I tell myself, patience New, patience whoever you are – I don't remember any more. Perhaps it doesn't matter. Perhaps it never did. I aerate further with a single rotation of the wrist, then satisfied the elements have made their mark, tip the glass towards my mouth. Yet, as it approaches the lips, I pause. I'm not quite ready to imbibe. I open my journal and write these words – the epilogue to pages and pages of notes. Do I want them to be my last? I've caught up with myself, just as events have caught up with me.

I wander to the window, glass in hand, and look out into the night. I wonder what's happening out there. Is the town peaceful because the restaurants have closed and the shops are shut and the nigh on imperceptible street illumination has put off the elderly and the vulnerable and the fearful, or is there something more to it?

I've walked around Perrangyre many times after dark and often you could be mistaken for thinking that the only thing left alive was the ocean and the occupants of the hotels that line the crescent. Somewhere, I know, at this time, there's a man alone on the beach walking his dog, a drunk teenager and his unfortunate girlfriend shouting at each other as they wait for a bus that's never going to come, and somewhere a wizened old dear is lying in bed, wondering if she made the right choice to come here all those years ago. Yet I'm sure that soon the quiet will be punctuated by hysteria and screams, by desperate cries for help, and those cries will be chased by sirens, and soon after that the slamming of car doors outside my home and the frenzied thumping of vengeful enforcers.

If you're still reading you know I had plans and they meant everything to me. Many were hurt, but that's the game. They chose to play; I didn't ask them.

If you've learned anything about me at all, you know I could never be beholden to the thrupenny schemes of others. If they're enough for you that's your choice; be a stranger in your own life if you wish, just don't presume to tell me I must do the same. Many have tried to keep me down. All have failed. Thoughtless, degenerate people who wouldn't have amounted to anything, tried to dilute me with their mediocrity and thought terminating world view. Ultimately they had to go: Petra Zealot, Fred Spoor, Robin Eep, Anthony Courcier.

I sit down and the cat jumps on my lap. He looks up at me then brushes his nose against mine, but says nothing. I look to my glass and realise that if I'm denied my liberty there'll be no one to look after him, no one for him to identify with. I think how awful that will be and, before I know what's happening, tears are creeping down my cheeks and soaking into my T-shirt.

Beyond this room Perrangyre remains silent, as though poised. Everyone and everything is looking to the next moment, needing to learn if any of this can count for something after all. I listen to the cat purr and I know my mind is made up. I pour the toxic contents of the glass on to the scuffed, uneven planks of this overpriced, unkempt rental. Keir Rothwell cannot go on; he's finished, just as Petra surmised, but New Shockley has more to do. New Shockley is leaving.

VI

Point of Departure

Seconds now had the character of tools, chipping away at my freedom. There was no telling when Murgatroyd would come, no way to know how close he was, so I didn't waste precious minutes dwelling on it. There was no time to be precious about anything, no time to sentimentally trawl through accumulated artefacts of a long and fruitless student life. No time at all.

I took a few clothes, modesty covering essentials, and reusable drapery – baggy, holey jumpers and washed-out jeans – and swept them into a rucksack with the cat settled on top like a cake decoration, the elastic pulled taut to keep him in place.

He looked annoyed and somewhat ridiculous, as animals often do; his eyes following me as I rifled through the remnants of Keir Rothwell's occupancy. Rothwell's passport was stowed, his birth certificate folded and pocketed, some loose change and a few crumpled notes retrieved from a pot on the kitchen top. No money was taken from the shop, I'm not a thief. Finally, my journal and pens. Whatever happened next I'd want it on the record, whenever I had the chance to document it. I wondered where I'd be when that moment came. A café, a hostel, a cell? Depending on how things ended, would it be better to tell all or leave the reader hanging? Part of me liked the idea of a cliffhanger, that sublime point of departure when anything's still possible. Life is at its most magical in such moments, before the tyranny of choice and consequence.

I allowed myself a moment to look at pinned-up photographs, grabs from a life now over. This was the stuff I couldn't take with me; things I'd never see again: Kerry with her arms wrapped round me; Robin standing cocksure and pointing; a figure, reminiscent of me, wading into the water, gallivanting on the beach. Whoever this man was he was carefree – not a concern in the world. He'd licked the happiness bowl clean. He was a man with a career in front of him; a man with great friends and a potent lover.

As the streets were pounded, my breathing becoming shallow and heartbeat frenzied, the cat kneading my back, I realised what an infinitesimally small period separated hope from panic, confidence from desperation. I was nimble and sprung, conscious of every step as I tore up overgrown alleys, vaulted over decaying walls and crouched to avoid the glare of passing cars, progressing path by path, road by street walk, to the railway station, my back damp with sweat, my pits musty, the expelled air from parched lips becoming thinner and thinner.

It was late, but how late? Any delay could result in being stranded. When the last train left the station, meandering up the branch line to Truro, there would be no more for several hours. I recalled Murgatroyd's observation that Petra couldn't have left by public transport on the night she disappeared because services shut down after eleven. Missing that train meant a long and potentially fatal wait to depart – hours in purgatory – more than enough for a determined police force to sweep a town and find a fugitive.

My fatigue had forced me to slow, my senses alert to any sign of a police presence. As I approached the verge that lead to Station Approach, I heard the hourly chime of the town's church clock. I'd left Robin and closed the shop around 9.45 p.m., rushed home, brooded and scribbled. That must have eaten another hour. Now I contemplated the horrifying possibility that it had just gone eleven, which meant the last train, my way out, was a few minutes from departure at best.

My muscles hurt, the tension in the calves being nigh on unbearable, as the single light of the station platform grew ahead. My energy gone, the weight on my back crushing and dragging, I forced each step, imagining the landscape had a rope running across it that I could use to pull myself along. I gave myself aural prompts, 'come on!' 'nearly there!' and my body responded with derision; pain radiating in all directions, my chest and back squeezed by an invisible sadist who would not relinquish their grip. More power, more momentum, and still the station wouldn't come.

Such was my determination to break through and reach the pathetic two-carriage shuttle, its engine choking as it readied itself to depart, the interior lights so inviting, that I nearly missed the elephant trap. Yards from the station office, alone in the adjoining car park, was a vehicle. Its lights were off, but the illumination of the train created a pair of silhouettes; quiet figures waiting in the driver's seat and front passenger's side.

Stopping to get a better look, I stuck myself to the long wall that lined the car park, separating it from the beach below. The train was revving hard now, but I couldn't move; I didn't dare. I swore under my breath and felt the cat kick, like some bestial parody of pregnancy, as I tried to get a fix on the car, squinting to see the detail. I dared to move a little closer, keeping as low as possible, content that the pitch darkness was sufficient camouflage for now. On the wind I could hear a beeping sound; the train doors were locking. I wasn't going to make it. I let out an exasperated groan, a sound from the darkest nook of a hollowed heart and watched as my ride began to pull out of the platform, snaking its way along the cove and off into the night. With the car park shrouded in darkness, both car and passengers remained motionless. The police were here and now, for the next seven hours, so was I.

Why, you ask, did I not simply backtrack fifty yards and take my chances at the nearby bus station? There was no reason to suppose there wasn't a car there too, but the question betrays an ignorance of what passes for public transport in this part of the world. There was no bus out of town at this time. There was nothing. The bus station was open, well-lit and on a main road, not a secluded area like the remains of Perrangyre's once opulent Victorian rail hub. The shoreline below the station was expansive, dark and deserted. Carefully, I wound my way down the incline that led to the sand.

Taking stock, it felt like geology and circumstance had conspired to keep me imprisoned in this provincial dumping ground. Perrangyre was built on a crescent, a hollow, carpeted with beach and flanked by unassailable cliff and rocks as tall as overpriced three-storey houses. In night's gloom all one could see were lights from whatever life remained after dark. There was a hotel with a glass annex and a red hue, like an Amsterdam brothel, with figures backed to windows. I could see a guest house, with a woman drawing her curtains in the top window, pausing for a moment to take one last look at the glass sea and the moon's blue torchlight.

Then there was the weak glow from the railway station office; distant now but clearly visible. The last train was long gone. One couldn't see the track lining the curve or the tunnel into which my last, best hope of escape had disappeared a short time ago. I stood on the beach, taking in the gentle swish of low tide and noting the perilous geological formations that effectively sealed each end, making escape impossible, and wondered if the few hours left to me would be enough to think my way out.

Though it was hopeless, I had no choice but to contemplate an escape route on foot. With the cat mocking, mewing his disapproval, despite my frequent warnings that his whining would give us away, I paced the length of the curve, looking for a line through the edifice. There were nooks, crevices and alcoves, going nowhere; dead ends flanked by rocks that offered nothing but slimy footholds and pools that soaked feet up to the ankles; missteps that soiled the air with choice insults, directed at no one.

Emerging from one of the beach's natural hides, I saw a light, some distance away but closing, held at chest height – the careful approach of a man. In a minute he'd be standing next to me, and not for the first time in recent days, I contemplated the worst may be necessary.

Hushing the cat, who groaned like a bored child, I bent down and picked up the biggest rock I could find. It had a smooth, rounded base but a sharp tip – it was a giant teardrop. I clutched it tight as the figure moved closer – he was just twenty yards out now and fully formed. His light wasn't aimed at me, though only a few feet separated the cat and me from its footprint. I psyched myself for the blow to come, squinting hard to get a semblance of the man's build and height. He was closer still, seconds away, the rock awkward in my hand, when I saw the second figure, lower down, trotting – a dog – and instantly backed on to the cliff face, the cat obscured from view. The man, just a dog walker it seemed, continued on his route, his animal leading the way. 'All right there,' he said, nodding in my direction. I nodded back. On he went and I dropped the rock, content that this benign old duffer, fond of his nighttime walk, had ridden his luck. Someone had to be lucky. Why not him?

The hours on that beach were long; so long that I contemplated handing myself in. I was desperate to know what was happening in the world above. The night was punctuated by brief spasms of life from the town beyond. The cat and I were alert to momentary yelling, laughter from young lungs, at least two people, and most troublingly, a scream, faint but loud enough to carry, that rang out, hours into our wait, impossible to place and impossible to ignore. I struggled to get a clear line of sight to the station office, straining to see the illumination of car lights or any sign of movement, but there was none. Everything remained still and the long, lonely night went on.

My hope was to get out on that first train; scope a route to the platform, beyond the peripheral vision of the waiting police officers, one of whom could, for all I knew, have been Murgatroyd, then ride my luck. If I could get to Truro, I had a chance of making it to London and from there anything was possible. New Shockley only needed a break, just an opening, and he could change the world.

My scheme had been too grandiose for this geographic outhouse. I'd tried to introduce the future to a place where the past was the stock currency. The plan, I now realised, never had any hope of succeeding because the stifling self-interest of a narrow and intellectually pauperised local population was too well practised and too committed. I'd been the best thing that ever happened to Perrangyre, but I'd been forced out. I sat on the rocks and wondered if there'd be anyone of insight left to appreciate this irony once I was gone.

The sun was coming up and the dark was recast as gloaming as I stood at the base of ascending rocks; a natural, if inhospitable bridge between the sand and the wall separating the cove from the railway line. I was wondering if a climb was possible, when my eye caught movement on the nearby coastal path and my nasal cavity was filled with the stench of rot.

Perhaps he'd been there all night, there was no way to know, but the presence of this vagrant, wretched though he was, seemed providential; indeed, for the first time in my life I felt serendipity as something tangible. In my universe there's no God and no fate, just one thing after another, yet here was deliverance – scraggy, with clothes hanging from a malnourished frame; filth and facial hair saturated in decay and hopelessness.

This foul derelict, swaying rather than walking,

seemingly pulled towards the water, looked like my ruin personified. I took a moment. Was he familiar? Had I seen him at the school on the day of Maisie's summons? He'd worn a sandwich board adorned with 'SAVE THE WORLD'. Well perhaps he could save mine.

It would be wrong to say I overpowered him; there was nothing to overcome. He dropped like the stone used to relieve him of his troubled consciousness. The cat approved of the second blow, insurance, but seemed less enamoured at being attached to a figure overlaid with torn clothes that barely qualified as rags. The stench was unbearable, it was like being wrapped in dead flesh, but the disguise was perfect. Who, but the most committed officer, would wish to get too close to this wretch? The telltale stink of disease preceded him and he left a trace in the air that would have the more fortunate retreat to a safe distance, keen to put yards between them and their broken liberal conscience.

★★★

The first train of the day was clanking along Perrangyre's crescent, the fresh morning air polluted by the departing unfortunate that walked slowly towards the train platform, his pet cat in his rucksack – his only friend. The vagabond didn't look at the police officers, though he could see from the corner of his eye that they gave him a momentary, dismissive glance. He was surprised to see others on the platform so early – a family with a suitcase and a few locals who'd come to see them off. They barely gave the shuddering man a second look. He kept his distance. The ticket master, who'd travelled with the train, approached him cautiously, asking if he intended to board. A gravelly, weathered voice said 'yes', and produced a few tattered notes, enough for the fare to Truro. A ticket was duly dispensed from the machine around this disgusted official's neck. Moments later, with the broken man in one half of the carriage and his only fellow passengers, a girl and two tired looking adults, in the other, the train's engine whirred into life.

The social reject, forsaken by the self-important cretins outside, hunched by the window. His cat was on the seat next to him, head poked above a sand-flecked rucksack, looking up to him – the only creature that would. The outcast, with no home and no prospects, stared through the grime and saw a man he recognised – Howell Murgatroyd, in rude health, surveying the platform and having a quiet word with the train conductor, who gave him a reassuring pat on the shoulder.

The lost soul turned away and allowed the policeman to walk straight past him, scratched glass separating them. In his peripheral vision he saw the officer give him a fleeting glance, but angled his face in the other direction, content it was flecked with muck from the beach and largely obscured by the hood of his dirty coat.

This loser, this anonymous afterthought, held his breath as the doors beeped and the engines stirred, and the train, finally, shuddered forward, pulling out of the station, beginning its short journey to the mainline. Only now, with the beach he'd grown to know so well blotted out by tall grass finally passing out of view, did he allow himself a smile and a sharp expulsion of breath. He was free. Murgatroyd hadn't boarded the train. The traveller would never know why but it didn't matter, it was behind him.

★★★

The guard now walked through, ignoring me – unwanted of Perrangyre – moving to the family grouped around a table at the end of the carriage. I saw him lean over to the presumed mother, a woman who looked drawn and nervous, and heard him say, 'You're all right now madam, there'll be someone to meet you all at the other end; I'll just clip your ticket, if you don't mind.' The woman acknowledged him with a nod and turned to the girl on the adjacent seat, giving her knee a reassuring squeeze.

'Nothing to worry about now, honey,' she said. I looked at the cat and we both agreed this was curious talk. I moved the cat to the window seat and swapped places, hoping to get a better look at the girl so anxious to leave town that she'd caught the 6 a.m. train; a service usually reserved for shift workers and escaped killers.

Now I saw her and she saw me, and the atmosphere, already pungent, thanks to my attire, changed in an instant. I was looking at the teenage brat from the shop; the girl who'd stabbed me with her umbrella and paid for it with a visit to the cellar and a cold dose of reality. She studied me for a moment, then recoiled. She was shaking violently, pulling her mother's sleeve. I stared at her, conscious that this was, as they say, a make or break moment. The cat was rubbing his head against my arm.

'Don't worry, Puss,' I said, 'I'll think of something. When I think I win.'

POSTSCRIPT

Reprinted from *Vanguard* with their kind permission.

Revisiting Perrangyre
By Hugo Morley

The critic and essayist Hugo Morley grieved with the residents of Perrangyre, following Keir Rothwell's murderous assault on his former home. Then, six months on, a man claiming to be the killer-at-large sent him a chilling account of the crimes and a plea for acceptance.

If you'll forgive the old age martyrdom, I'm senior enough to remember when Perrangyre, before modern tourism was invented, was just a market town with a nice line in Snoek (an oily, foul smelling fish that no one eats any more) and the odd disgruntled teenager who talked about moving away. I was one of them, and I did.

I took a job at the *Express* under Derek Marks and buried my provincial origins. Today, they're typically worn as a badge of pride, and few places conjure up romanticism like Perrangyre. The town no longer struggles to hold on to its youth. It's become a creative powerhouse. The kind of picture postcard place where they paint the pictures you see on the postcards. Students flood in and flourish there. It's a mark of the town's revival in the last few decades.

Perhaps that makes the source of its new notoriety that much crueller.

Since twenty died there, amidst a bizarre and unprecedented sequence of events, for which British crime has few direct correlatives, this beautiful town has been stained by tragedy. The outrage is still acutely felt.

Hungerford, Soham, Perrangyre; towns hijacked by violence and transformed utterly. In my life I've been proud, if embarrassed, by the generous accolade of 'favourite son'. For the record, Awen Hammett, the physicist, has always had a far stronger claim in my view. No one associated with the place ever doubted there'd be a third name adorning future histories, not to mention a fourth, then fifth, and so on. But now we have it, we can hardly bear to utter it.

Having avoided mentioning Keir Rothwell as long as possible, one has to deal with him and with his legacy. Assuming tabloid epithets like 'monster' aren't too crass or reductive, a fruitless question perhaps, Rothwell's company does indeed look monstrous – Brady and Hindley, Christie, The Wests – even Sutcliffe. Once again society's been infiltrated by an offender whose deviance makes the rest of us a little less secure, more fearful of what the seemingly ordinary man and woman in the street is capable of. And we're all asking the same questions – how could it happen? What mistakes were made? Who's to blame? And the big one: why?

As a Perrangyre boy – particularly as a Perrangyre boy – I asked these questions in the months that followed. For me this was more than dinner party conversation, it was an assault on a community I care deeply for; a town that's always welcomed me home. It's more urgent still, as the fox had raided the chicken coop and escaped. Without answers, without capture, there can be no resolution, no catharsis. Someone, it seems, agreed, and wrote a memoir filling in the blanks. They sent that book to me.

I call it my Wearside Jack moment, recalling the tape sent to police from a man claiming to be the Yorkshire Ripper. John Humble wasn't the Ripper, of course, but police wouldn't know that for two years, or the hoaxer's identity for another twenty-five. George Oldfield, the detective taunted on tape, wasted resources and focus looking for him, enabling Peter Sutcliffe to go on killing. Such a warning from history conditions one's scepticism about the Rothwell manuscript. But the moment I saw this loose book, bound with string, a truly awful present, with its cover letter from a man purporting to be the alleged killer, I understood how Oldfield must have felt. This was Jeffrey Dahmer's secret journal, Jimmy Savile's diary found under the floorboards.

Inflation since the 1970s being what it is, this confession was of a different order of magnitude from the short message posted to Oldfield. It had a somewhat pulpy title, *Murder by the Bottle*, and ran to some 75 000 words. It was, the author told me, 'the truth', in a letter that attacked press coverage of the crime and cruelly blamed the people of Perrangyre for their fate; an example of the kind of grandiloquent grandstanding that would characterise the next few hundred pages. The author had chosen me because of my favourite son status, goading me as his inspiration for choosing Perrangyre. This barbed aside would be typical of the text. If the author wasn't Rothwell, they'd successfully parodied his presumed sadism.

The police took the original text and the envelope it came in for evidence. I took my scanned copy to Vanguard editor, Bob Peak, an honourable man whom I knew would resist any temptation to monetise the contents. We close read it together and established first principles. We'd put the full text in the public domain, and treat every line and syllable with the utmost scepticism, until its veracity could be established. We agreed it was a fascinating document, inhabiting the subjectivity of a calculating dissembler. The narrator sought to rationalise his actions, he was unapologetic.

Bob thought I had to write about it, not to indulge its lurid content or give the author the attention they craved, rather to evaluate its authenticity. The book made many claims that could be tested. Then there was what it represented; a ghoulish piece of parasitic literature, feeding on tragedy. That someone had taken the trouble to write it was a source of fascination for both Bob and me. If Rothwell wrote it, the impetus was clear enough – approval, narcissism, a chance to self-mythologise. Churchill's boast, 'History will be kind to me for I intend to write it', sprung to mind. If the book's an authentic killer's memoir, it's a stream of mitigation – providing motive, reframing personalities to suit the author's outlook, providing a definitive cut-off; a preferred ending. If a hoax, an attempt at art from artlessness.

The detail in the book, a risk for any hoaxer, forced Bob and me to admit that we knew very little of what had actually taken place, beyond the headlines, platitudinous editorials and fifteen-second clips on the evening news. As an interested party, I'd imagined myself to be a burgeoning expert on the subject – I could quote chronology, correct friends on minutiae misreported or misremembered, but the book featured characters I'd never heard of – Brain Haemorrhage Guy, Obnoxious Katherine. Who were they? Did they exist? Bob put it thus: 'If you're a hoaxer, assuming you weren't close to Rothwell, you'd want to stick to details in the public domain – publicised stuff like the shop's interiors, a million pictures of which are available on Google, or those who've appeared in newspapers and magazines. So bringing in people who aren't well known is audacious, because you can't know what you're writing is true. For me, that says the author's either Rothwell or a close acquaintance.'

When the story about the book broke, I declared that as the recipient, and for the sake of the town, I intended to go back to Perrangyre and either debunk or authenticate it. I was in the invidious position of having the answers people craved, while not knowing if I could trust them.

By publicising my intention to write this piece, in fact by giving the book any credence at all, I risked playing the dutiful stooge. But it was also a strategic decision. I hoped to prick the conscience of the author, making the comparisons with Wearside Jack explicit and talking openly of my fear that by going to Perrangyre and asking questions, I was facilitating further hurt for people who'd already suffered a great deal. And I praised the text, noting it was 'darkly compelling', hoping an endorsement would serve a hoaxer's purpose well enough, and they'd feel emboldened enough to claim ownership of their work, building a profile as the faker who piqued the country's curiosity. To date, no one has come forward.

It's worth noting that if *Murder by the Bottle* is the killer's work, then it's not a book without precedent. The Moors Murderer Ian Brady famously wrote *The Gates of Janus* from his cell; essentially a study on serial killers through the ages, presaged by self-analysis (though with no direct reference to his crimes). It found a publisher and an audience who looked past the moral implications to the first-hand insight being offered.

O J Simpson, who must be classified as an alleged murderer, wrote, though ultimately did not profit from, *If I Did It*, a bizarre pseudo-confession and case study in cognitive dissonance, in which a man who couldn't admit to double-murder, it seems either to himself or the public, attempted a half-hearted plea for their understanding while simultaneously maintaining he had nothing to do with it. There are murderers and there are those who make killing part of their story, and the Rothwell text, if authentic, would belong to this tradition.

Murder by the Bottle is, at least, unequivocal. Keir Rothwell, the character that inhabits the book, ultimately admits to everything while passing responsibility on to his victims, whom he insinuates forced his hand. Petra Zeller, the woman belatedly found in the cellar of In Vino Veritas, the shop where Rothwell worked as an assistant, is alleged to have instigated her own destruction, and this kind of victim blaming is one of the text's structuring themes.

The other victim found on the premises on that fateful morning, Robin Eep, is depicted as a show pony who betrayed Rothwell and subsequently became the poisoner's guinea pig (though after the toxic wine had been shipped out). How does the author reconcile the poisoning with this forced-hand narrative? By referring to it as 'decapitation'; the idea that a closing net could be cut up if you killed witnesses, wiped out the investigating officers.

It's an absurd fantasy but read as a hoax, a work of fiction, one can see the logic of the imagining. Poisoning a town is not a rational act or the work of someone who understands legal processes, the methodology of detection, and so on. Rothwell the killer is now twenty-one, if he's alive. Such naivety and self-delusion seems plausible, along with other unfortunate youthful follies such as flippancy, arrogance and self-absorption, all of which the book captures with great fidelity, either inadvertently or by design.

This is a memoir of escalation, positing the notion that Rothwell flipped many years before Perrangyie, only to be destabilised by events, then forced to fight a rearguard action that pushed him to greater extremes. It's important to the character that narrates this story that we understand his lack of cruel intent. But perversely, the events described are bookended by two acts of boastful premeditation. The end we know is justified in-book as an act of revenge and self-preservation. But the beginning is where any examination of authenticity must start; the disappearance of Anthony Courcier.

A Rothwell hoaxer might have learned of the case from a story written by the *Guardian*'s Aka Weiss, who reported that police investigating Rothwell during the Petra Zeller missing person inquiry uncovered his link to a forgotten disappearance at his junior school, a decade earlier. Rothwell and Courcier, both eleven, were in the same year at the Silus School in Chalk Farm, when the latter vanished during a playground break. He was never found and a friend of the boy, Wye Stammers, mentioned Rothwell to police, saying Courcier had chased him into nearby woodland. There was never any suggestion Rothwell had anything to do with the disappearance, but the character who narrates the book imagines this incident as transformative.

Those who've read the text will know the scene, recreated from Rothwell's point of view, has him enacting revenge on the boy he says bullied him relentlessly. He cites Stammers as an enabler. The question of whether he did more than knock Courcier unconscious in the wood is left dangling until the chapter 'Drinking Alone', when the author, with the manipulative instinct of the novelist, appears to confess to the boy's murder, mentioning him in the same breath as those whose deaths he's described first-hand. The chilling implication is that Courcier and Stammers conditioned a sociopathic outlook that led to an early eruption of violence; a volcano that would bubble up again in Perrangyre, years later.

If that part's untrue then one's minded to say the entire memoir is a fraud. But here, the police are unhelpful. When I ask, in light of Perrangyre, if they've re-examined the case, a source confirms that nothing new has been uncovered. The area around the school was searched, on the basis that Courcier might be buried on site, but no grave was unearthed. Wye Stammers, the boy that allegedly suspected Rothwell, who later, somewhat unfortunately, chose Perrangyre for his Art degree, did indeed take his own life, though many sources, including his GP, confirmed he suffered from depression and had done for many years.

Did Courcier chase Rothwell beyond the school's borders? Possibly, but young children chasing one another is common enough and does not usually lead to murder. Rothwell's antagonistic relationship with Courcier has not yet been corroborated. Classmates, perhaps fearful, neither saw or heard. What's reported in the book is either first-hand experience or invention.

Later, when I talk to Rothwell's friend Kerry Lasky, she maintains she only knew who Stammers was after he died, and that Rothwell never mentioned him. It's not what the book tells us, but disputed conversation isn't enough to disprove the author's recollections. Many of the narrative's 'errors' can be placed in this category.

There's much in the book that isn't disputed. Rothwell did have a turbulent relationship with the school's retired Dean, James Trevenna, who sanctioned him on several occasions for aggressive behaviour. Rothwell did wreck a studio, reportedly following a heated argument with noted artist in residence, Maisie Rae, and was subsequently ejected from the art school. But Rothwell the character, who starts with this incident, omits earlier work-related conflicts, and alleges the end of an affair between Rae and himself catalysed his outburst.

Trevenna, in this version, is recast as a hypocrite who forces Rothwell out rather than dealing with the fallout from an exploitative and therefore inappropriate relationship. The author adds a scene in which he humiliates Rae with a meat effigy, depicting her, during the school's end-of-year degree show. The school denies the affair and by association any act of vengeance. Rothwell did present at the show, three days before he was formally ejected, say fellow students, but what he produced was, for many, 'abstract', 'with no commentary', according to witnesses.

Its meaning was withheld by the artist. Is the detail in the manuscript a belated reveal?

Petra Zeller, styled as the 'wine seller in the wine cellar' by excited red tops (a phrase adopted by the book's author), signifies the tension between reported incident and attributed motive. Officially Rothwell's first canonical victim (Anthony Courcier is unproven), the book reproduces many widely published details. She was killed first, at least a fortnight before Rothwell fled, he hid the body on the shop's premises, in plain sight, given the proximity to those working there, and it was discovered part-skeletonised in a freezer used for ice bags the morning after the poisoning. The coroner's report suggested that the poor condition of the freezer, a broken rubber seal lining, a thermostat set too low, might explain the poor condition of the body. No cause of death could be ascertained.

But Rothwell the character, brazenly, matter-of-factly, attributes the condition of the body to its use as food to feed a feral cat – an animal that has a great degree of agency in the narrative, goading him, just as the Son of Sam, David Berkowitz, took 'instruction' from his pet dog. Rothwell had no pets, according to acquaintances. The idea a cat 'told him to do it' won't be confirmed as a rationale until he's captured. The inclusion of it in the Rothwell character's story is either normalised in-text – an honest reconstruction of the author's subjectivity (who never questions his sanity) – or a writer, familiar with the likes of Berkowitz, perhaps signalling their affection for Bulgakov's *Master and Margarita*, having fun at our expense.

Bob Peak, whose knowledge of popular culture far exceeds my own, found an altogether more low-brow allusion in the cat–human dialogue, *Little Shop of Horrors*. Rothwell, the character, acknowledges he's a fan of Roger Corman, who directed the 1960 cult film. This, for Bob, was a possible tell that what I had was a work of fiction informed by other such works. But could it not, I said, equally be indicative of how such works shape the imagination? If the killer is the author, would his cultural influences not condition his storytelling – not least, if he was a fantasist?

The facts don't give us the cause of Zeller's death but the book does, laceration of the carotid artery with a broken bottle. It also outlines the aforementioned motive, mocking the detective investigating her disappearance, Howell Murgatroyd, for failing to understand it. The threat to 'The Project', an attempt to turn the shop into a clandestine work of art, and much discussed when the text was published online, drove Rothwell to kill when Petra Zeller decided to fire him. The artist could not bear to be separated from his studio.

A hoaxer's either been lucky or has done their homework. Ian Zeller, who movingly spoke about his wife in numerous interviews, said Petra had labelled Rothwell 'rude and uncooperative', 'lazy and disinterested'. She had indeed been shocked when the summer attack on the former manager [in which he was violently beaten by an abusive customer] hadn't roused Rothwell to change his behaviour. She subsequently talked about dismissing him.

But talk is all that can be corroborated and so the book's version of the story provides a psychologically deeper, more nuanced explanation for the disaster that followed. With it comes some unkind allegations – suggestions of marital discord. Petra's widower has dismissed that as fiction. Proof that the whole text is a lie. One's natural inclination is to believe a broken man. The caveat of course is that on the chance that Rothwell the character and Rothwell the killer are the same person, one could understand why no living relative of his victims would want to vouchsafe any of his judgements. Whatever the ups and downs of his relationship, Ian Zeller loved his wife. His very public grief is testament to the scale of his loss. Writers who talk about the spectrum of misogyny, as one columnist did, and the right of the police to ask questions about the quality of the relationship, demean themselves with such piousness and hypocrisy.

Is there any evidence that Rothwell's project existed? Again, this seems fundamental. In theory, the book identifies a litany of witnesses who could have seen it, without knowing what they were looking at – investigating detective Howell Murgatroyd, the shop's customers, the former manager, and the girlfriend of Robin Eep and Rothwell's friend, Kerry Lasky, whom he employed in the weeks preceding the poisoning. Lasky, who gave an early interview to the BBC, in which she said she had no idea what Rothwell was planning to do, was never asked about his motive, beyond the usual fishing about whether he'd said anything that might have revealed his psychological disposition in the days and weeks prior to the murders.

Looking dazed and quite incapable of processing the enormity of what had occurred, as though she'd been struck by lightning and hit by a bus on the same day, which figuratively speaking she had, she could only say that her former peer had wanted to 'come back to the school', 'was lost without it' and 'talked about lots of ideas', but nothing involving his shop job.

When news of the manuscript broke, including the suggestion that Rothwell had been driven by some kind of misplaced artistic imperative, I travelled to Perrangyre, contacted Lasky and asked her if the passages in which Rothwell the character identifies her as a confidante, even someone who might have encouraged him to use the shop that way, had any truth to them. It is, she says, bunk. 'I knew nothing about his plans or what he was feeling – he was secretive, he didn't talk about his work.' Was it a fact that she knew nothing about Petra Zeller's fate? 'Nothing – he didn't let us down there [the shop cellar]. Nobody knew.' The book says this exactly. Had she read it? 'Bits, not the whole thing.' Did it read like her friend? 'It's imperious like he was, yes. But I've got none of his writing to compare it to.' Why describe him in the past tense? 'Wishful thinking.'

Was she witness to the scene, late in the book, where Rothwell dragged Hannah Menkin to the cellar; the fourteen-year-old girl whose chilling account of being showed Zeller's body, led police, finally, to the tip of the iceberg? Here, she's less certain. 'We did have trouble with some girls and Keir did take one out back, to call the police I thought, but she soon ran out. I was there. I don't remember what was said. It wasn't something I ever thought I'd have to think about.' This, one realises, is the problem with most of the testimony I'm going to get. Too many memories informed by hindsight; conversations and asides half-listened to, half-remembered, now deemed crucial.

One of *Murder by the Bottle*'s asides refers to April Zucarro, the forty-six-year-old Dean and artistic director of Perrangyre's art school, who now finds herself battling the worst public relations crisis in the institution's history. Rothwell the character threatens to relegate her to a footnote, and so he does – she appears in one scene. But she's also identified as someone who was invited to view the project at its shop location. The innuendo that she had a larger role in actual events, and could support the version written, made her a must see on my visit. I confess because of my ties to the place and guest lectures at the school in past decades, I was quite unprepared for how reluctant an interviewee she'd be.

I meet her in the office where she and Rothwell allegedly tussled on the day he murdered Robin Eep and sent out his toxic shipment. She's guarded, almost gaunt from stress, but opens up about Rothwell when I quote the 'you'll just be a footnote' passage.

'He said it,' she confirms, 'but unfortunately for you [when assessing the book's authenticity] I reported it to the police, as I interpreted it as a threat, and I've subsequently seen it in print, so it's been in the public domain for months.' Was she a bigger part of Rothwell's life than the book implies? 'It doesn't hurt me, if that is the official version,' she says, 'quite the contrary, but from the extracts you've shown me, it looks like he's substituted a lot of our tutor/student relationship for an imaginary sexual one with Maisie Rae. Part spite, part fantasy, I suppose. We discussed his ideas a lot in private. I used to hold regular tutorials with him; sometimes we'd go for coffee. He'd talk about himself, about his family – his father bullied him, he said, and his mother turned a blind eye. I was stupid enough to believe I knew him very well. We argued about art, about philosophy; he was intelligent. Difficult at times. But I never thought he was dangerous. Half the kids here are troubled in some way; that's their creative spur. It's like finding a stressed medical student. Show me a placid one.' But what of the project? 'He did invite me, after he'd been ejected, to see something he was working on – and again, that's widely reported. He didn't tell me what it was.' Zucarro didn't keep the invitation. 'I wish I had, but we're all wise after the fact, aren't we?'

But how wise? Bob Peak was very excited when I told him that, thus far, the only inconsistencies between book and evidence were those he said/she said questions – nothing of substance. But we both knew that the pivotal witnesses were the story's two biggest characters – Maisie Rae, who'd agreed to a single television interview in the direct aftermath of the tragedy but nothing since, and the man Rothwell the character had portrayed as his nemesis, Howell Murgatroyd, the detective vilified in some quarters for failing to arrest Rothwell when it might have made a difference.

Rae's staff have built a bunker around her, but she eventually agrees to talk to me by phone. In the five-minute conversation that follows, she filibusters for the most part, acknowledging receipt of the manuscript and dismissing the idea of a sexual relationship as 'a masturbatory fantasy'. She challenges me to explain how a long affair could be kept secret given the level of media interest in her work and personal life, her time off-campus, her commitments. There's exasperation at the mention of Rothwell's name, which she doesn't use herself, and as I thank her for her time I'm asked, in the piece to follow, to help her by uncoupling the two of them as she feels she's become 'like Bruce Ismay and the fucking *Titanic*'.

Afterwards, I reflect that without the affair, which opens the author's account, frames his discovery of the wine shop and motivates him on, the story as written is demonstrably fiction. How can one push Rae on this point? She has no responsibility for the book and couldn't admit these portions were true without destroying her reputation. This is the bind that blights all my witnesses, all my biographical characters. None of them want to be part of this story, let alone be immortalised in word and deed, by a young man whose characterisations, if authentic, threaten to outlive them all. Who wants Keir Rothwell as their biographer?

This question looms large when I'm finally confronted with Howell Murgatroyd. If it wasn't crass to say it, one could call him Rothwell's final victim. Murgatroyd, portrayed as a sprightly eccentric by the author, cuts a forlorn and quiet figure when we meet in his modest Perrangyre home. He's lived in the town all his life, joining the police when he was eighteen, working his way up ever since. Until last year, he was well-liked and well-respected in a community where everyone's connected, particularly in the social media age. Murgatroyd's wife is a local business owner, his two children attend the secondary school named after Awen Hammett. He's never wanted to live anywhere else, he says, but staying now has its complications.

'I'm the Rothwell detective now,' he tells me, 'the one who let him get away. That's not fair or true, it's a view that doesn't understand police practice, but people get their view of detectives from Sunday night drama, movies and crime novels. They also know who did it and how, of course, which I didn't know and couldn't have known. So, it's very hard.'

Murgatroyd's read the manuscript and finds the character with his name whimsical and insulting. 'He's much more interesting than the real me, in that he's like a Cornish *Columbo* [in reference to the TV detective played by Peter Falk] whereas I'm just an ordinary person. But he's also, in keeping with all the tabloid hysteria and daytime TV vilification, assumed to be ultimately incompetent. The author manages to stay one step ahead of him, by wit and luck, but I'd argue that Rothwell was more lucky than smart, and he benefited from the fact that the Petra Zeller inquiry was not a homicide investigation. The public need to be reminded, we didn't know she was dead, and that he rapidly escalated his offending in a period that is, in my experience, unprecedented. Only he knew what he planned to do. And people forget that as soon as we had a witness we issued a warrant for his arrest. We weren't to know, could not have known, that he'd already poisoned the wine batch and had it delivered. Try to imagine it from my point of view. Late one evening we get a report that someone's been shown a body in a shop basement – Rothwell's shop. We subsequently discover a double homicide. Within an hour we've found a third body [Fred Spoor, the shop's owner] at the offender's home. And a few hours after that reports of hospital admissions, some fatalities, and so on. He even sent a batch to me. By morning, it's a disaster. The previous day it was a missing person inquiry.'

I share with Murgatroyd my theory that his characterisation is just part of the mythologising that runs throughout the text. In fact, I note that an episode of *Columbo*, 'Murder Under Glass' is alluded to early on and by the author's chosen title – a story that featured, presciently, wine injected with poison. Another tell that the book's a fake?

'I wouldn't like to say,' is Murgatroyd's verdict, 'in case I'm blamed for getting that wrong too. Though, these exchanges between us are rubbish – they're inventions. I talked to him in the shop, of course I did, and we interviewed him, because we had reason to think he was involved in the disappearance, but it's nothing like verbatim – we have a video recording to prove it. Not just audio, as written. Plus, he was interviewed under caution, as the law requires. We don't do informal chats under those circumstances.'

But what of the crucial substance of the investigation? The press have criticised Devon and Cornwall Police for the apparent errors and omissions in Murgatroyd's investigation, revisited in the text. Why wasn't the cellar searched properly? Why didn't the police take a DNA sample when investigating the break-in and assault on Lewis Gray, the man beaten in his holiday home, 300 yards from the wine shop? Murgatroyd sighs.

'The body in the cellar was missed, I accept that, but unfortunately these things happen, even when the circumstances are more favourable to proving guilt. For example, think of Tia Sharp, the girl killed by her grandmother's boyfriend, wrapped in a sheet and hidden in the loft of the family home. Officers missed it the first time around. They only found her when they searched again a week later, and they'd been posted outside for God's sake. In that case, a child was missing, which is treated as a de facto murder investigation, and the offenders were living under the same roof as the body. Think of Helen Bailey, the children's author. Ian Stewart put her body in a cesspit under their home; she wasn't found for three months, and the killer was under investigation the entire time. People ask, how can it happen? Well, this isn't Sherlock Holmes. Real investigations rely on evidence, reconstructing events, building a case, and sometimes a bit of luck. But when we begin, we know nothing. You don't guess a novel's ending on page one.'

So why wasn't Petra Zeller found sooner? Did Murgatroyd make a mistake? 'Petra Zeller was an adult, so the way we investigate differs from a child going missing. The wine shop was a place of business; there were people in and out each day in the weeks following her disappearance; they traded every day; and consequently it was not looked at immediately, as no one had screamed the place down. The killer worked there, we now know, but so too did others, and they saw nothing. I took a look at the shop; I didn't check the freezer. I have to live with that. The condition of the cellar, as described in the book, is correct. The author, if they're a hoaxer, will have read about the flies and the stink from it, which half the world thinks was like a neon sign that read 'body here', but actually there was a dead animal down there, behind the wall, and it predated the disappearance by weeks, which was checked. So there was no smoking gun. A DNA sample was taken from Rothwell in relation to a nearby assault. Unfortunately, the day we got the result was the day he fled. By which time we knew who we were looking for.'

Murgatroyd, having read the manuscript, is familiar with the narrator's abrupt ending – a cliffhanger foregrounded in 'Drinking Alone', in which the author speculates as to whether it's better to provide an idealised conclusion rather than a truthful one. For Rothwell the character this is consistent with a person intent on placing himself at the centre of his own narrative, controlling his own destiny. For a hoaxer, it's a convenient device for managing the unknown – Rothwell's ultimate fate. I ask Murgatroyd if there's any reason to believe the final passage, in which the killer attacks a vagrant, disguises himself in his clothes and boards an outbound train, only to be confronted by Hannah Menkin and her family. The detective looks despondent. Since the manuscript became public, it's a question he's been asked many times.

'No body was found on the beach,' he recalls. 'It could have been washed out to sea, certainly, and if the victim was a tramp, or whatever, then that would explain why no one has reported him missing. However, I think your author has once again picked up on one of the stories surrounding the case and used it. So, there was a piece by a *Times* journalist, who'd spoken to Hannah Menkin's family, and was told that she saw Rothwell on an early morning service – the one we put her on with her mother and father, to be interviewed by colleagues in Truro. She alerted the guard and the man she'd pointed out, who was a vagrant, was understandably spooked by it and got off the train at the next stop. That was an unmanned station, just a single platform, and he ran off.'

Was it Rothwell? 'There's no reason to believe it was,' says Murgatroyd, with more than a note of irritability. 'People have to understand that Hannah Menkin was highly traumatised by her experience. Rothwell threatened her life. So, she was fearful that he was following her, and would seek her out. I don't believe he had any intention of doing so; I think he lost it, then tried to intimidate her. What the *Times* didn't tell people was that Hannah had seen several men whom she thought was Rothwell – one waiting on the street outside her house, a man hanging around the police station, who we quickly identified as a plain clothes officer. This vagrant wasn't the first. It's not unusual for people who've been subjected to that kind of threat to have false sightings of their attackers afterwards. The *Times* got over excited and I think your writer did too, intuiting that was as good a conclusion from the killer's perspective as any.'

'Because he or she has no more idea than we do where he went?'

'Exactly. That, for now, is where the trail goes cold.'

Does Murgatroyd think Rothwell will be caught? 'I do,' he says confidently. 'I'm surprised it hasn't happened already, frankly. He's been very lucky to stay hidden for so many months. He must have help. But one thing we do know is that this guy doesn't have Lord Lucan's resources. Eventually, someone will give him up, or he'll give himself up – or he'll be found dead. It wouldn't surprise me if by the time you've published your piece, he's reading it from a cell.'

But two months after that interview, Rothwell isn't in a cell. He remains at large – a folk devil. Despite thousands of man hours and a hunt that's crossed borders (he's been sighted as far afield as Sweden), the anthropoid who consigned Perrangyre to the status of a punchline in stand-up routines has not been found. The book he might have written is all we have of him; either that or a work of fiction based on a largely imaginary figure – a ghoul who left nothing behind bar pocket change, a few old photos and broken lives.

I went to Perrangyre, I talked to those who were prepared to talk, who could be found, and I moped around a town that seems to have had all the colour drained out of it. And I still don't know if *Murder by the Bottle* is fiction, non-fiction or a bit of both.

In the manuscript Rothwell the character, already more lifelike to online literary critics than the real thing, suggests that history will forgive him. 'They forgave Eric Gill,' he deadpans. Well, I'm not sure we have forgiven Gill for his incest and bestiality, even if Rothwell has. What's certain is that the kind of moral shift the author longs for, allowing for the Perrangyre murders to be excused as collateral damage in the name of art, is a long way off. Assuming some standards are inviolate, like empathy and compassion, what happened in this town will always be attributed to deep and irreparable human failure.

One day, we may get the story from the killer directly. But leaving Perrangyre I came to the view it hardly matters. A first person account would be no more or less reliable than the book I had in my hand. The rest is data – forensics, reports and chronologies. That's the only truth we'll ever have, and it will never be enough. For as the Rothwell character notes, 'We don't really know anyone, do we?'

Acknowledgements

Murder by the Bottle was brought to you with the backing and support of Iain Maguire, who liked it so much he put his name on it. Both Keir and I thank you. If you didn't enjoy it, you can send your letters to him.

My thanks to the friendly team at RedDoor Press – not just the home of brilliant books but also lovely people. Clare Christian's faith in the novel was truly humbling. I'm indebted to Heather Boisseau for getting me through the editorial process unmolested, and to Carol Anderson, my editor, who spared Keir's syntactical blushes. I'm grateful for Anna Burtt's work on the cover, and to Lizzie Lewis for her expertise in promoting my wares.

Honourable mentions to some of the novel's early readers – David Whitfield, Sandie Byrne, Kris Kenway, Bryony Pearce, Hayley Longster, Matthew Knight, Sherrie Barnes and Jay Coleman. The raw data from these readings was enough to persuade me I had a story worth telling.

Finally, my thanks to my family – Mum, Dad, Guy – whose belief never wavered even when mine did. Sometimes a bit of optimism and encouragement is all you need.

About the Author

Ed Whitfield is a film and theatre critic, who occasionally blogs on popular culture. To pose as a novelist he undertook an MLitt in Creative Writing from the University of Glasgow, and Faber's Writing a Novel Programme. He enjoys long walks, dining, dining on ashes and faux self-deprecation. He splits his time between London and Cornwall, but has heard good things about the rest of the world and hopes to see it someday (provided there's a good bus service). *Murder by the Bottle* is his debut novel.

edwhitfield.wordpress.com

MAGUIRE
CRIME

Maguire Crime is an imprint created by
RedDoor Press, in association with Iain Maguire
of High Spirits Press, in which we showcase
the very best in debut British crime fiction. We
select our titles to represent exciting new voices
who push the boundaries of the genre and we
are delighted to share these compelling reads
with you. We hope you enjoy them too.